Mistletoe and Mulled Wine at the Christmas
Campervan

Caroline Roberts lives in the wonderful Northumberland countryside with her husband and credits the sandy beaches, castles and rolling hills around her as inspiration for her writing. Caroline is also the Kindle bestselling author of the 'Pudding Pantry' and 'Cosy Teashop' series. She enjoys writing about relationships; stories of love, loss and family, which explore how beautiful and sometimes complex love can be. A slice of cake, glass of bubbly and a cup of tea would make her day – preferably served with friends!

If you'd like to find out more about Caroline, visit her on Facebook, Twitter and Instagram – she'd love to hear from you.

carolinerobertswriter.blogspot.co.uk

 facebook.com/CarolineRobertsAuthor
twitter.com/_caroroberts
instagram.com/carolinerobertsauthor

Also by Caroline Roberts

MISTLETOE AND MULLED WINE AT THE CHRISTMAS CAMPERVAN

CAROLINE ROBERTS

One More Chapter
a division of HarperCollins*Publishers*
1 London Bridge Street
London SE1 9GF
www.harpercollins.co.uk

HarperCollins*Publishers*
1st Floor, Watermarque Building, Ringsend Road
Dublin 4, Ireland

This paperback edition 2022

2

First published in Great Britain
by HarperCollins*Publishers* 2022

A catalogue record of this book is available from the British Library

ISBN: 978-0-00-848351-7

This novel is entirely a work of fiction. The names, characters and
incidents portrayed in it are the work of the author's imagination. Any
resemblance to actual persons, living or dead, events or localities is
entirely coincidental.

Printed and bound in the UK using 100% Renewable Electricity
by CPI Group (UK) Ltd

For Harry and Rowan

Chapter One

Lucy and Jack were both singing 'Ruby' at the tops of their voices as the vintage campervan swung along the coastal lanes in the autumn night.

Jack's impromptu suggestion – 'Let's head for the beach ...' – had set them off on their way after a cosy supper of fish and chips at the local pub. Lucy couldn't help but get caught up in Jack's spirit of adventure; though she was now back-tracking slightly, thinking that it'd be pretty damn chilly out there on the sands tonight in Northumberland.

'Umm, are we really going to do this? You do realise it's October, it's past ten at night ... *and* it's pitch black,' Lucy said, suddenly hesitant as they finished their song. Her sensible shell couldn't be kicked off quite that easily. It had been a lifetime in the making, after all.

'Hey, no worries, there's a full moon, plenty of light ... And just look, it's one of those still, beautiful nights, Luce.

There's no backing out now.' He was grinning at her from the driver's seat.

He pulled the deep-red, chianti-coloured campervan into an off-road area beside the dunes. They were the only ones there, unsurprisingly. Stepping out into the cool night air, Jack took Lucy's hand and guided her along the track between the tickling shafts of marram grass. Her eyes began to adjust, and yes, there was an almost-full moon, gleaming pale-silver, pearlescent like the inside of a shell.

The rolling hush of the waves breaking on the shore could be heard as the dunes ended, revealing, in the half-light, an arc of sandy beach.

'You coming in then?' Jack was already removing his trainers, his socks.

'You're kidding? I thought we were just taking a stroll …?' Lucy's voice had a beat of panic. Her boyfriend of three months might be gorgeous but he was bloody crazy!

'A stroll … a dip … whatever takes your fancy?' A cheeky grin was plastered across Jack's face.

Was he teasing her? She still wasn't quite sure when he was quipping.

'I will, if you will …' he continued.

'The sea'll be freezing.'

'Nah, it's not that bad. It's the time of year when the water temperature is actually warmer than the air.'

'Okay, Mr Fount-of-All-Knowledge.' Lucy pretended to be grumpy, but her lips were curving into an involuntary smile.

'So,' he quirked an eyebrow. 'Are you in?'

'Ahm … I'll paddle. Up to my ankles only. And that's it.'

What was she saying? How had a walk on the beach morphed into some kind of cold-water dip?!

Boots off, socks, okay and yep, jeans – no point getting them all wet. Jeez, the sand was bloody freezing, and she daren't think about the water they were about to hit.

And they were off. Two sets of footprints running down to the shoreline. Jack's hand warm around hers. All in the half-light of an October moon.

Holy cow! They were in, all in a dash before she could back out … and yep, it was f-f-freezing!

'Wahey!' whooped Jack.

'Argh …!' screeched Lucy. Icy droplets were splashing up around her shins, the current making a swirl around her ankles. This was crazy. Jack Anderson was bloody crazy. But you know what? She hadn't felt so *alive* in a long, long time.

'Come on. Jump aboard. We'll go out a bit deeper.'

What was he on about now?

'I'll give you a piggy-back. Come on, I'll take the strain. I'll not go too far, I promise.'

So she clambered aboard. Hugging him tight, her arms around his shoulders. 'You're nuts, and that's official.' But still, she found herself giggling.

Jack suddenly dipped down, just a bit, to take the hit of the next wave. She screamed. The chilly waters swirling up in a froth around her legs, splashing her thighs. 'Enough, enough. I'll get bloody pneumonia at this rate.'

It should have felt scary, out there in the murky night waters. Yet, Jack felt strong, steady beneath her. And it was exhilarating. He stood up taller again, leaving just a lap of waves around her dangling feet. And then, he managed to angle her around so that she faced his front and they were chest to chest, with Lucy still clinging on. He pulled her in even tighter, and placed his lips against hers, salty fresh. A lingering taste of chips. And a kiss so deep, so tender, that in spite of the cold it actually managed to ignite her whole body.

A few minutes later, as he set her back down at the sandy shoreline, Lucy wasn't quite sure if it had been the cold waters … or Jack … taking her breath away.

Chapter Two

S traw-coloured October sunshine streamed through the gap in the cottage curtains. Jack came to, lingering in a happy-sleepy haze, with Lucy next to him; her gorgeous conker-coloured hair spread out like a fan on the white cotton pillow, her floral-fresh scent all over the bedclothes, and her warm body nestled close. He trailed a fingertip ever so gently over her lightly tanned forearm where it rested across his chest, not wanting to wake her, not yet. Memories of last night's love making stayed tender within him.

He took a long, slow breath. This was what lazy morning Sundays were all about. Yet it was all so new for Jack – this being together – that it felt fragile as well as precious.

He'd never imagined it could be like this. So much more than fun flings, and flirty nights out. And yeah, he had to admit it, it still bloody well scared him, all this relationship stuff. But *this* ... he glanced down at Lucy lying there, her long dark lashes resting closed, so trusting ... and found that, in spite of his fears, his soul was singing. He was drawn to her, captivated by her … Yes, okay, the voice in his head chipped in (and dammit, he wasn't sure if it was in warning or celebration), he had to admit he was falling for her, big time.

He placed a gentle kiss on the top of Lucy's head, her hair soft and ticklish under his lips. As he did so, his gaze was drawn to a strange step-like contraption placed next to the shabby-chic chest of drawers to his side of the double bed. It was made up of three carpeted steps. Hmm, it didn't look like any exercise step he'd seen before; they were usually rigid plastic and a different shape altogether. Hah, it looked more like something an old lady might have to help her climb into bed. And well, Lucy had certainly leaped into bed with him last night – and the other nights before that – with no difficulty at all. What the hell *was* that?

He was pondering this when Lucy came to with a soft sigh and a feline stretch.

'Hey, morning, sleepy head.' He smiled.

'Hi, you.' Her deep-brown eyes connected with his. It hit him right in the pit of his stomach, every time.

He leaned to kiss her gently on the cheek, stirring all kinds of emotions and 'morning physicalities'. Wow, how did she manage to look so sweet yet so damned sexy all at once?

Luckily, perhaps, the step contraption distracted his gaze once again. 'Luce…? What *is* that thing?'

'What?'

'The weird step thing over there?'

'Hah, right. It's for Daisy.'

Daisy was Lucy's dog, a characterful Dachshund, who

was currently in her bed in the kitchen, no doubt awaiting her breakfast.

'It's *Daisy's*?' That fact was even more confusing.

'Yeah, sure, she uses it to get up on the bed with me ...'

'*Really?* You have furry steps for your Dachshund?'

'Yep,' Lucy answered, matter-of-fact about it, 'it's because of their short legs. Dachshunds shouldn't jump much. They have really fragile backs.'

'O-kay. So, does she sleep in here most nights, then?'

'She used to, yeah ... when you weren't around so much.'

'Hah, well that'd certainly put me off my stride. A sausage dog in the mix.' He laughed.

And as if in response to them chatting up there without her, Jack heard her pitiful whine drifting up the stairs.

'No wonder she looks at me as if I've put her nose out of joint.'

'Hah, yes, she will do. And you *have*, by sneaking into my bed and my life.'

'Oooh, that's dangerous. Hope we don't get back to her nipping my ankles again.'

The little dog had taken an instant dislike to Jack when they'd first crossed paths, though to be fair, she'd mellowed an awful lot since then. 'So, do you think a dog biscuit or two will bring her around? While I make coffee for us?'

'Hmm, it might help. But ... a bit of bacon or sausage would work even better, from the butty you're about to make for me, too ...' Lucy laughed, as she angled for some cooked breakfast.

'Hey, don't get above your station, madam.' Jack moved in closer, grinning rakishly. 'I've only offered to do a coffee trip.' He proceeded to tickle her ribs. 'And this is your house, so you should be serving me, I do believe.'

'Stop, stop.' Lucy was giggling. 'Okay, I surrender. Coffee's fine, honestly.'

He drew back, still smiling. 'It's alright, I'll make them, the sandwiches. I'm feeling a bit peckish too, now you've mentioned it. Is there bacon in the fridge then, and bread?'

'Oh yes, we've got some rashers. But hmm, now then, I'm not so sure about the bread … it's perhaps not that fresh.'

'So now I've got to go out and get fresh bread from the village shop too. Jeez, you are getting so high-maintenance.'

Lucy knew he was joking, and lay back on the soft pillows, grinning at his rant.

'Right then, well I'd better keep this lady in the lifestyle she's accustomed to. And go and face Devil Dog Daisy while I'm at it.'

Jack sprang out of bed, his late-twenties body firm and end-of-summer tanned. Totally unfazed at being naked in front his girlfriend, he reached for his discarded T-shirt and boxer shorts from the night before.

❄

Wow, Lucy took in that gorgeously toned, manly view and pinched herself once again; Jack was really here, in her bed and in her life, after all the painful ups and downs she'd endured over the past few years. How fabulous was that body to wake up next to in the morning. To have him there beside her, and last night so very close against her … eek. Her skin tingled just remembering.

It felt almost too good to be true. But it *was* true. They'd become an item, for now at least. Jack was here in her bed, in her head … standing beside her right now, in fact, giving her his trademark broad grin. And that was in fact *all* he was wearing, hah. With his floppy blond fringe and surfer-style ruffled hair, a touch on the long side, he oozed a confident, happy-go-lucky beach-style vibe. She watched as he began to dress, then headed out of the doorway to make her breakfast. Lucy gave a contented smile as she rested back against plump pillows. If she could purr, she might well have found herself doing just that.

※

'Hey, there … Dais.' Jack had learned (the hard, heel-nipping way) that the best way to greet Dachshund Daisy of a morning was to let her know of his presence *before* he launched in through the kitchen door. She was probably just being protective of her owner, but Jack was sure there was a hint, well a big dollop, of jealousy in there too. And after seeing that bedside step, no wonder. He must have well and truly put her out – out of her cosy sleeping zone beside the lovely Lucy! Even as he pushed the door ajar, a barrage of barking exploded.

'Hi, it's only me. Okay, o-kay,' he soothed. The smooth-haired black-and-tan dog eyed him suspiciously, *still*. He'd stayed over a dozen times now at least. 'Hey, don't you think it's time we learned to rub along a little better, young lady?' They were getting there, step by step, and paw by paw, but it had been slow progress over these past few months. 'I'll fetch your food then, shall I?' As he approached the cupboard where her dog kibble was kept, the barking ceased. Well, some things were worth calming down for. But she lifted her long nose to give Jack one more big brown-eyed yet steely look. It was like she was telling him not to mess with her mistress's heart.

'I won't, promise,' he said out loud. *What was he doing, talking to a dog?!*

Blimey, the pair of them were definitely getting under his skin. And he'd be damned if there was anything he could do about it at this point. Best to give in, go with flow. Dish out the dog food, and go fetch the fresh bread and maybe some croissants too. He gave a smile, then he frowned ever-so-slightly. This was getting way too domesticated for a guy like Jack Anderson. He felt an unwelcome ripple of unease rifle through him. Was he getting in too deep?

Chapter Three

J ack was greeted by a glorious, if slightly chilly, October morning, as he stepped out of the door of Lucy's terrace cottage. The fresh salty sea air swirled around him in a light breeze, and halfway along the street at a break between the houses opposite, he could see the pewter-grey tones of the North Sea.

The coastal village of Embleton was nestled a mile inland behind the dunes of a long and sweeping golden-sand bay. A typical Northumbrian settlement of traditional houses and cottages, with a primary school, two pubs, hotel, golf course, village shop and café, it was small and friendly and the place that Lucy had made her home just last year. That was, he'd learned, after some kind of relationship breakdown. It seemed to be a great little community. And now, a couple of months into their relationship, Jack was finding it was beginning to feel a little like home for him too. This was mighty strange and uncharted territory. He'd never stuck with a romantic relationship before in his life – well, not since an early and very sweet teenage crush. He'd been far too busy trying to avoid being tied down to any one person, or indeed pinned to one place. A month, two tops – well, mostly one or two nights, if he was being totally honest – and he was up and off, back enjoying his single life. That was until the thunderbolt of meeting Lucy at the start of this summer, which had shown him just how empty and hollow that single life had become.

He strolled along the street, giving a little whistle as he went. Said a cheery 'hello' to an old chap, who doffed his flat cap with a friendly smile. He'd evidently just called to collect his morning newspapers. The shop wasn't far, only around the corner, and on the next street.

He then passed a dog walker on the narrow flag-stoned pavement. A middle-aged man who bid him a friendly hello, and a 'Lovely morning.' The accompanying Labrador sniffed Jack's ankles with interest. Perhaps 'Eau du Dachshund' was lingering there. Hah, he hoped to goodness the little devil dog hadn't taken a revenge pee on his trainers that he'd left in the cottage hallway.

'Good morning,' Jack said, responding with a smile.

And it was. The sun was shining. Life was good … and precious … and could be swept away when you least expected it. And boy, he knew about that more than most. With everything that had happened to his brother, his family … Every damned moment was precious.

He pulled himself back to the here and now. He needed a positive hit today. It wasn't the time to dwell on the past. It was a beautiful autumn day. He had a gorgeous girl waiting in a cottage by the sea for him. And all he needed to do was to buy some fresh bread and rustle up some tasty bacon sandwiches. The beach then beckoned for a stroll on the sands. He had a hand to hold, lips to kiss. A life to live. Today was going to be a good day.

❄

As she lay in bed, now alone, Lucy's happy glow was tinged with an odd feeling of unease. A sorrow, she realised. She had fallen hook, line and sinker for Jack, there was no denying that. And they were getting on really well. He made her smile, made her laugh, in fact, her confidence seemed to have soared since they'd got together. She loved that he'd managed to infuse her life with a spirit of adventure and fun, that she'd been missing for so long – she was learning to enjoy the moment.

But … and why was there always a damned 'but'? Jack, many years ago now, had briefly dated her close friend Becky, and he had messed her about, seriously denting Becky's heart and pride. Of course, that was all in the past. Lucy had tried to explain to her friend how Jack was a very different person these days, and that yes, he'd admitted he had been a bit of a player in his youth, trampling on a few girls' hearts. He'd even sent a message to apologise to Becky directly, to try and clear the air, but Becky was having none of it. And sadly, over the past few weeks, the friendship between the two young women had become extremely frosty. This was devastating to Lucy. They had always been so close, right from being little girls at school together. It was hurting her – and no doubt Becky too – but Lucy knew she had to give her relationship with Jack a chance. Get to know him even more, prove that her instincts were right, and to somehow show Becky the truth of the man she had fallen for.

Words kept jumping back into her head from the argument they'd had only yesterday:

'Hey, how's it going?' Lucy had asked her friend, clutching her phone to her ear.

'Fine,' Becky had responded coolly, which didn't in fact sound *fine* at all. 'So, you're still seeing him then?' she'd bit, launching right in.

There was no need to ask who Becky was referring to.

'Yes.'

A frustrated blast had launched back at her: 'You're crazy, Luce. And I can't believe you're not listening to me. Don't you get it? He's toxic.' A short pause and then she'd slammed back in with, 'Well, don't come running to me when it all goes tits up.'

Lucy hadn't known how to respond and had floundered, feeling like piggy in the middle, not wanting to have to lose either of them. Dammit, could it really come to that? That losing one or the other was the only way? 'Well, I'll catch you soon. Take care, Becky,' she'd ended up mumbling, before saying goodbye. Switching off the call with trembling fingertips and a heavy heart.

She understood that part of Becky's frustration was rooted in the fear that Lucy would get hurt, but another big part was rooted in the vulnerability of her friend's teenage past. Jack's two-timing had come at a time when Becky's parents were on the verge of splitting up. Lucy was sure this had something to do with why it had hit so hard. The million-dollar question was: would Becky be able to move past this? Could their friendship survive?

Lucy clung to the hope that it could, and she was determined to try everything in her power to save it. Although one thing she knew for sure was that she absolutely couldn't toss Jack aside now – he meant far too much to her. She gave a slow sigh as she sunk back into pillows that had Jack's salt-and-citrus scented cologne all over them. Time would tell, and she had to accept that not everything was in her control.

Well, for now, she'd better get up, take a quick shower, and get ready for the bacon butty breakfast that Jack would soon be making. It was unusual for her to lie in, but life had been all go these past few weeks. Having finally built her catering reputation, after setting up her new pizza business in the spring, she was now getting loads of new bookings, and she hadn't dared turn any of them down. Which meant she'd been dashing across the coast and countryside of Northumberland with All Fired Up, her fabulous dove-grey-painted converted vintage horsebox, working like a trojan.

After a turbulent couple of years, and a broken engagement, Lucy had dared to dream, to step out from her comfort zone and steady life, and to make that dream a reality. She'd followed her heart and her passion for cooking, very much inspired by her wonderful Italian grandfather, Papa, who sadly was no longer with them. Her family, her friends and yes, Becky, had all given her their support. Lifting her up when, at times, it all felt a little impossible. There was no way she was going to let it fail now. Not her business, not her friendship, and not her relationship with Jack. She should be happy that she'd achieved so much. But why did it all suddenly feel like a house of cards?

Wafts of sizzling bacon were soon drifting up the stairs, drawing Lucy down to find her gorgeous sandy-haired boyfriend, frying pan in hand, with a rich coffee aroma on the go. Now that was a sight to please any food-loving and warm-blooded girl.

'Hey, this is great, thank you.' It was wonderful to be spoilt. In six whole years, she'd only known her ex, Liam, cook her breakfast once. (Hah, yes, and that had been when his parents had stayed over with them, so to be fair the effort was more for them than for her. No doubt in an attempt to make him look good.) With Jack, this was the fourth time in four weeks! They were getting quite homely indeed. Lucy felt a surge of happiness and stepped forward, slipping her hands around Jack's taut waist, from behind.

'Hey, careful you. Watch out.' Jack brandished his metal cooking tongs menacingly, whilst sporting a grin. 'I have hot instruments to hand.'

'Hmm, and don't I know it.' Lucy was thinking very much about last night, and gave a mischievous giggle.

Jack laughed raucously, then turned away to continue his culinary task. 'Now then, behave, you.'

'Do I have to?'

'No, absolutely not. The naughtier the better.' His grin widened.

Lucy loved their daft banter. Jack's sense of fun was catching. He was like a breath of fresh air. Like a stirring sea breeze, in fact, after sensible, staid (translate to *bloody boring*) Liam.

Jack was soon serving up, and the two of them sat on stools at the kitchen counter, enjoying bacon butties made with soft doughy bread from the village stores, teamed with strong coffee and zesty orange juice. Daisy the Dachshund was poised beneath them anxiously awaiting any stray crumbs that might just come her way.

The autumn sun beamed in through four square panes of the kitchen window as they ate. Deciding to make the most of the fresh, sunny morning with a walk on the beach, they were soon clearing the cups and plates to the sink and getting their trainers on. With Daisy now sat in the hallway, tail wagging, keen to join in.

It was about a mile from Lucy's cottage to the beach. Past the golf course, and on through the winding track to the start of the dunes. Strolling the pale-golden sands, hand in hand with Jack, with Daisy trotting about amusingly, trying her best to avoid the salty puddles left by the receding tide, Lucy felt the warmth of contentment.

If it wasn't for the Becky situation, life would in fact be pretty perfect. She loved her cosy coastal cottage home, having moved in a year ago after selling the new-build house she'd lived in with Liam. A break-up that was probably long overdue, but was barrelled into action by his affair. A bomb in the already damaged building of their relationship, but still damned hurtful nonetheless. Yet having Jack beside her these past weeks, staying over and sharing her beachside life, being able to talk things through with him, be it personal or business … to touch, kiss, make love with him, well … it was hard to put it into words. But somehow life glowed. It felt so much fuller, joyful.

The bay was particularly beautiful this morning. A

crescent curve of golden sands, with the far cliffs rising to the ruins of Dunstanburgh Castle as its backdrop. Though the blue of the sky was autumn-muted, with pillows of white-grey clouds beginning to gather on the horizon, the sun still peeked through, giving silver-gold light that danced on the crests of the waves that rolled to shore. They chatted as they strolled along. The breeze was life-affirming, fresh and invigorating, rippling through Lucy's dark hair which fell loose. The chill of the wind just meant they walked a little closer, warming each other. Enjoying the touch, the togetherness, of their clasped hands with fingers interlinked.

Yet, after yesterday's call with Becky, there was still one nagging concern that dimmed all this … one dark cloud in an otherwise bright, hopeful sky. Lucy must have gone a little quiet.

'You okay?' Jack slowed his pace, pausing to face her.

'Yeah, I'm fine.' Lucy didn't want to spoil the moment, didn't want to burden him with her worries about having fallen out with her best friend.

'You sure? You just seem a bit subdued this morning, Luce.'

'Ah, I'm okay.'

'Well, you know, if there's ever anything you want to talk about …'

She felt the squeeze of Jack's hand around hers, protective, caring. But this was between her and Becky. She didn't need to burden Jack with any of it. She should be able to deal with it.

And, looking out over the bay, hearing the rhythmic

18

rolling hush of the sea, the timeless tide, she really didn't want to spoil the moment.

'Thanks, I appreciate that.'

In no way did this new relationship feel 'toxic' – as Becky had described it. She *couldn't* have got this so wrong. But they'd always been a team, her and Becky, they'd faced the worst together, fought the same battles. Now it seemed they were on totally different sides.

But hey, whoever said life was easy? When had it ever all run smoothly at the same time for her? But she had her family, her friends – with a little Becky blip, that was all – plus the lovely support of her new village community. The people who had held her up through some very tough times in the past, and the ones who were helping her back on her feet now.

Hmm, perhaps it was time to thank them all properly. The only thing was how? She couldn't afford some big posh do, or a meal out for everyone. There were rather a lot of them, for a start ... And she was still finding her feet with the new business, her savings having gone into that and putting a deposit down on her cottage. But a get-together might also help bring Becky back to the fold. It might be a chance to get her friend and Jack to meet up casually, in a bigger crowd. Get to know each other *now*, rather than dwelling on the past. Yes, it was food for thought.

As they headed back along the shoreline, with Daisy skipping along at their feet, Lucy mentioned her thoughts to Jack. 'You know what, life's looking up just now, and I think it's high time I thanked everyone who's helped me these past couple of years. The ones who saw me through that shitty break-up, and everyone who's helped get All Fired Up running and off the ground.'

'Yeah, that sounds a good idea. So, what are you thinking? Some kind of party?'

'Yeah, maybe … but the cottage is tiny. I'd never fit everyone in. And a "do" out is going to cost an arm and a leg – though I'd love to be able to do that for everybody. Hmm, I'd better not sink the pizza business I'm meant to be celebrating by pushing the boat out too far and spending the last of my savings.'

'True.'

'Oh well, I'll have a think on it. Maybe come up with something on a smaller scale.'

They had turned around by this point and were making their way back, tracing the damp sands of the shoreline where little rushes of frothy waves broke.

'So, what's lined up for you this week?' Jack asked.

'Pretty quiet, to be fair, other than my market slot in Alnwick on Thursday. Seems to be a bit of a lull, which is a bit of a worry.'

Unusually, after the end-of-summer rush, the pizza van bookings for the next couple of weeks had begun to dry up quite noticeably.

'Yeah, it does shift a bit at this time of year. With the change in the seasons and the weather, outdoor catering doesn't quite have the same draw for your birthday parties and suchlike, but I wouldn't worry too much – I've been there before – and it picks up again come November with the Christmas Markets and festive events slotting in nicely.'

'Ah, that's good to know. And, I do have that wedding booked, in three weeks' time.'

'Meet you there!' Jack grinned.

'Brilliant.' She always enjoyed it when they were at the same events. It made the bookings more fun, and she had to admit (to herself, if not him! No need to boost his ego any more) she liked watching him in action as the campervan barman – it was how they'd met, after all. And, it was great to know she had that extra bit of support if needed. She knew that he liked to watch her back, quietly and in the background, at these things.

As the dunes ended, they retraced their steps along the sandy track that turned into grass, and then were soon walking back up the characterful coastal street towards Lucy's stone cottage, with Daisy trotting alongside. The pizza horsebox was parked up there in its usual spot to one side of her property.

'That's it! Of course.'

'What's *it*?' Jack was bemused.

The dove-grey-painted antique horsebox, with its signage, *All Fired Up – pizza just like Papa used to make*, was stationed invitingly at the side of her little house. An idea was forming. Pizza … for everyone … served right here. And, as well as her friends and family, if she asked along some of the village community too, then hopefully no one would make a fuss that a bit of a bash was going on in their street! It'd be a lot of work, but hey-ho, it'd be well worth it.

'Yess! I can hold the party right here. It's still reasonable, if slightly chilly, weather. And well, if we all wrap up a bit, we'll be fine. Pizza and prosecco!' She was used to making pizzas by the dozen. And she could knock up a few salads and some garlic breads too … Her mind was buzzing, and in party mode already.

'Now you're talking. And, if you need a dashing prosecco server with a very charismatic campervan, well … look no further …' Jack was grinning, catching on to the idea.

'Do I get a discount?' Lucy gave a leading smile.

'Hmm, there might have to be some clauses attached to that …' Jack tried his best to look serious, but a cute smile was lifting the corners of his mouth.

'Hah, payment in kind, I wonder?'

'Something along those lines …' Cocky barman Jack was back, but the twinkle in his eye just made her smile.

They both laughed.

'You're on.' Lucy grinned. In fact, that was no hardship at all. Payment in kind would be a delight! 'Thank you, Jack.'

'It would be my pleasure.'

Lucy quirked an eyebrow.

'No really, it sounds a cool idea, the party. I get it,' Jack followed up.

Lucy could picture the pizza horsebox all lit up with its pretty fairy lights. Ruby, Jack's red classic VW campervan with her hatch up, globe bulbs beaming almost as brightly as Jack's smile. And her little street abuzz with conversation and laughter. What a lovely and personal thank-you that would make.

A pizza and prosecco party it would be, then. She couldn't wait to fix a date and send out the invites. She gave a smile, and then a little sigh – all she needed was for her closest friend to agree to come along too.

Chapter Four

With the invites drawn up, and cards and messages sent out to friends and family, Lucy waited anxiously for the return of Becky's RSVP, or even a message from her. But there was still nothing two days later, and she was feeling antsy.

She sent a further text:

Hey Becks, hope you are fine? And hope you can make the thank-you bash at mine on the 23rd. It would mean a lot to me if you could come …

Well, God loves a tryer, that's what her mother always used to say. And she was trying her best here. Though it felt very much like she was banging her head against her stubborn friend's brick wall right now.

Book Club night was coming up at the Driftwood Café this week, too. A rather wonderful cake-and-coffee fuelled affair, held monthly with a gathering of between six and twelve of them, depending on commitments, the Book Club was held after-hours in the pretty tearooms on the next street in her village. Would Becky show at that, Lucy wondered? She'd been a few times with her. Who knew? Argh, it was such a shame that all the lovely things they did together had become tainted by this daft rift.

Lucy scrolled through her phone and framed a further chatty-toned message:

And don't forget it's Book Club this week. Have you read The Midnight Library yet? I thought it was great. Be lovely to see you there. X

Maybe the party was a step too far, but doing something normal – and non-boyfriend related – might be just what they both needed to put things back into perspective. Lucy found she was looking forward to that friendly bookish gathering too. It was a real pep-you-up kind of evening. Each month she'd got to know the members of the group a little more; beginning to feel a real part of this village community she now called home.

She'd loved this month's book too, and couldn't wait to hear what everyone else thought about it. Reading had always been a pleasure for Lucy, and an escape. And boy, had she needed some escape these past two years when life had gone topsy-turvy in all kinds of painful ways.

❄

The little tinkly bell as she pushed the white wooden door open never failed to make Lucy's heart lift, and sounded just like a 'Welcome to The Driftwood Café' jingle.

'Hello!' Lucy announced herself with a smile.

A friendly chorus of 'Hi's and 'Hello's chimed back.

Several members of the Book Club were already gathered about the big round table at the centre of the café. Lucy spotted Glynis, Paul and Sarah. Cathy was often a little late, dashing in after closing the village stores for the night. Hmm, no sign of Becky as yet – and no answer to her message from a few days earlier either. Louise, the café owner, was bustling towards them with a tray of goodies. Heads bobbed up and smiles widened with an air of expectancy about what baking delights might be on offer this evening. Louise was renowned for baking the moistest, scrummiest cakes in the county – well, she had to be up there with the best of them anyhow.

Tonight's tray held … a host of orange cupcakes with spiderwebs, freaky eyeballs and sugar-paste bats on, as well as chocolate-dipped treacly flapjacks.

'No tricks, just treats here,' homely Louise announced with a grin. 'I know it's a little early, with a week yet to go until Halloween, but I couldn't resist.'

'Oh, they look great.' Sarah beamed.

'Chocolate cupcakes with an orange-flavoured frosting,' Louise explained.

'Ooh delightful,' commented Paul, reaching forward to take one. 'Sorry, I know it should be ladies first, but really, I can't help myself.'

The group chuckled.

'She's a witch, that's what she is,' Cathy said cheekily as

she burst through the door before pulling up a chair, 'drawing us in with her spellbinding cakes. Evening, all!'

'Hi, Cathy. And don't listen to a word she says. You lot are here voluntarily every month like clockwork. There's no need to put a spell on you.'

'It's because you make us feel so welcome,' said Glynis.

'Ah no, it's because of the cakes,' chuckled Paul.

'Cheeky!' Lou pretended to bat him with her hand. 'Oh, and there's a carrot and ginger cake yet to come too. Abby's just slicing it up in the back there, and brewing a pot of tea for you all. Got to the "boil and bubble" part yet, Abs?' she asked, joining in the puns.

'Watch out, she'll be cackling next,' Cathy laughed.

Abby, who was Lucy's pizza horsebox assistant, also doubled up as waitress here in the village café. Well, to be fair, after some early staffing issues, Lucy poached her services from Louise (under mutual agreement to boost the young woman's hours) on the odd weekend and evening for her busier events, and the eighteen year old was proving invaluable. She was delightfully professional, friendly and a hard worker.

'Sorry I'm late,' Helen blasted in through the jingly door next. 'Had to wait for me mam to arrive to mind the kids. Said the traffic was terrible coming over on the A1.'

'No problem, my love. We haven't had chance to get going, anyhow,' said Lou.

Abby came through with the tray of carrot cake, and an enormous pot of tea with a selection of spotted and floral vintage mugs. They seemed to be all set.

'Well then, I think that's it. Time to talk books.'

'Oh, have you heard from Becky at all?' Lucy ventured.

'Yes pet, she let me know about an hour ago that she had something crop up with work tonight. Had to stay late or something,' responded Louise.

With that a little ping of a vibration came from Lucy's phone. She pulled her mobile out discreetly and took a quick peek.

Sorry can't make Book Club. Held back at work. Crazy busy just now. Catch up soon. B

At least her friend had messaged, Lucy supposed, but she experienced a dull, disappointed feeling within; it felt very much like it might be a cop-out.

'So, have you all had chance to read *The Midnight Library*?' Louise's voice brought Lucy back to the here and now. 'Any comments?'

'I thought it was great,' Abby started. 'It's a book that really makes you think. Kind of asks as many questions as it answers, with all those alternate lives.'

'Yeah,' Helen took up, 'tells you to stop messing around with regrets, and just get on and live.'

'I think the author wanted to show that everything in life isn't perfect,' Lucy added, 'that all those worries we have … the what-ifs, the regrets, yeah … are actually pretty pointless. It's about choosing life and being brave enough to live it, warts and all, as it's *never* going to be perfect. I loved it.' The book had resonated so much with Lucy. She had even shed a few tears for the protagonist Nora Seed and her lonely journey.

'I liked that it was messy, like real life, but that it was positive overall, too,' Cathy added.

Lucy took a bite into a moist orangey cupcake. *Delicious.*

'It was a really clever idea,' added sixty-something Glynis, 'and it was beautifully written.'

'Yeah, it *was* a really cool concept,' agreed Abby. 'All your different choices played out. It is quite scary at times, wondering if you are doing the right thing.'

'Life's just bloody tough,' added Helen. 'And we all know about that.' Her recent tricky divorce was obviously still fresh in her mind.

'It was a quick read, easy to engage with,' chipped in Paul. 'Though it was a bit like those *Groundhog Day* plots, I found. Quite good, but not my normal kind of read.'

'No, not for you with your Mills & Boons addiction, my lovely,' quipped Cathy.

'Hey, I've been dipping my toe into a bit of crime lately,' countered Paul.

'Ooh, get you.' Louise laughed.

'Well, I thought it was quite unique. About choices, regrets and embracing life,' added Glynis.

'And that sums it up well, Glynis, thank you. I did enjoy it too,' added Louise. 'Certainly made me think. More cake, anyone?'

'Well, I think I might well regret not having some of that carrot and ginger cake,' Sarah said with a smile.

'And I think I might regret *having* a slice when I next hit those scales. But hey-ho, it's there for the eating. I'll just have to put in an extra mile on the dog walk in the morning,' added Helen.

'You might have to jog the whole beach, looking at the size of those slices.' Sarah flashed a grin.

The chat turned to village and family life, with the

upcoming Halloween activities for those with children. Lucy making a mental note that she'd need to buy in some sweets for the trick-or-treaters, and get herself a pumpkin to carve. This led to a discussion about recipes for pumpkin soup, or if in fact it was actually worth it, with the little pumpkin flesh that came out of those big orange things. And then they all revelled in the delightful toffee chewiness of Driftwood's divine flapjacks.

The next Book Club, Louise announced, was to be a 'Christmas special', with it falling in late November. They were to bring and discuss their favourite festive reads – with several of the club offering to provide homemade Christmas cake, mince pies and their best festive bakes, too, happy to take the strain off an already busy Lou and her team.

'Aw, that sounds lovely folks, thank you,' Louise looked genuinely touched. 'Though I may not be able to resist rustling up a little festive something myself, you know me. But yes, that'd be wonderful, and I look forward to it.'

'Sounds great.'

'Brilliant.'

It had been a lovely evening, and all too soon Lucy was walking the short distance home with her breath misting in the dark frosty night air, her tummy full and her mind still buzzing about *The Midnight Library* and all the questions it raised about life, friendship, regrets and more …

She hoped to goodness she wouldn't live to regret her decision to stay with Jack. She really wanted the chance to get to know him more. And she desperately hoped her friendship with Becky could find a way back. Instinctively, she crossed her fingers inside of her woolly gloves.

❄

You are invited to

Lucy's Pizza and Prosecco Party

With All Fired Up & The Cocktail Campervan

At Cove Cottage, Embleton

Saturday 23rd October

From 6 p.m.

I'd love to see you there!

Please RSVP

❄

Chapter Five

Guests were due in five, oh yes, *five* minutes!

It had been an afternoon of bunting hanging, fairy-light stringing, pizza dough balling and tomato paste stirring. All the while, singing along to some classic 80s rock courtesy of Jack's iPhone, including a blast of Bon Jovi's 'Living on a Prayer' with some improvised air guitar from them both, accompanied by a cheeky glass of prosecco – just the one, as it was going to be a long night yet. The sky had bubbled up with grey cloud in the last hour, but the late-October evening was thankfully looking to be balmy. Fingers crossed, it would stay dry.

Some of the villagers had even pitched in to help, with Cathy's husband (from the village stores) bringing around a tall ladder and helping to fix a strand of lightbulbs from the cottage eaves across to the horsebox roof. Helen and her two children had arrived mid-afternoon with two carved-out pumpkins they'd made to add a little autumn cheer to the proceedings. Lucy put them in pride of place; one on the pizza counter hatch, the other by the front door of the cottage to greet everyone. Tealights were scattered and ready to be lit as soon as dusk fell.

Lucy hadn't wanted to offend any of her neighbours so had posted a little handwritten invitation through every letterbox in her street. Well, it was one way of getting to know people! She'd also invited various other locals she'd got to know since moving in, including of course all the Book Club members. Whilst being a friendly gesture, she also hoped it might help to avoid any complaints about noise. Being a relative newbie to the village, Lucy really didn't want to upset anyone. And, with her cottage being so small, and the food and drink being served outside from the pizza horsebox and the campervan, the event was bound to spill out onto the flagstone pavement of the street.

The pizza oven was loaded with logs and heating up nicely, as bottles of prosecco, local ales and Italian lagers were cooling in the fridges of Ruby the campervan. Back-up drinks supplies were resting on ice in plastic horse troughs – borrowed from and brainwave of Sarah from the Book Club, who as well as being an avid reader, also kept two ponies. Genius.

Lucy had set out jam-jar posies of flowers next to coloured glass tealight holders on the gathering of put-me-up tables; white village-shop-bought carnations mixed with clusters of small pale-pink roses, picked from the prolific climbing rosebush that was still giving a last blast of autumn blooms in her back garden.

'Right, that's Ruby all set. Are you ready over there?' Jack called from his parking spot beside the cottage. He was stood inside the converted bar area of his pride and joy, the buffed and gleaming Chianti Red Westfalia T2 VW Campervan. Two trays of flute glasses were lined up on the chrome counter with a measure of limoncello in each, ready to top with the chilled prosecco as a welcome Limoncello Fizz Cocktail. An Italian-themed touch guaranteed to start proceedings with a sparkle.

'Think so.' Lucy's smile felt a little tight. She was anxious for it all to go off well. It was her chance to showcase All Fired Up to her community and to her family and friends, as well as making it a big thank-you to everyone. She so wanted her guests to have a really good evening. And she knew that her pizzas and her hosting needed to be tip-top.

'You'll be fine,' Jack said reassuringly, spotting her nervousness. 'Remember, everyone here this evening is a friend.'

'Yeah, that's true.' That did help put things into perspective. 'And thanks for all your help here too.'

A toot sounded from the street as a dark-blue hatchback turned the corner, announcing the first arrivals. It was Lucy's brother Olly along with partner Alice, and toddler Freddie. Her nephew, who after being let out of his car seat, was looking extremely serious as he concentrated on carrying a box of thank-you chocolates across to 'Annie Lucy'. Bless him, he struggled to say 'Auntie'.

'Oh, thank you, Freddie.' Lucy stepped forward to give him a big hug. 'Now they look rather scrumptious.'

'Freddie have one?' He looked up with a cheeky smile.

'It's a gift, Freddie. They're not yours,' his dad interjected.

'Hah, having to hold all that chocolate is far too

tempting, bless him,' Lucy couldn't help but grin. 'Of course. We'll open them in a minute, shall we, and share them out?'

The little boy's smile grew wide and he nodded.

'And there's lots of delicious pizza coming soon too,' Lucy added.

Daisy trotted up to greet her favourite little pal. The Dachshund was dressed in a cute orange jumper designed to look like a pumpkin, though her long sleek figure stretched it out to appear more like a small marrow. Oh well, you can but try to be seasonally attired.

'Daisy!' Freddie was as delighted as she was to be meeting up again, and there were licks and hugs aplenty.

Just two minutes later, and hot on their heels, came Lucy's mum, Sofia, who'd driven the twenty miles from her hometown of Rothbury, bringing Lucy's grandmother 'Nonna' with her. Nonna had offered to help with some baking, and got out of the car proudly bearing her family-favourite Chocolate Mousse Cake. A large Italian-style chocolate mousse-topped sponge, decorated beautifully with strawberries, raspberries and chocolate curls. A real party showpiece of a cake. Now *that* was guaranteed to go down a treat with the guests a little later.

'Aw, thank you so much, Nonna. That looks divine.' Lucy took the cocoa-and-cream laden delight from her grandmother's slightly wobbly hands.

'You're very welcome, pet. There's another one in the car too. I hear you're expecting quite a crowd … And ooh, doesn't this all look so very pretty here.'

It was the first time the old lady had seen Lucy's pizza horsebox up and running. Its fairy lights twinkled welcomingly along the hatch front. The Italian-flag bunting was hoisted, and a mouth-watering selection of pizza toppings were lined up on the wooden shelf inside. Set out on the countertop were two recycled kilo-sized 'San Marzano' tomato tins that had been filled with red-checked napkin-wrapped cutlery, alongside a large jug of fresh basil, and – of course – Papa's old and much-treasured pepper mill from his restaurant days in pride of place.

The tiniest hint of a tear crowded Nonna's eyes as she said, 'Oh, Lucy, it looks wonderful, pet. Papa would have been so proud of you.'

Papa had sadly passed away ten years ago now, leaving a huge gap in their hearts and lives. Lucy's mum, Sofia, stood nodding nostalgically beside Nonna and Lucy, with a bittersweet smile cast over her lips. There they were, three generations – all once with the same beautiful dark hair that Lucy sported in long lustrous waves, Nonna's now cut short and white, Sofia's salt and pepper and shoulder length. All hard-working women, feisty at times, and fiercely loyal.

'Yes, Papa would have been very proud … and so happy to see this,' Sofia added. 'You've done well, Lucy, getting this up and running and off the ground. It looks fabulous.'

Lucy felt her nerves begin to settle and she had a lovely warm glow inside.

'Hello there. Can I offer anyone a glass of prosecco, or a Limoncello Fizz Cocktail? Or there are lime sodas to kick off with?' asked a smiling, yet unusually nervous-looking Jack, who appeared with a tray of freshly poured goodies to hand. He was dressed smartly for the occasion in beige chinos, a black turtle-neck jumper and his logoed Cocktail Campervan apron.

'Oh yes please, young man.' Nonna was straight in for a Limoncello Fizz. 'I used to love this stuff back in the day.' She took a sip, 'Ah, Limoncello, that takes me right back! They used to serve it after your meal … in tiny glasses. Moonlight over Sorrento Bay. Magical memories …' The old lady paused for a moment, with a breath of a sigh, then seemed to bring herself around. 'Oh, and you, young man, must be Jack, the one who I've been hearing so much about, yes?'

Lucy felt herself blush standing beside them. *So, this was it,* time to meet the family. Well, her mum and Nonna. (Jack had already met Olly, when her brother had helped at an event back in the summer.) This was yet another reason for her ragged nerves this evening.

'Ah, yes … well, it's lovely to meet you.' Jack sounded a touch awkward.

'Jack, this is my grandmother, Nonna, and my mother, Sofia,' Lucy made the introductions.

'Well, very nice to meet you, and have a wonderful evening.' He looked as though he was about to dart off, relieved to spot some new arrivals.

'And it's lovely to meet you too, *finally,*' said Nonna, the old lady giving a warm, yet discerning, smile that managed to keep him grounded beside her. And she gave a knowing nod in Lucy's direction; in Nonna's eyes, inspection time of Lucy's new boyfriend was well overdue.

With the introductions now made, at least Lucy was able to breathe an initial sigh of relief. They all chatted politely for a while longer, along with Olly and his family, talking about the weather, Lucy's new venture, and how wonderful the horsebox looked since it had been converted. With plenty still to do, Lucy was soon excusing herself, ready to go and prepare her garlic pizza breads. Jack seemed relieved to be stepping away at that point too, glad to be getting back to familiar ground serving his cocktails.

He caught up with Lucy over at the horsebox, a few minutes later, with a roll of his eyes. 'Ah, I didn't know you were going to bring out the whole family tonight.' It sounded like a jokey quip, but his furrowed brow revealed some anxiety. With all the party preparations going on, she hadn't thought to warn him that her mother and grandmother would be there as well as her brother's gang. In fact, it hadn't crossed her mind that a 'warning' was needed. Family was such an integral part of Lucy's life.

Lucy didn't have time to dwell on this, as old friends and new then started to arrive in clusters, with plenty of laughter and chatter. Of course, almost all the villagers knew each other already, and they were soon making themselves acquainted with Lucy's family and friends. As the gathering grew, gifts arrived of yet more prosecco, Northumbrian ales, cakes, bakes and flowers, along with smiles and hugs.

Lucy enjoyed a glass of the zesty Limoncello Fizz, stepping out from her pizza station for a while to mingle with her guests as they arrived. She was clinging to the hope that Becky might be able to bury her hurts and would be turning up to join them, too. It was early evening yet, still plenty of time for her old friend to make an appearance. Lucy understood that this would be hard for Becky, seeing Lucy and Jack together socially as a couple. But surely it was time to let bygones be bygones? And fingers crossed, this was the time for them all to move on.

Apron on, and back at the vintage horsebox once again, ready to start topping her next round of pizzas, Lucy watched Jack work his way through the growing crowd, pouring yet more prosecco with a steady hand whilst making pleasant banter with the guests. He was always 'on it' when he was in his bartender role, whereas she could still feel quite shy in a large group.

She then saw him pause to stand with Nonna for a while, fetching her another Limoncello. Jack stood nodding amicably to start with whilst her grandmother had her serious face on. Hmm, Lucy had the feeling that Nonna was giving him the once-over, bless her. Hah, she could imagine him being grilled. Jack looked up, giving Lucy a frown, followed thankfully by a quick wink from his interrogation position. She really hoped Nonna wasn't giving him too much of a hard time, and she couldn't help but wince at the scenario. Nonna had never been known to mince her words.

❈

'So, young man?' Nonna's discerning grey eyes fixed on Jack's. 'I do hope you're going to look after our little Lucia in the way she deserves?'

Jack shifted on his feet. *Oh my word*, he was fully expecting the elderly lady to follow up with, *And are your intentions honourable?* The conversation had the air of Victorian era interrogation.

'She's had a particularly tough time lately, has Lucy,' Nonna continued, 'and she doesn't need any more messing about. Not like she's had with that louse of a Liam …' She shook her head sadly.

Jack wasn't quite sure how to counter this. 'Ah, well …' he floundered. Of course, he wouldn't want to hurt her. But what exactly did her grandmother want him to promise? It was very early days for the two of them, after all.

'Well, that's the trouble with you young men nowadays. No backbone … and you can't seem to commit to anything.'

Damn, was she some kind of a mind reader?

'Umm.' He'd suddenly lost his tongue along with his usual charming banter.

'*Lightweights.*' Nonna tested the word as though she didn't use it much, and then gave a nod, as if happy with it.

Jack felt his cheeks flush. 'I . . . I do think an awful lot of Lucy,' he said, quickly trying to backtrack and fill in the gap, to find the words that he really meant, as well as those that might soften the old lady's opinion of him.

Nonna gave a small, slightly wary smile, and then stared at him, taking his measure. 'Well, we'll see. We only want what's best for Lucy, that's all.' Her tone softened.

To Jack's relief, someone approached, taking a cocktail from his tray, and with that Nonna turned to talk to Lucy's brother; little Freddie then taking her hand, ready to lead her away to show her the 'spooo-ky' carved pumpkins.

✹

A short while later, yet more family arrived with Lucy's dad turning up with partner Jo. Lucy smiled. It was good to see him there, as he hadn't been at all keen on her giving up her secure job at the accountant's office, and he was still somewhat cautious about her new venture.

Taking a slice of freshly cooked margherita pizza, he bit into it. 'Hey, this is really good.'

'Of course it is, don't sound so surprised,' Lucy replied with a small grin. 'It's made just like Papa's.'

Her dad's face softened; he'd always been fond of Papa and Nonna. 'So it's going alright then, is it? Your business? You're making a go of it?'

'Well, I'm giving it my best shot, and yeah, it's broken even so far … with more bookings coming in now too. I'm definitely starting to build a name for myself.'

'Yes, I saw that clip in the local press … and it looks great, the horsebox, all painted and all set up. I wish you every success.' He raised his beer bottle as a toast.

'Thanks, Dad. That means a lot.'

'Yes love, and I hope you do really well,' Jo chipped in with a smile. 'It looks gorgeous, the pizza horsebox, really unique.'

'Thank you.' Their support, even if it had come a little late, meant the world.

'Hey, I only want what's best for you, Luce. That's all any father wants.'

She nodded, suddenly feeling a little emotional. 'Right, well, I'd better get back to it. Party to host, more pizzas to bake, and all that …'

As dusk began to settle, the fairy lights on All Fired Up and Ruby's golden-globe bulbs began to twinkle like festive stars against the darkening deep-grey and fading peach tones of the October evening. Music spilled out from a speaker that Lucy had rigged up outside: a mix of easy listening current pop, with a bit of 80s soft rock thrown in for good measure. She stoked the logs that were molten orange in her stone bake oven, ready to bake another round of pizzas. And, looking out and seeing her friends, the villagers and her family, all together in this place that she now called home, hearing their chatter and laughter, seeing children playing – oh, and Helen and Sarah from the Book Club now swaying – it gave her the happiest of glows.

❄

Jack looked across from Ruby's countertop where he was pouring more cocktails which seemed to be going down a treat. It had been a bit full on meeting the extended family like that, and even Lucy's dad had turned up, which had caught him unawares. But he conceded it was lovely to see Lucy looking so happy. Her deep-brown eyes were all a-sparkle and her gorgeous smile widened as yet more people arrived. In fact, how many people *had* she asked along this evening? They were still arriving in their droves. Luckily, Ruby – aka The Cocktail Campervan – was loaded up with plenty of prosecco, his gift to Lucy for this evening – but blimey, he didn't think he even had that many friends. It looked like half the village was here.

Ah … that was it. Lucy really *had* invited half the village. He remembered her saying something about dropping invites into the street doors. Oh well, this was certainly a great way to say hello to her new community, and to say the big thank-you she had wanted to all those who had helped in establishing All Fired Up.

Jack felt so proud of her; leaving her steady job and

taking this plunge into the unknown, and thankfully, *his* world of mobile catering. If she hadn't taken that leap they might never have met. But now, unbelievably, this gorgeous woman was now *with him*. Mind you, he had been given the low-down by her grandmother just before, hadn't he! Nonna's words were still ringing in his ears, settling into his soul … He just hoped he could step up to the mark.

※

'Need a hand here, boss?' Abby stepped forward with a sunny smile, prosecco glass in hand. 'Happy to help, as always.'

'Oh, but you're not here to work today, Abby. Tonight's about me thanking you all. And anyway, isn't your Callum coming along soon too? You don't want to be tied up cooking pizza all evening.'

Callum was Abby's new flame. They'd met – rather hilariously – when he was the bottom half of a cow, in fancy dress, at one of the events Lucy had been booked for in the summer, and things had been 'moo-ving' on very well for the pair ever since.

'Yeah, he'll be here in a while, but he'll be fine. He knows a few of my mates from the village, anyhow.'

'But you're meant to be here to enjoy the party.'

'I *am* enjoying the party … but you can't take it all on, Lucy. You're supposed to be having some fun too. Anyhow, I'll enjoy it just as much, topping pizza bases here in the horsebox for a while, as long as I have a glass of fizz and you by my side. I can catch up with Cal later. We're bound to be here dancing and drinking 'til the early hours, after all.'

'You sure?' Lucy had prepped as much as she could earlier, but lots of the pizza bases still needed hand-stretching and topping before going into the wood-fired oven to bake. They were working at a good rate, but they still needed to feed the ever-growing gathering.

'Yeah, 'course. Come on, give us an apron. We can people watch and catch up on the gossip.' Abby was insistent.

'Well, thank you, my lovely. That'd be brilliant.'

'Oh, and my little sis Freya is here too. When this next lot of pizzas are ready, we can rope her in to do the rounds, offering them out. I've already told her that's her job.'

'Aw, thanks.'

'Yeah, she's hoping to get some work as a waitress, so it'll be good experience for her,' Abby grinned. 'So, Team Pizza are go!'

With that, brother Olly, who'd been listening in, rolled up to the horsebox counter. 'Hey, I'll take an apron too. Don't forget I'm your No. 1 Pizza Topper.'

'Hah, he helped me *once*, Abby.' Lucy rolled her eyes and laughed.

'Yes, and you did say I was a super sauce spreader.'

'Hey, I was just buttering you up to keep you onside for the night, Bro.'

'Now she tells me. Anyway, let me help … I have an ulterior motive.'

'And what might that be?'

'I'm bloody starving … Alice wouldn't let me snack before we left, so this is supper. I'm relying on you, Sis.'

Lucy gave a grin, and they continued to banter like pros. A sibling tennis game of words they'd kept up since the two of them had learned how to talk.

'Okay, perch yourself next to Abby. We also need some more garlic pizzas, folks, so the dough balls are ready to stretch and there's a big tub of herby garlic butter all made up. Pop an extra drizzle of olive oil over them too, and afterwards we'll sprinkle on some chopped fresh parsley and rosemary.'

So, with her helpers on hand at the topping station, and the oven up to temperature, they were ready to crank up the pizza party magic.

❄

A short while later, Lucy spotted Nonna seemingly getting on well with Glynis from the Driftwood's Book Club. They were stood just a few metres from the pizza oven, no doubt benefiting from the warmth it was throwing out. The creases around their eyes as they chatted showed a wealth of years and experience between them.

Lucy caught snippets of the conversation drifting over on the evening breeze. A mention of 'Papa', accompanied by exaggerated pointing at the signage on the side of the pizza horsebox. Nonna most likely sharing her Geordie/Italian history, regaling Glynis with tales of Papa's family's restaurant all those years ago, down on the Newcastle Quayside.

And then came Nonna's voice, loud and clear: 'Oh yes, he was a real Italian stallion, my Antonio!'

Abby looked up from the horsebox counter with a

huge grin, as Olly spluttered out a cough. A few of the nearby guests turned to stare at the old lady in amused surprise.

'Oh, my goodness,' Lucy muttered under her breath. That was far too much information. She could feel the colour rising in her cheeks, and it wasn't just from the heat from the pizza oven. Crikey, Nonna had definitely been enjoying far too much of that Limoncello Fizz that Jack had been serving out!

Glynis, however, seemed totally unfazed by the comment, letting out a raucous giggle. 'Well, lucky you!'

❄

The celebrations rolled on. Friends and family chatted, danced in the little courtyard of the cottage, tucked into some delicious food and sipped their cocktails. But as the time ticked away, Lucy couldn't help but feel a little anxious, still looking out for Becky. It was now past nine o'clock and she still hadn't arrived. The strand of hope of her turning up was thinning with every passing minute.

As ten o'clock came and went, with several guests starting their merry walk or taxi drive home and Nonna safely whisked away with Mum (smiling broadly and waving out of the car window), it became heart-wrenchingly obvious to Lucy that Becky was going to be a 'no-show'.

There hadn't even been a message from her close friend; no *Sorry, I couldn't make it*, no last-minute explanation of a crisis. The only thing in crisis seemed to be their friendship, and that gave Lucy a sad, dragging feeling in the pit of her stomach. She couldn't work it out, this really wasn't like Becky at all.

There had to be more to it. And Lucy was determined to find out what.

Lucy fired off a short text:

Sorry you couldn't make it this evening.
Hope everything is okay. L x

She had to try …

❄

'Well, that went off well, didn't it?'

It was after midnight with just Jack and Lucy left, tidying up.

'Yeah … really well.'

The smallest hint of disappointment came through in Lucy's tone.

'You must be tired. Listen, we can finish clearing up in the morning. I'll put these glasses back in their boxes and pop them in Ruby. I'll take them back to dishwash at Matt's like I usually do after events. No need to do them now.'

'You sure?'

'Absolutely. It's been a long day. Hey, is it okay to stay?' Jack asked softly.

'Of course, I kind of hoped you would.'

'Well, I haven't had much to drink, so I could still drive; I've been far too busy serving.'

'No, stay. I'd like that.' Lucy was tired for sure, but she wanted him close. For some reason, after the buzz of the party, she was left feeling a little vulnerable. Maybe she was overtired after such a long and hectic day, even if it had worked out brilliantly.

'Your friend never showed then?' Jack said, intuitively grasping the situation.

Lucy marvelled at how in tune they could be.

'Ah, no ... I'll speak with her tomorrow, I'm sure, find out what's going on.'

Jack stopped his clearing up, put down the glass he was holding, and gently took her hand. 'Look, I'm sorry if it's anything to do with me. How I was back then ... I'd never have wanted to make things difficult for you.'

'It's okay, it can't still be about you, not really. That was all years ago. She's stubborn, but honestly, there's got to be more to it than that. I just need to get her to open up a bit.'

'Yeah, I hope it sorts itself out soon. Hey, how about I make us up a nightcap? What do you fancy? Espresso Martini? Baileys on ice?'

'Hmmm ... Just a cup of tea would be perfect.'

'Hah, you sound like Nonna,' Jack grinned.

'No way, Nonna would still be in the Limoncello Fizz if she had half a chance.'

'Hah, you're probably right. You saw I had the Nonna showdown?' He pulled a grimace.

'Yeah, I guessed so,' Lucy winced. 'She had her serious face on. I used to get that look when I'd been a bit naughty as a kid.'

'Hah, it was a bit awkward. But it's obvious she cares about you, Luce. And hey,' he took a breath and looked right into her eyes, 'so do I.'

Lucy felt herself melt a little.

'Come on, let's just sit a while.' Jack's voice was gentle. 'It's a gorgeous night.'

Lucy looked up. In her rush to be the hostess with the mostest, she hadn't quite registered all the stars that had come out and were glittering right above them, as well as the luminescent arc of a crescent moon.

'I think I'll have a little tot of whisky myself, and I'll go fetch you that cup of tea.'

Daisy gave a small bark.

'Okay, can't be missing you out, I suppose … and a dog biscuit for you.'

Her thin black tail started wagging happily.

'Sorted, then. Sit down, and I'll fetch you that throw you put out earlier. We can snuggle up on the two-seater bench!'

'Now that sounds like my kind of nightcap,' Lucy smiled.

And they sat under a starlit sky, talking away, with Lucy's head leaning against Jack's supportive shoulder, Daisy tucked under the blanket with them, until Lucy began to nod off.

Jack looked down at her head nestled against him, those glossy dark waves. 'Hey, time for bed, sleepy head.'

There was no answer. So, he shifted position, slowly got up, and carried her up the cottage stairs in his arms, Daisy skipping along after them. After carefully taking off Lucy's shoes and jeans, which caused her to stir just a little, he tucked his sleepy girlfriend in. Then, weirdly, he even found himself pulling the little step contraption up close to the bedside ready for the Dachshund, muttering to himself, 'Can't believe I'm doing this for you, devil dog.'

Jack undressed and snuck in under the crisp white

covers himself, breathing in the gorgeous warm floral (if slightly pizza-toned) scent of his rather fabulous new girlfriend. Daisy twirled in a circle, settled, then let out a contented doggie sigh, and they all cosied up for the night.

Lucy stirred momentarily. 'Hmm, shame Becky didn't make it …' In the dark, the words trailed along with her disappointment. It was the only thing that had felt wrong with the night for her. And it had cast a shadow over Lucy's happiness.

Jack stroked her hair gently, then placed a tender-sleepy kiss on her forehead. 'It'll all sort itself out, somehow.'

Lucy closed her eyes. *He was right, of course he was.* It all sounded so easy, put like that.

But … as she drifted back off to sleep, the thought lingered … what if it didn't?

Chapter Six

The next morning arrived bright and fresh and Lucy sat in the courtyard garden of the cottage, wrapped up in a cosy cable-knit jumper, jeans and boots, with a hot mug of tea to hand. An empty prosecco bottle was lurking in the flower bed, a sign of the party last night, and Jack had now gone back to his lodgings. She took a slow breath and took out her mobile, scrolling down to Becky's name … and dialled. It rang, and then rang some more. No answer. The inane voice of the mobile phone company's answerphone clicking in. *Oh.*

Had her friend heard it ringing? Was she in the middle of something? Was she determined not to speak to Lucy? Lucy gave a troubled sigh. She had witnessed Becky's stubborn streak over the years, it was part of who she was. It meant she was a fighter, she stood up for what she believed in, and she'd stood up for Lucy many a time … in the playground, in night clubs, and pulling her out of her despair when her ex, Liam, did the dirty on her. It was a quality she usually loved about Becky – but now the weapon was being wielded against her.

✳

Lucy pursed her lips and dialled again, determinedly. One ring, two rings, three … She was holding her breath, wondering whether to call off, when … on the fourth ring, there was a click.

'Hel-lo.' Becky's voice at the other end of the line sounded cool, but at least she had answered.

'Hey-y, Becks,' the relief in Lucy's voice gave itself away with a tremor. 'How are you?'

'Yeah, I'm okay. You?' Her friend's tone was guarded. Lucy felt like she was walking on thin ice, one false step and … 'Look, please don't tell me you're still with him?' There they were, at the crux of the matter straight away. Well, that was good, Lucy conceded. There were things that needed to be said. They both needed to be honest with each other.

'Yes, I am. But, Becks, please hear me out …'

'Okay, you have one minute to justify why on earth you are still with that cheating little git of a player … when you know he's not trustworthy. You know how much he hurt me.'

The bitterness was still there, even though Jack and Becky's fleeting 'romance', fling if you like, was over nine years ago. Oh yes, frustratingly, that girl, like the proverbial elephant, certainly didn't forget, and definitely hadn't forgiven. But there had to be more to it than that, surely?

'Look, he's changed, Becks. Jack is not the guy you met

back then. His brother had just died when it all unravelled, he was going through a bad patch back then …'

'Luce, you've told me all this before,' Becky cut her off. 'This isn't news. Guys like Jack Anderson *do not* change. They use people, they're players, and they can charm the birds from the bloody trees. I can't stand back and just let this happen. Can't see you get hurt all over again. And I can't believe *you*, of all people, are being so bloody naïve.'

'Just give him a chance. Give *us* a chance, Becks, please?' Lucy paused, feeling her throat tightening with emotion. 'He means a lot to me.'

'Hah, another one he's managed to pull the wool over their eyes. Lucy, I can't stand by and say nothing. And if you're not listening to me, I can't pretend it's all fine between us … when it's not.'

'Look, why don't we meet up for a coffee? Chat this over, like we always have done when we've had a problem?' Lucy pleaded.

'Why don't you call me when you've seen sense, when you've dropped him? I'll be there for you then,' Becky retorted, her tone determined with a steely note to it.

'Becky …' was all Lucy could say, as she felt her heart nosedive. She couldn't leave Jack when everything she felt was telling her that he was the best thing that had happened to her in a very long time. That what they had already was special. She *had* to give him, *them*, this chance. 'I can't give him up, not now.'

A second or two of awkward silence followed. 'I've got to go … Bye then, Luce. You take care.'

'Bye …' Lucy's voice trailed, dismally. She didn't know what else she could say.

Lucy stared into space, the bricks of the garden wall blurring slightly before her. She gave a sniff. Daisy trotted over, rubbing her smooth black-and-tan fur against Lucy's ankles and looking up at her with deep-brown eyes, as if to comfort her. Lucy lifted the little dog carefully into her lap.

'Oh, Daisy. What's for the best? What am I going to do?'

Just when she'd thought she'd found a love worth waiting for, this was the flipside. Lucy felt torn, but there was no way she was going to give up on Jack. *But*, she sighed, could there be a grain of truth to what Becky was saying … was Jack the sort to give up on her?

❄

Come along to

The Warkton-by-the-Sea Autumn Food Festival

Saturday 30th October

From 12 noon

Fabulous food, arts and crafts, live music

Fun for all the family!

Free Entry

❄

Chapter Seven

As much as her failing friendship hurt, Lucy knew she had to keep going, moving forwards with her new business and her life. The following week rolled on, and it was now only two days' time until the Warkton-by-the-Sea Autumn Food Festival – a coastal celebration of all things Northumberland. Being her first year with the pizza horsebox, this was a new event and experience for her. Her emotions were a mix of anticipation sprinkled with fear – of messing up, not having enough stock, or some suchlike. A while back, Jack had given her the nod about it being well attended and was going to be there with his Cocktail Campervan. That gave her a little frisson of excitement, too.

First things first, she needed to make enough dough for *one hundred* pizza bases, no mean feat, with the special 00 flour just like her Papa used to use, and the dough would then need a couple of days to prove. Hopefully, that amount would provide enough pizzas to last the day. It was always hard to gauge with these kinds of events; she couldn't afford to waste too much, but equally she didn't want to run short. With it being held on a Saturday and a reasonable weather forecast, she was hoping it would be busy.

Organisation was key. She'd need to decide which flavours to concentrate on and then she'd source her fresh toppings. Her most popular being her tasty tomato margherita with mini mozzarella balls, a spicy nduja Italian sausage, local goat's cheese and rocket, and Northumbrian ham and mushrooms. Hmm, perhaps something with prawns might work well too, she mused, with it being a seaside festival. Locally caught prawns with peppers and olives, perhaps – Northumberland with a Mediterranean twist. She'd make some garlic bread pizzas too; her melted mozzarella, garlic and fresh rosemary speciality was a belter.

Lucy was humming away with the radio on in the background as she measured out the flour, salt, yeast and water. She'd invested in an industrial-sized mixer, which had to be kept in the spare room when not in use, as it took up so much space in her little kitchen. Soon she was kneading, then rolling up the large dough balls ready to prove, using the same recipe that Papa had shown her all those years ago when she was a little girl. Papa – which actually meant 'father', not 'grandfather', but had stuck nonetheless – had passed away several years ago now, bless, but she still smiled as she thought of him. Lucy loved her scrummy childhood pizza suppers, sat around her grandparents' old wooden table with brother Olly, munching on the tastiest pizza slices ever. Aw, how she wished Papa could have seen her take this new direction, striving for her dream inspired by his love of good food, good ingredients and his family. That strong sense of love that always came through in his cooking.

As Lucy rolled and kneaded yet more dough balls, her thoughts turned to Nonna and all those years she'd had to spend alone since, left on her own. How she must have missed him. They'd had such a happy marriage. Yes, they had bickered, but it was always good-humoured; Nonna flicking her tea-towel at Papa when his teasing got too much. They were a team; even to little girl Lucy that much was obvious.

But you never knew where life would take you, the twists and turns of the road ahead, each one of our journeys different. When you found that special someone, you couldn't let them go … not unless they were taken from you, like Papa, like Jack's brother, Daniel. Her mind stayed firm. She wouldn't give up on Jack, whatever Becky might think. No-one said it would be easy, falling … being in love, and she really didn't know how their particular journey as a couple might yet pan out – they were only just starting out, after all. But what she did know was that it was absolutely worth fighting for.

❄

Saturday morning, 6 a.m., and Lucy's phone alarm sprang to life. It was still dark outside, but she leaped out of bed, ready to head down and make all those last preparations – chopping her topping ingredients, packing up the cool bags, the kiln-fired logs, and loading the horsebox.

Three hours seemed to fly by, and with trusted assistant

Abby by her side, she set off along the country lanes with All Fired Up in tow, winding down the coast to the village of Warkton.

'Ready to "dough" this, boss?' Abby asked.

'Ooh, it's too early for such "punny" jokes, Abs, but yes, absolutely!'

A sense of expectation and animation filled Lucy as the row of old stone cottages and the shops of the quaint main street appeared before them, leading down to the harbour and sea. Bunting flags in yellow and red – the colours of the Northumberland flag – criss-crossed above them as they drove down the cobbled street, and fluttered in the late autumn breeze.

Turning up past the little harbour, Lucy could see several stalls were already setting up. They pulled into the grassy field that had been designated as the main festival location. It was a hive of activity, with catering vans and trailers of all kinds, from farm shops with sausages and pies, to coffee stands, puddings, ice creams and cheeses from the local dairy, a bakery, and even a delightful-looking chocolate stall (scrummy!). And there she was: the gleaming deep red of VW Ruby. The two girls smiled as Jack gave them a welcoming wave.

As they pulled into a space towards the top of the field, indicated by a marshal in high-viz, the view out across the harbour and bay was stunning. It was a cloudy day, but that only made the mix of slatey-sea greys, greens and blues stand out more. The harbour down below them was small and rectangular, with just a few fishing boats bobbing within the shelter of its ancient walls.

This had been a thriving fishing community in the past, with Warkton-by-the-Sea becoming known as one of the kipper capitals of England. Over a hundred years ago, the North Sea was teeming with herring. At certain times of the year, the little village would welcome the Scottish fishwives, and twenty or more boats would go out daily to fetch their catch. The seas could be perilous at times. Today, beyond the harbour's stone boundary, the waters merely rocked and rolled in fluid peaks and troughs. The odd seabird bobbing up and down, happily riding the swell.

Today it wasn't quite kippers, but at least pizzas were on the menu. Cooking them in the wood-fired oven was an art and with, hopefully, many orders coming in at once, time-consuming. With big functions and festivals like this one, Lucy didn't get much chance to chat with her customers whilst she cooked, as taking an eye off the ball often meant a burnt pizza, but having Abby was a godsend. The teenager was very much finding her feet with All Fired Up after just a couple of months of helping out. She was good with the chitchat and taking orders, as well as creating the tasty toppings with just the right amount of tomato sauce and cheese. The two of them worked well together.

Lucy proceeded to light the oven and, leaving Abby to keep an eye on things at the horsebox, went off in search of a couple of coffees to keep them going, intending also to take the opportunity of saying a quick hello to Jack before things became more hectic. Wandering past the various stalls, although it was only late October, there was already a Christmassy feel to the festival. Strands of red, silver and gold tinsel wafted in the sea breeze at one stall, catching the light. And the craft stands were very much in festive mode, with gifts galore on display, cute wooden toys, baubles and cards, and gorgeous appliquéd Christmas stockings.

Lucy decided she'd better give All Fired Up a touch of festive magic too, and bought a few strands of silver tinsel to drape around the serving hatch. After all, with the shift of the seasons and the darkening autumn skies, she figured everyone needed a little sparkle, cosiness and fun to look forward to.

And there, stood in front of his bulb-lit halo of campervan light was sandy-haired Jack, giving her a warm smile from behind the chrome countertop of Ruby as he set out his glasses, spirits, and cocktail shakers. Oh yes, she was looking forward to some cosy nights in with this gorgeous man over the coming weeks. How would Christmas feel being back in a relationship this year, she mused?

Crikey, the last couple of Christmases spent with ex Liam had been rather dire affairs. Both pretending that everything was fine. That the perfume and presents made up for a lack of closeness. The cracks, had she been looking, were already so apparent. The engagement ring she was wearing, and the house they still shared, the only glue that was left.

And Christmases past, years ago back when Mum and Dad were still together. That fizzy excitement of childhood. The anticipation of the Advent calendar. School plays and party days. The ripping open of gifts on Christmas morning. All that festive magic.

But then, of course, Mum had ended up on her own. Gosh, that must be over seventeen years now, and well … everything changed. Life rolled on and moved in waves, like the sea. A constant flow, sometimes up, often down, sometimes choppy. You couldn't always stay on the crest of a wave. But, while things were going well, right here, right now, she was determined to enjoy them.

'Hey.' Jack beamed, his slate-blue eyes sparkling at her.

'Hi. It's looking good here,' Lucy commented. And it wasn't just the gleaming VW Ruby that was all set up beautifully. Jack was looking rather dapper in a crisp white shirt, tweed waistcoat and dark jeans, teamed with his black Cocktail Campervan logo apron.

'Cheers. Yeah, I went for a "smart with a touch of festive" feel.' There was indeed a bunch of classy coffee-and-cream-coloured baubles sat at each end of the counter top, placed artfully alongside a sprig of real holly and pine. 'Ready for a busy day?'

'Yeah, hoping so.'

'Well, the food festival was really well attended here last year. It must be getting quite a name for itself by now, so I'm sure it'll be a great day.'

'Fingers crossed.' Whilst business was doing pretty well, Lucy still had her start-up loans to pay off and Abby's wages to find, as well as funding all her own living expenses. Finances had been tight for a while, and she had the cottage and its mortgage to keep up. 'Well, I'd better finish getting set up. Catch you later.'

'Yeah, me too. Looking forward to that catch-up,' Jack said, and he gave a cheeky wink.

Lucy couldn't help but grin. They hadn't seen each other for a few days now, and her body was already missing his touch.

As she headed over to the coffee van, Lucy spotted a

fabulous stall piled high with cocoa delights; little foil boxes and bags sealed with curls of colourful string, filled with truffles and fudge. Oh, yes, it was The Chocolate Shop by the Sea's stall. She recognised the wonderful handmade chocolates that Jack had bought her back in the summer. Lucy couldn't resist going over to take a look.

'Hello, there,' said the auburn-haired lady behind the trestle-table, giving a warm smile. 'Was it your pizza horsebox I spotted coming in earlier? It looks gorgeous – love the grey paintwork. Is it vintage? Oh, I'm Emma, by the way. I don't think I've seen you around before, have I?'

'Hi, Emma. I'm Lucy. And no, I'm actually pretty new to all this. Just started the pizza business back in May.'

'Ah, I see, fresh on the scene!'

'I'm a … a friend of Jack's,' Lucy continued, 'the Cocktail Campervan guy. Oh, and your chocolates, I had some a while back, they were amazing.'

'Aw, thanks. So, how're things going for you?'

'Great, yeah. Finding my feet. It's all starting to come together, I think.'

'That's good to hear.'

The catering community that Lucy had met so far seemed to be supportive rather than competitive, which was lovely.

'And you?' Lucy asked politely.

'Never been busier. I have a shop and café here in the village, and our little mobile stalls are always abustle. So I can't complain. Well, only about not having enough hours in the day …' she grinned.

'That's brilliant.' It was nice to hear of other local

businesses doing well, and it gave Lucy hope for the future. Adding to the grain of belief that she'd made the right decision six months ago when she gave up her steady accountancy office job. Of course, that belief needed to be teamed with a big pinch of hard work and a sprinkling of determination.

'Well, if you're looking for bookings, I've a tip for an event not too far away. It's a really gorgeous do, and held early December in the lead-up to Christmas: the Claverham Castle Christmas Fayre. Not to be missed.' She gave a broad smile. 'Here, I'll jot down the castle's number for you.' She quickly scrolled through her phone, wrote the number on the back of a business card, and handed it over. 'Give Ellie there a ring … check if there are any spaces left. You might just get in.'

'Oh, thanks so much.'

'I wouldn't leave it too long, mind you. They get booked up quickly. Oh, and mention my name if you like. We all remember what it's like being the newbie.'

'Aw, that's so kind. Thank you. And it's held in a castle, you say? That sounds cool.'

'It is. Yeah, it's a really pretty place, tucked away in the hills. It's not that far away.'

'Thanks. Claverham Castle,' she read aloud. 'Yeah, I think I've heard of it, but I've never been. Right, well, I suppose I'd better get back to the pizzas. Abby, my assistant, will be wondering what's happened to me … *and* her much-needed coffee.'

'Hah, yeah, it's a bit nippy this morning. Autumn's in the air.'

'It is for sure. Well, one thing I have in my favour,' Lucy grinned, 'the pizza oven'll warm me up nicely.'

'Lucky you!'

'Have a good day.'

'You too, my lovely.'

Lucy set off for the nearby coffee stall with a spring in her step. How nice it was to be welcomed so warmly as part of this newfound catering community. When she'd started out with her pizza venture, one tentative foot at a time, she hadn't realised there'd be a whole new gang to support her too. It was a very pleasant discovery.

❄

After a few hectic hours over lunchtime with the pizza production line at full blast, Lucy and Abby finally paused for breath, refreshing with a delicious glass of something cold and thirst-quenching served from The Cocktail Campervan. Jack appeared, forging his way through the food festival throng, with two cut-glass tumblers with a dark-pink liquid in each.

'Roll up, roll up for a Cranberry Crush. The first taster of my Christmas drinks selection. No alcohol in this one, naturally. Need to keep you two on your toes. No snoozing on the job, or any of that.'

'Ooh, that looks good, and just what I need. I'm parched.' Abby took a glass gratefully and gulped back a large swig. 'Bliss.'

He was apparently testing out his new festive-style mocktails, and wanted their opinion. Lucy had a feeling that he was also looking out for them too, after seeing how non-stop busy they'd been – oh yes, beneath that cocky barman veneer, she suspected he was a sweetie really.

'Yum, so what's in this one? Besides the obvious cranberry juice,' Lucy asked, after taking a zingy sip.

'So, there's the juice, a twist of lime, topped up with soda over crushed ice. And some fresh cranberries, blueberries, and mint to garnish.'

She gave a thumbs up. 'A bit like a Cosmopolitan then, a non-alcoholic festive fizz. I like it.' She took another sip, 'Mmm, very much.'

Jack grinned. 'The Cocktail Campervan at your service, ladies. And don't forget to spread the word …' He gave a wink. 'Better get back to it. Don't want to be missing out on any customers.'

'Thanks, and best of luck.'

'Cheers.'

❄

By the end of the festival day, Lucy found herself starting to get the festive feels. What with all this tinsel, the twinkling fairy lights coming out en masse from the various food stalls as the sky deepened towards a late-afternoon dusk, the winter-spiced drinks wafting by with woody-cinnamon scents, and customers clutching bags filled with gifts galore. And it made her think of family … and friends … bloody hell, she hoped she and Becky would be talking to each other by Christmas. The two of them often had a girlie shopping day together with a celebratory tipple or two at lunchtime. And there was *always* a festive and fun drinks night out along with their friend Katie. It was all part of the tradition – it wasn't one they could break, was it?

Christmas Day, these past few years, had been spent with her mum and Nonna over at Sofia's house in Rothbury. A family affair with Olly and Alice popping by, and last year, an overexcited Freddie tearing open his parcels like a whirlwind, leaving heaps of discarded wrappings as he dived into his new toys. Turkey dinner followed by mince pies, noisy games and laughter, with the backdrop of the old fake-fir Christmas tree that had seen many a year and better days, but they still wouldn't let Mum get rid of it. Plus, of course, a visit to her dad and his partner, Jo, on either Christmas Eve or Boxing Day, whichever fitted them best.

She glanced over to The Cocktail Campervan where Jack was winding down for the day as he served out the last of a jug of mulled wine, and she couldn't help but wonder what the landscape of Jack's Christmas might look like; realising that it would be a difficult day for his family. Losing a son, a brother, like that? How could you ever enjoy Christmas in the same way again? Her heart had broken for Jack when he'd told her all about his brother Daniel dying at just twenty years of age. A student on a football pitch, playing a game which both brothers loved, unaware of the dangerous heart condition that had hidden itself for so many years, but which cruelly stole his life in a matter of seconds. But somehow Jack's fractured family must have found a way forward through the years. It all must have been so difficult, though.

She sighed, feeling for them all. However messy her

own family had ended up being after her parents had split, it still managed to be joyful at Christmas time.

❄

That evening, after packing up at the festival and then dropping Abby home, Lucy cleared and cleaned the horsebox, finally collapsing on the sofa around eight o'clock with Daisy and a much-needed cuppa. Wow, it had been such a busy day, and profitable too, judging by the looks of the bulging cash tin and card receipts.

There was a rat-a-tat at the door, which caused Daisy to jump down off the sofa with a bark. It was Jack, bearing a bottle of red wine and a smile, ready to join Lucy at the cottage for a late supper.

Lucy got up, meeting him in the hallway. He was already in through the door.

'Hey, still okay to drop by?'

She still managed to melt every time he walked in … however tired she might be. His handsome face, dusty-blond hair with its slight wave, that little bit of stubble on his chin. Oh my, she'd got this thing bad.

'Of course. I've got an easy supper in mind. Hope that's alright?'

'Absolutely, I'm not expecting you to start cooking after a day like today.'

They were soon curled up and cosy with the bottle of red wine, and the coffee table laid out with a selection of fresh bread rolls from the bakery stall, local cheeses from the Doddington Dairy stand, plus some Northumbrian 'Italian-style' charcuterie. The two of them chilling out in front of the open fire, with Daisy's nose twitching at the delightful and tantalising smells wafting just above her.

Lucy let out a slow yawn.

'Tired?' Jack smiled at her, his hand reaching to brush away a strand of dark hair that had drifted down in front of her eyes.

'Yeah. I'm all pizza'ed out.' Lucy's feet were throbbing from the long hours stood by the pizza oven, and her arms were aching from constantly working the pizza paddle and stretching out dough balls.

'Went off well, though, didn't it? I did a storming trade with the campervan this afternoon. The punters couldn't get enough of my Toffee Apple Cocktails.'

'Ooh, you'll have to make me one of those. They sound delightful.'

'Autumn gold in a glass.' He grinned, slipping into his campervan barman patter.

'Scrumptious.'

'Well, I'm afraid you'll have to make do with this glass of Merlot for now, as all the ingredients are back at my digs. I've emptied out the van.'

'Ah, typical …' she said with mock indignation, then leaned back against him. 'It was a good day, though, yeah. So many people there … lunchtime was crazy busy. Me and Abby could hardly keep up.'

'Yeah, it was a good call.'

She gave a thumbs up. 'And what a setting. It felt kind of Christmassy too, didn't it? I loved that. Can't believe we're nearly at the end of October already.'

The year was indeed flying by. With the new business,

and this new relationship, there was so much to take on board, and much to be thankful for.

'So, what do you and your folks do for Christmas?' Lucy asked. The words came out before she had time to think.

'Ah … it's usually a pretty quiet affair. Just the three of us …' Jack gave a tight smile. 'Oh, and the biggest bloody turkey ever. I think Mum's been over-compensating for the past ten years. Me and Dad daren't say a thing. Stuck eating cold turkey for days … and then there's the vat of turkey soup.'

Lucy was worried that she'd spoilt the cosiness of the moment. 'Sorry …' She rubbed the back of his hand instinctively.

'What for?'

'Bringing that up … I should have realised Christmas wouldn't be easy for you … your family.'

'It's okay. We've had a long time to try and get used to it.'

'And do you … ever get used to it?' She held his gaze.

His slate-blue eyes seemed to hold that hurt. 'Nope. But I don't want to forget about him – about Daniel – either. Sometimes it's good to talk about him. Remember him. I don't want my brother to be forgotten.'

Lucy's heart seemed to squeeze. Just thinking of her own brother …

'Hah, yes, there was that one Christmas …' Jack launched into a memory. 'Yeah, we must have been young teenagers. Mum and Dad had gone off out … to the supermarket, I think it was, and we were home alone. It must have been about a week before Christmas.

'Well, our curiosity got the better of us. We knew their

gift hidey-hole – top shelf of their big bedroom wardrobe. So, there we were, perched in turns on a stool, rummaging through. Well, we found some stocking fillers and the pair of new trainers we'd asked for – ace, and the Xbox that was to share – brilliant, and a couple of games for it, a footie one and the newest *Call of Duty*, which we were bursting to try. Well, we had plenty of time, but we thought we'd better not push our luck.'

Lucy snuggled closer to Jack, enjoying the tale, picturing the two young lads up to mischief.

'Anyway, evidence all tidied up, chair back away in its place. And Mum and Dad came home none the wiser. And then came Christmas Day … and the big unwrapping. The Xbox, the trainers, selection boxes – you always need a selection box – footie game, bits and bobs … everything unwrapped, nothing left under the tree, but no *Call of Duty*.

'Dan and I were giving each other quizzical looks. Big thanks, hugs, quiet chat between me and Dan about how it might be being kept back for later, like an extra "surprise". Well, we were about fit to bursting by the end of Boxing Day. We daren't say anything, of course, or they'd know we'd been snooping. And yes, though we no longer believed in good old Father Christmas, the last thing we wanted to do was jeopardise our future Christmas presents.'

Lucy couldn't help but smile, as the story rolled on. She and Olly had had some capers in their time, too.

'Well, in the end, we had to wait until my birthday at the end of February. That was when it finally came to light. Hilarious. Mum must have forgotten about it, and then found it again. Hah, she couldn't work out why we kept giggling when I opened it. Do you know, I don't think I've ever told her to this day … Hah, the stuff of legends. It might be high time I shared that memory … this Christmas time. Mum would love it.'

'Aw, that's so funny. You two must have been a right handful.'

'We were pretty good, actually … most of the time.' Jack gave a cheeky grin, which then dipped a little.

Lucy felt for him. When someone you loved died so young, it must shake up your whole life. Unsettle everything. There was a whole deeper side to Jack that she had yet to get to know. That was, if he'd let her …

Talking of loss made her yearn for physical contact. To be close to him. She propped her feet up against the coffee table, with its now-depleted nibbles, and snuggled up. 'Ah, can't wait for a rest, and a lie-in tomorrow. That'll be bliss. It's been a long day.'

'Yeah, I'm pretty bushed too. Ready to turn in, myself.' Jack smooched a little closer, his thigh leaning against hers; a sensual hint of things to come.

Hmm, bed-time was calling, and perhaps she wasn't *that* tired after all …

❄

Later, Jack's breathing had slowed to the rhythmic hum of sleep, whilst Lucy lay awake wrapped in his arms, her body still tingling from his caresses. This with Jack, it felt so beautiful, so powerful, and yet something scared her about the depth of her feelings. Was it almost too good to be true? With this evening's poignant conversation and the echo of

Daniel's death in her thoughts, she pondered about how life could change in an instant.

Yes, they were so very in sync in bed, but was it more about the physical for Jack than the long term? A flurry of questions were left milling in her head, like the glittery flakes in a snow globe. Where *would* life fall for her and Jack?

Chapter Eight

Two weeks later, and Lucy was winding her way back from Alnwick, where she'd called for supplies from the local butcher and farm shop. She needed to stock up ready for a market day stall event the next day. Plus – and she was excited and a little nervous about this – the Winter Wedding event she was booked to do this coming weekend. She had to pass Jack's village on the way home and so, on a bit of a whim, she decided to loop off the main road and do a drive-by, just to see if Ruby was parked up outside. After all, it would be an ideal chance to call in and say 'hi'.

Jack lodged with an old friend, Matt, whom Lucy had met once or twice. He was a really nice guy who worked as a vet locally. She'd even taken Daisy in for a visit to the surgery when her pooch had had a bit of an upset stomach that didn't settle – much to Daisy's disapproval, being poked and prodded like that, and then having to take that foul medication and fasting, all very undignified. Anyway,

Matt was lovely with her and the Dachshund, and his medicine did the trick.

Lucy turned the corner to see the row of semi-detached houses of Jack's street, and yes, there was Ruby, parked up and gleaming in the morning sunshine. Jack had obviously been giving her a good clean and a buff; he liked to keep her sparkling and ready for action. Lucy pulled up at the roadside, and with a spring to her step, headed for the front door, giving the bell a hopeful ring. Even with Ruby here, there was still a chance Jack might be off out cycling or doing something sporty. However, the door opened and there he was, dressed casually in knee-length khaki shorts and a white T-shirt.

'Hey, did anyone not tell you it's now November ... in Northumberland?'

'Hi there ... and no, I'm living in some tropical clime radiator zone. Jess likes the heating up high, as in sauna level.' Jack's smile was warm. 'Good to see you, I know it's been a few days.' His eyebrows were also raised a little in surprise.

'Yeah, I was just passing by after popping to Alnwick. Thought I'd come and say hi.'

'Well, that's nice.'

And he gave her a smacker of a kiss, right there on the doorstep, which left her with a tingly frisson of surprise. 'I did wonder if you might be off out jogging or cycling or something?'

'Nah, not today. Trying to catch up on some good old admin on the computer. Accounts stuff, and I need to apply for the next round of licences for events. All fun ...' He pulled a grimace, as if that was actually the last thing he wanted to be doing. 'Needs must, and all that. Coffee?'

'Well, only if I'm not interrupting?'

'It's fine. I could do with a little interrupting, to be honest … break the monotony of the Excel spreadsheet and the council website.' He gave a cheeky smile.

'Okay then, coffee sounds good.'

They headed through to the kitchen where Jack had evidently been working; his laptop lay open on the table, alongside a used coffee mug, pad, pen and his mobile phone.

'No Matt at home?' Lucy asked; the house seemed really quiet.

Jack was still renting the spare double room. But he had mentioned of late that it was at times a little *too* cosy with Matt's fiancée, Jess, staying over more often than not nowadays. Three's a crowd and all that. So, if the two of them wanted to spend a night together, Jack tended to stay over at Lucy's cottage, giving both couples a little privacy and saving them from the slightly awkward foursome situation in the kitchen in the mornings.

'Nah, he's off out with Jess … they're looking at wedding venues. He's on the final countdown now. Well, more like a two-year warning. They have to book soon, or they'll not get anywhere decent, or so he's been told.' Jack rolled his eyes. 'I think Matt'd be as happy with a bash and a few beers at the local rugby club. But that's not going to do for Jess, no way.'

'Ah, right …' A weird pang stirred within her. Hmm, Lucy wasn't even sure if it was a pang, or more a shard of memory hitting awkwardly, as an image came to mind of looking online at reception venues herself … the year that Liam proposed, and the year after, and the one after that … it had never, somehow, been the right time to take anything forward, in Liam's eyes. His spiel being that they needed to save up for the house together, the new car, new sofa, foreign holiday, pensions. All those things were higher up the list compared to their actual relationship. That should have been warning enough for her, really … but she'd been so damn naïve back then. Anyway, that was all in the past. And thank God for that.

As Jack turned to fill the kettle, Lucy took a seat at the kitchen table. Scanning the room, she tried to pick up on any vibes of Jack's day-to-day life here – white units with a mottled-grey Formica top, practical and not untidy, with just one mug sat on the drainer that read 'Yoda Best Vet' with a picture of the *Star Wars* character on it, evidently Matt's. It didn't give much of Jack away at all, seeming more of a base for the two lads than a homely spot. The table where he'd been working seemed slightly more personal with his ballpoint pen, a notepad with a few handwritten dates of upcoming events bordered by some arty doodles – a campervan, clouds, a curl of a wave, or so it appeared, amongst various squirls – with his iPhone to hand. Lucy's eyes were then drawn to what was currently on the laptop screen, a gorgeous view of mountains and blue skies … first she thought it was his screensaver, a view like that would be a typical screen image for Jack. But then she realised it was a website page. Her gaze snagged on the tag line over the picture: 'Backpacking in New Zealand – adventures of a lifetime.'

What?

Jack stood scooping instant coffee into cups, as Lucy's heart took a nosedive. *Was he thinking of going away?* Upping sticks halfway across the world. Heading off on some new travels again? Yes, he was an adventurer, a free spirit, that was part of who he was, and she had to admit, part of what made him so unique, attractive. She knew he'd loved going travelling in the past, spending several years away from the UK. Was he thinking of heading off again? And why had he not said a word to her, his girlfriend? Her mind was whirring, like the swirl of coffee in the mug he was passing to her. She didn't know what to think, let alone say … so said nothing.

'Hope instant's okay? Sorry, we're all out of the good stuff,' Jack's voice broke in.

'Ah, yeah, fine.' Her calm tone surprised her. She took a sip, far too soon, and scalded her lip. Dammit.

Just when was he planning on telling her about this? Her mind was still on spin mode.

And there *she* had been, planning to get to know him more. Looking forward to Christmas together, New Year, and so much more. Well, by the looks of it, they might just about get this Christmas in as a couple, but then what?

'So, what were you up to in Alnwick?'

'Ah, just getting a few supplies in, ready for my market slot, and stocking up for the Winter Wedding bash this coming weekend.' She managed to get the words out, her mind still whirring.

'Yeah, that should be a real nice event. Me and Ruby are booked in at that too, of course.'

'Yeah, the couple sounded great over the phone. It's Warkworth way, isn't it? At her parents' place. The house overlooks the sea, apparently.' She found herself wittering on, a cover for her frenzied thoughts. 'I haven't seen it as yet, as the two of them called at my cottage to discuss the booking, wanting to take a look at the horsebox. It sounds as though it'll be lovely, though.'

'Yeah, it's an amazing spot. Real lord of the manor stuff, with a stunning sea view. Such a cool location. I met them there to talk about the drinks options.'

'Ah, sounds great.' She felt a little twist of anxiety about the event; she so wanted to make sure it all went off brilliantly for them. A wedding was such a special day.

She then saw Jack's eyes catch on the open computer. He swiftly closed the backpacking page and after a couple of quick clicks, shut down the lid. He didn't say a word.

Should she ask him about New Zealand right now, or at least before she left? Find out if there was anything to this? He might just have been browsing, after all. But then, it'd mean admitting she'd been snooping at his computer. And might her quizzing end up sounding a bit possessive, controlling? She felt like she'd been punched in the gut, but didn't know how to react next. Oh goodness, might Becky be right about him after all? Was Jack, the wanderer, about to make his exit?

❄

You are invited to

the Winter Wedding of

Benjamin Hamilton and Sarah Gregory

At East Grange, Warkworth, Northumberland

At one o'clock in the afternoon

Saturday 13th November

Reception to follow

❄

Chapter Nine

Sparkling flute glasses caught the sunlight lined up on Ruby's chrome countertop as Jack concentrated on putting the finishing touches to his tableau of Classic Champagne Cocktails – adding chilled fizz to the drinks made with angostura bitters, cognac and a sugar cube. Oh yes, champagne and cocktails were going to kick off these winter wedding celebrations, with the bride and groom and their guests about to spill out of the gorgeous country manor house where the ceremony was being held.

Campervan Ruby, parked just off the gravel driveway to the front of the old sand-stone hall, was polished even more so than the glasses; buffed with care and pride to a deep and shiny chianti red. Her stage-light bulbs were aglow, and a pretty strand of ivory linen wedding bunting flapped lightly from the lifted hatch in the afternoon breeze. A small cut-glass jug of fresh ivory roses teamed with milky-green-leaved eucalyptus sat beside Jack's treasured antique silver cocktail shakers, completing the classy look.

Both Jack and Lucy were delighted to be catering at this winter wedding. The ceremony and traditional wedding breakfast were taking place within the beautiful coastal hall, with its glorious views out over the bay. Jack had been thrilled to be asked to take on the bar facilities. And with some quick thinking after a request for canapés to accompany the welcome cocktails, he'd contacted Lucy, who'd come up with a great idea to give the welcome nibbles a Northumbrian–Italian twist.

Jack had also suggested that the wedding party might want to consider hiring a quirky-quaint horsebox pizzeria that could help with the evening catering too. And, that was that! The job was a good'un. They were becoming quite the team.

Jack glanced over at Lucy; dark hair piled up in a bun and full of focus as she put the final touches to her Italian-inspired platters of canapés. When she finally looked up, he gave her a steady smile and a thumbs up, mouthing, 'Ready for the off?' His heart couldn't help but lift at her warm smile back.

Around them, the shrub-bordered gardens were clinging to their last leaves of late autumn bronze, and beyond that a grassy-green field rolled down to the coast. The view from the 'bar' was amazing, with grey-gold winter light settling over a silver-hued North Sea. They were near enough to smell the salt in the air, to hear the cry of a gull. Despite it being a touch chilly (he was glad of his thick tweed jacket beneath his apron), it was a stunning location. Jack was determined to do his utmost to ensure the wedding couple and their guests got the truly special day they deserved. Like every event since he started The Cocktail Campervan, he'd give it one hundred per cent, and he had a few special tricks up his sleeve for later, including some mixology magic with bespoke cocktails, plus his fun 'Pimp the Prosecco' hour. In fact, the two of them had plans to turn the evening into a pizza and prosecco extravaganza.

❄

Lucy was feeling a little nervous about the event, but Jack's broad grin and supportive thumbs up helped to calm her somewhat. Crickey, she glanced down at her watch, there were only five minutes left to go. She'd not made canapés professionally before, so this was a bit of a first, but when Jack had mentioned the couple's request, it had seemed far too good an opportunity to miss. Her reputation might yet rest on it – eek.

And her head was still swimming about his New Zealand dreams. Or could they in fact be concrete plans? A punch of anxiety hit her. Argh, she just needed to focus on the here and now. It would all be fine, she told herself as she took a slow breath; she was well organised. Her platters had mostly been pre-prepared at home this morning, and just needed some last-minute assembling to ensure the crostini and bruschetta bases stayed crisp. She had basil-and-tomato bruschetta to serve, plus Northumbrian goat's cheese and olive tapenade crispy toast bites. A trio of bite-sized mini pizza garlic breads were also ready to quickly bake off in the wood-fired oven: traditional garlic and herb butter, melted mozzarella cheese, and some with caramelised red onion.

Abby was with her too, thank goodness, the pair of them

ready to waltz between the guests and offer little ivory napkins along with their bite-sized tasty snacks.

'They look great, Luce,' Abby commented, as she gazed down at the platters.

'You think?' Lucy was still in the clutch of her nerves.

'Ye-ah, absolutely. My mouth is watering already.'

'Well, don't drool all over them,' Lucy joked.

They both laughed, taking the edge off the tension.

And then the heavy wooden doors of the hall flew open and out fluttered a smiling bride and groom. Her in white lace, him in a smart navy suit, and a whole host of hope, promises and dreams ahead of them. A happy gathering of family and friends followed, with cheerful chatter and confetti in their wake.

'Aw, doesn't the bride look beautiful,' cooed Abby. 'Love that dress.'

'Oh yes, it's gorgeous.'

Bride Sarah was wearing a stylish sheath of ivory satin, which had diamanté jewel detail across the bandeau neckline, and a warm furry stole covering her shoulders. It looked rather Audrey Hepburn, thought Lucy admiringly.

'And, he's not so bad either,' Abby added; her eighteen-year-old assistant's eyes widening at the rather dishy dark-haired groom.

'Hey, eyes front, you. Hah, he's taken, and what about your cute-as-can-be Callum?'

'Hey, I'm only noticing what's on view.' Abby was grinning. 'I'm more than happy with my lush local lad. We were out on a date last night, in fact. Drinks at the Dunstanburgh, followed by a fish-and-chip supper.'

'Ooh, sounds very nice. But back to the task in hand.

Let's get cracking here, we have work to do,' Lucy chided, but she couldn't help but smile along with her assistant. And yes, the groom was pretty dishy, to be fair, but of course not a patch on that gorgeous bar guy who'd been smiling over at her before.

Once the bride and groom and family and friends had had a chance to catch a champagne cocktail, the two girls – dressed the part in black skirts, white blouses (hah, with thermals beneath) and their All Fired Up aprons – set off amongst the suited and booted guests with their platters of canapés.

'Can I offer a tomato and basil bruschetta, or a goat's cheese crostini?'

'Mini garlic pizzas for anybody?'

'Do take a napkin.'

Lucy found herself slipping into a rather posh tone. Perhaps it was the sense of occasion and the imposing manor-like venue getting under her skin.

She spotted Jack giving her a supportive wink as she neared the campervan. My, the gathering were buzzing like bees around those nectar-like champagne cocktails. Ruby did look rather splendid with her wedding theming. And Jack had scrubbed up pretty well too: smartly dressed, blond hair slightly ruffled, that cheeky sparkle in his eyes as he chatted to the guests, and those 'guns' on display. She noticed he'd discarded his jacket now that he was busier, his muscles flexing as he shook up his cocktail creations. Hmm, if she was All Fired Up, then he seemed to be 'All Shook Up' right now! She couldn't help but stare for a second, and smile … along with several of the guests. As always at these events, she wasn't the only one who noticed his charms.

Thankfully, the canapés seemed to be going down well, with the platters emptying fast, and appreciative mutterings of 'Delicious' and 'Mmm' filling the gaps between the buzzy chatter.

With it being a November wedding and a discernible chill in the air, the guests soon began to drift back to the warmth of the hall with its roaring log fires for the afternoon reception. Lucy had taken a look earlier and noted it was styled beautifully; each round table set out with cutlery, napkins and glasses, posy bowls filled with ivory flowers and greenery as centrepieces, and deep-green garlands of fir and eucalyptus with delicate trails of white roses were feathered along the top table. With candles aplenty, and wine ready to pour, it looked like it was going to be stylishly cosy in there. The perfect winter wedding.

✳

Daytime shifted to a purple-hazed dusk, and a further flurry of guests began to arrive in their fancy frocks and smart suits for the evening 'do'. Lucy had reloaded the pizza oven with logs and was stoking it up ready for action. Jack in the meanwhile was very much back in action preparing for his 'Pimp the Prosecco' part of the proceedings. A bit of fun to be had by all, with all sorts of prosecco cocktails conjured up using flavoured gins – raspberry and elderflower were always popular, with fizzing mini bombs, garnishes of edible gold flakes, fruits and herbs and more. The new arrivals were having a great time experimenting with their drinks, and once again there was a real buzz around Ruby. From her pizza baking post,

Lucy overlooked the grounds which appeared transformed in the dusk with loops of sparkly lights softly swaying between the trees, and delicate trails of twinkling mini bulbs threading their way through the florist's greenery that had been carefully swathed along the balustrades of the steps, all the way up to the main hall door. Guests milled about with some spilling out of the hall, still swaying to the beat as the music and dancing cranked up.

Lucy was thinking how pretty it all looked when out strolled a young couple arm-in-arm, followed soon afterwards by a man seemingly on his own. *Oh, bloody hell* … there was something *awfully* familiar about that dark cropped hair, a certain squareness of his neck and jawline. He was dressed in a smart navy suit that, oh yes, she'd seen him wear before at that works Christmas party, the one just before …

A gaggle of guests brushed past him, then he was stood alone. Hovering halfway down the steps and seemingly perusing the grounds. Lucy felt distinctly uncomfortable, the hairs rising on the back of her neck, until the smell of burning caught her nostrils and her attention. Shit, she'd only gone and burnt the first lot of pizzas. What an idiot! She couldn't afford to waste her ingredients like that.

Bugger it. She then burnt her arm trying to use the paddle to lift the bases out quickly, but it was already too late. The first two pizzas were charred and inedible; they'd have to be binned before anyone noticed. So much for showcasing her fabulous food and creating a good reputation.

'Ah, you okay there, Luce?' Abby's head bobbed out from the horsebox's hatch.

'Er, all fine, no worries. Just a small technical hitch.'

An effin' ex-boyfriend of a technical hitch, in fact.

What the hell was Liam doing here?! She wondered how he even knew the bride and groom. She certainly hadn't recognised them when they'd met to discuss the booking several weeks ago.

Lucy felt herself prickle. There was a time when she and Liam had still been talking about their *own* bloody wedding … the one, of course, that was never going to happen. Oh Christ, he was coming her way … and she had *nowhere* to hide, other than facing the blast of the oven. Might he already know about her new business venture, her pizza van? It was all over Facebook, after all. Did he know she'd be there? She felt herself flush with heat, and it certainly wasn't just from the log flames.

From the corner of her eye, she traced her ex's steps … dammit, he was coming right towards her. His eye then caught hers, and she was trapped like a rabbit in headlights.

'Hey, Lucy?' Despite the greeting, Liam's smile looked tight.

'Hi,' she echoed feebly.

All those memories: the good times, the bad times, the getting to know yous, the breaking up … they all started to fizz back to the surface. She stood there, frozen.

'Nice to see you, Luce.' His smile broadened, but there was something disconcertingly cynical in his tone.

Well, it didn't seem very *nice* to her. It didn't seem very nice at all. Movie-clip images struck her of a mutual friend sharing the devastating news of his fling – 'if it was me, I'd want to know …', the hammering noise of the 'For Sale' sign being banged up outside their new-build/new-hopes house, like the final nails in the coffin of their engagement and their future together.

Words were lost to her initially – only 'wanker', 'tosspot' and 'dickhead' coming to her. She managed, *just*, to keep them in. Reminding herself that she was here in a working capacity, and that it was someone's special wedding, after all. The last thing she wanted to do was to cause a scene.

'Well … I didn't expect to see you here,' was all she could manage.

'Yeah, well I know the groom, Ben. He works with me at Arnott & Co.' That was the solicitor's where Liam practised, specialising in property transactions. 'Joined us six months ago. Nice chap.'

'Ah, I see.' Facing him now, she noticed Liam looked a little older; a few more crinkles around his eyes, a smattering of early grey threads at his temples. He still looked good, though; he was always very presentable. And suddenly she was aware of how hot and sweaty she was, no doubt all pink in the face and flustered, stood there in her not-so-glamorous yet practical All Fired Up work outfit.

'So, how are you, Luce?' It was hard to fathom his tone as he chatted. Was he just making polite conversation? Did he really care? 'And hey, look at all this.' He gestured towards the horsebox. 'Quite some turnaround for you.'

Was his interest genuine? Did it have a hint of his old put-you-down sarcasm?

'Yeah well, I picked myself up and moved on.' Her voice came out a little stilted at first. But she soon followed up with, 'Business is going great. Yeah, really good. Booming, in fact. I might be expanding, actually … Yeah, there could be a whole chain of All Fired Ups about soon.' Blimey, where had that all come from? He'd probably see on social media that nothing at all of the sort was happening. But there was no way she was going to let him think that life was anything other than fan-bloody-tastic without him. Oh yes, the protective wall was going up – it was like she'd just fitted those bloody thick industrial-style oven gloves right around her heart.

'Well then, I'm a bit busy just now. Better get on,' Lucy continued, lifting her wooden paddle, ready to load another batch of pizzas in. Either that or to smack him over the head with it. Hmm, that might be very satisfying indeed.

'Right, well, I'll catch you later then, Luce … I'm just going to find a couple of work colleagues,' he added, which seemed to be a hint that he wasn't here with a partner or girlfriend. But perhaps she was just being over-sensitive.

Her hands were shaking a little on the paddle. She tried to steady them, annoyed at herself for feeling so ruffled by it all. But seeing Liam out of the blue like this, it brought back all of the emotional rollercoaster she'd experienced at the end of their relationship.

He stared right at her then, an intensity in his dark grey-green eyes. The ones she used to gaze into. The ones she had thought she could trust. 'I've missed you.' And his words floated into the air, like weird nostalgic verbal confetti.

Chapter Ten

W ho the hell was that guy?

Jack had clocked that the tall stocky bloke in his designer suit had been staring across at Lucy for ages, even after having walked away from the pizza stand.

Something about the chap struck Jack as odd; he felt uneasy and he wasn't quite sure why. And when he'd started talking, she'd looked ... what? Perturbed? Uncomfortable? In fact, Jack realised, that guy hadn't even taken a slice of bloody pizza away with him, had he?

Ah well, he had enough on at the bar with his guests waiting for 'Pimp the Prosecco' top-ups, he just needed to crack on ... he was probably making something out of nothing. It was no doubt some harmless chit chat – perhaps the guy having a little too much beer on board. It was a wedding do, after all. And, Lucy had shown in the past that she was more than capable of taking care of herself in the odd tricky situation with customers, but still ... his eyes drifted back. Okay, good, the coast was clear, as the guy was now busy talking to another lad. Jack allowed himself to relax somewhat.

'I'll just be one minute, ladies,' he said to the three women gathered at the front of the queue, turning to quickly rinse out some glasses at the small sink behind him. The fizzes were proving popular.

Jack was doing his best to keep up with the prosecco cocktails, G&Ts and bottles of lager and ale that were flying out like there was no tomorrow. This lot were intent on having a good time, making the most of the celebrations and the free bar – courtesy of the bridal couple and her parents.

'Now then.' He turned back to the women, giving his trademark grin. He had a great smile with pearly-white teeth and those blue-grey eyes that sparkled expressively. 'Let me serve you with some more of my fabulous fizz delights.'

The trio of thirty-something ladies grinned back.

'You can certainly serve me up with some of *your* delights,' a false-lashed blonde moved in closer, leaning a more-than-ample chest against the counter top provocatively. The girlish group, who had gone all out with their wedding-day finery, dressed in bodycon pastel-shade lace dresses and bobbing fascinators, giggled raucously.

Jack continued unfazed; he'd got used to a lot of tipsy female attention. It was all part of the bar work, and it was generally pretty good-humoured. 'So, can I interest you in some lemon drizzle fizz? A burst of berry bramble, or maybe bellini-style bubbles, mango or peach? And there's always the gold flakes to add some extra sparkle to the fun. Get ready to "Pimp your Proseccos", ladies.'

'Ooh, could you make us something with the shaker, honey?' False-lash lass said, 'I really want to see you in action with that cocktail thingie. Never mind "Pimp the Prosecco", what about "Pumping those Pecs"?'

The girls hooted, and even Jack had to laugh at that one. He was glad the ladies were enjoying themselves, and after all, that was what The Cocktail Campervan bar was all about. So, he happily obliged with a fine display of his mixology skills, fixing up a trio of Cosmopolitans. He did indeed like to keep up with some gym work, as well as running and cycling in his spare time, which kept his 'pecs' in ample condition.

'There you go now, ladies. Enjoy! Meet your Craster Cosmopolitan. It has Northumberland vodka, cranberry and lime with my special rosehip garnish.'

False-lash lady took a long, slow sip. 'Mmmm. That, my friend, is bliss. Oh and the show wasn't so bad either ...' She gave a wink and off she toddled on four-inch heels, accompanied by her prosecco-sipping posse. Another happy customer. Jack did his best to keep his eye on the ball at the bar; he had a queue of thirsty customers ready to celebrate big time, after all, and 'Pimp the Prosecco' was still in full swing. But somehow his focus and his heart didn't seem to be in it. He couldn't help but scan the crowd of guests every now and again to see where that creepy guy might have gone.

Was he jealous, was that it? Seeing some bloke making a move on Lucy? But watching Lucy's face, her expression ... it didn't feel like the usual interaction between server and guest. Jack's protective streak was going off the scale. What *had* gone on over there?

He tried to make eye contact with Lucy. See if she was alright. But she wasn't looking his way at all. Jeez, whatever had happened, it was putting Jack right off his cocktail bar showman stride.

❄

The evening moved on, with Lucy forcing herself to refocus on her work. The festivities came to a close with a fabulous fireworks display, the night sky lit up with bursts of silver, gold and red, accompanied by the popping of corks of some final celebratory champagne. The bride and groom, looking so very happy if slightly dishevelled, came across to thank Jack and then Lucy for the fabulous catering.

'It's been such an amazing day,' Sarah beamed appreciatively, stood at the horsebox counter in her now slightly crumpled gown. 'Thank you so much for making this all so special for us.'

'Ah, that's what we're here for. You're both very welcome.' Lucy felt relieved and happy that it had gone off so well for them.

'And the food … your pizzas are spot on,' added Ben, with a big thumbs-up gesture.

'That's lovely to hear,' Lucy gave a grateful smile, 'and thank you. It's been a pleasure.' Well, the appearance of one particular guest aside.

Their thanks made all the hard work which she and Abby had put in so worthwhile. Her confidence in her business was growing with every successful event. A few merry stragglers were still wandering about the gardens as they cleared up, some tottering down the steps from the hall, whilst there was a backing chorus of 'Farewells' and 'Goodnights' and 'Thank-yous', and little peals of laughter echoing across the grounds. Lucy hoped to goodness that Liam wasn't hanging around – she so wasn't ready to bump into her ex again.

❄

Jack finally managed to catch up with Lucy under a string of white twinkly bulbs in the garden. 'Hey, Luce, everything okay?'

'Oh, yes, good thanks, such a gorgeous event, wasn't it?'

'Umm, who was that guy you were talking to before?' Jack asked with a slight strain to his voice. 'He seemed kind of … intense. Do you know him?'

'Ah … no, it was nothing,' she stammered.

'Oh …' Jack stalled. Had he been chatting her up? A surge of envy tightened across Jack's chest at the thought of someone making moves on her. Or, was it someone she knew or had history with? 'Well, I hope he wasn't bothering you?'

'No, it's all fine, Jack.' Lucy clutched her rubbish bag and moved swiftly on with her table clearing, thus closing the conversation.

'Right, well … As long as you're okay.' Jack caught up with her, touching her shoulder gently.

'*Really*, I'm fine,' she bristled.

Jack moved forward to give her a hug but she was off,

marching amongst the detritus-filled tables, disappearing into the night.

❄

Back at Cove Cottage, Lucy was wide awake and lying restless under the duvet, Dachshund Daisy by her side. Her thoughts were spinning, and old hurts were resurfacing after a long, confusing day. It was as if Liam had scratched the lid on a buried pot of frustrations and emotions.

Why had she lied to Jack when he'd asked her about the run-in? She hadn't wanted to keep it a secret, there was nothing – really – to hide. And Lucy knew full well that everything was over between her and her ex. But she did know that seeing him again had brought back a strange mix of feelings. The pain of losing someone you were once so close to was hard to shake off. That sensible anchored life she'd initially had with Liam – the settled routine of it, her old office job, and their very nice detached home – had all come rushing back. And although that life wasn't right for her – she *knew* that – it was a stark contrast to the crazy spontaneity she often experienced with Jack. What if he did up sticks and go off adventuring at any moment? She reached out to stroke Daisy's sleek, soothing fur.

Why do relationships have to be so complicated, Dais? Why can't men be more like dogs? Either they like you or not … and if they do like you, they stick around.

Life had changed so much in these past eighteen months. Stepping out on her own, taking the plunge with All Fired Up … meeting Jack. And though she was loving every exciting minute with her new flame right now, could she and Jack really work out? His free spirit, his sense of adventure, they were inspiring, enticing … And yes, he was gorgeous and funny and sexy and handsome, *but* was he ever going to be the kind of person who could truly settle down? And – after Liam – was that what she wanted?

Lucy gave a soft sigh in the dark of her room. It was all very discombobulating.

Chapter Eleven

Two days later, and Lucy's head was spinning once more – there was no rest for the wicked with Jack around.

'Come on. We're heading out!'

'No way! Leave me alone, you, I'm all cosy here.'

Lucy felt a dig to her ribs. She was lying snug as a bug in her comfy double bed, hoping for a lie-in next to Jack, who'd stayed over last night. It had been a restless couple of nights after the wedding event and the drama of seeing Liam and, boy, did she need a bit of extra sleep.

'Come on, lazy bones. I'm not taking no for an answer. I've just looked out of the window, and this morning is going to be glorious.'

Silence from under the duvet. It was definitely some crazy early morning hour.

'It's going to be amazing out there,' Jack coaxed.

'It's fine in here …'

'We need to catch the winter sunrise,' Jack persisted.

'We really don't …' Lucy felt Daisy snuggle in even closer too.

Daisy? What the hell was she doing up here? Yes, she often sneaked up and slept with Lucy when she was solo, and of course last year, she was always there when Lucy was on her own during those hard, lonely, post-break-up months. But she'd only once come up on the bed whilst Jack stayed over, the night they'd all crashed out in a bit of a daze after Lucy's pizza party. And well, Lucy had thought that would be taking things a step too far … a new lover *and* a Dachshund.

'Get up, lazy bones,' Jack said, sounding frustrated now. 'We'll miss the dawn at this rate.'

'Do I have to, really?' She tried opening one bleary eye at a time.

'Yes, really. You'll thank me for it later.' And with that, the covers were pulled back brusquely.

'Ugh.' Lucy's eyes blinked wide with the shock.

Daisy was most affronted too, giving a huffy snort, which summed up Lucy's mood perfectly.

'No time to shower, we'll head straight for the beach. We should just about make it.'

'Okay, okay …' Lucy swung her legs round reluctantly. Then grabbed some fresh underwear, teaming it with yesterday's jeans and a fleece top. All the while, thinking that this was crazy. She had a crazy boyfriend. She trailed down the stairs after Jack, who was bouncing like bloody Tigger – how dare he be so fresh at this hour in the morning?

'Do we have to walk *all* the way?' She was aware she

was sounding like a stroppy teenager, but fatigue was still washing over her.

'Yep.' Then, he took a glance out of the window and down at his watch. 'Ah, okay, so why don't we take Ruby down so far and then walk from there? I don't suppose you're in the mood to jog, are you?'

Lucy didn't need to say a word, merely raising her eyebrows.

'Alright, so we're set.' He picked up the campervan's keys. 'Let's go.'

Lucy crawled into the passenger side, fighting off a yawn.

They'd left Daisy in the house, still snoozing in the heap of bedclothes. *Lucky thing.*

It was a strange half-light outside, but the clouds that had gathered in the November morning sky had a beautiful, moody, soft glow about them, with gold and dusky pink hues amongst the silvery greys.

Jack parked Ruby up down the lane to the golf course, and they got out to trek the last half mile across the rough grass walkway over the golf course and to the dunes. The unusual winter light gave a muted golden hue to the landscape.

'Are we there yet?' Lucy well knew the route, but couldn't help but tease Jack as well as mocking her grumpy earlier self.

'Nearly … keep up, slowcoach,' Jack gave a wry smile. Then he took her hand in his for the walk through the dunes.

Up the first marram grass rise, and meandering up a high dune, sand shifting under their feet … and there …

with just seconds to spare, was the sweep of sandy bay, with the haunting silhouette of Dunstanburgh Castle behind. And *there* … they stood and watched as the sun rose bold and beautiful behind those ancient ruins.

It was timeless and stunning. A burst of molten gold glowed around that semi-circle and then, bam, a circle of bright, blazing, bronze sun. There were bold pinks and dusky oranges and mauve seeping through the layers of blues and greys. The dawn scene was so beautiful, it took your breath away.

'There, told you it would be worth it.'

Lucy nodded, taking it all in … the expanse of the bay … the glistening black-green of the rocks and pools, the cliffs that rose to the mystical-looking historic stone ruins.

She had to admit, it was quite a sight. And it was one she wouldn't have seen if it wasn't for Jack.

He moved even closer, cupping her head gently between his hands, and gave her the most beautiful kiss she had ever experienced. Even more toe-tinglingly awesome than that amazing sunrise.

It was a feeling and a moment that she didn't want to end. Oh God, her and Jack … But could she keep him here with her, when his soul was so free, so damned adventurous?

She couldn't put it all into words. But maybe that didn't matter.

Jack, Lucy, and Dunstanburgh at dawn … a magical moment that would stay in her heart forever.

Finally, after watching the sun rise higher, filling the sky with a myriad of colours that reflected down onto the wet sands before them, Lucy managed to speak. 'Yeah, I suppose this was worth getting up for.'

Jack just grinned knowingly.

This man who made her heart sing … he really wasn't like anyone she had ever met. She hoped upon hope that this, *them*, was the start of something, not just a drop in the ocean. That they might find their way together for a very long while yet. But why did her heart keep warning her otherwise?

❄

Come along to The Corbridge Christmas Tree Festival

& Christmas Market

Saturday 20th November

❄

Chapter Twelve

'Aw, doesn't it look pretty!' Abby exclaimed as they pulled into the cobbled market square at Corbridge.

Craft stands and catering, cards, candy, books and bakes filled the space. The stallholders were well on their way with the setting up, everyone putting on a fabulous show of festive displays and lights. Along the street, every shop and cottage had its decorations up, with swoops of gently sparkling coloured lights, and windows full of tinsel and treasures.

It was now mid November, and today was an exciting day, as this was All Fired Up's first ever Christmas event booking. And, of course, they had their own festive finery ready to festoon over the vintage horsebox. It was soon looking dandy with its twinkling strands of fairy lights, tinsel glistening around the serving hatch and bright-red baubles dangling from the top corners of the pizza menu blackboard. Even Lucy and Abby were sporting their Christmas jumpers. Lucy's featured a bright-red robin. She'd just pulled the jumper out of storage in the cottage's loft. It hadn't got an airing at all last year. She had only just landed in Embleton and was still feeling rather lost. She'd found solace over Christmas time with her mum and Nonna at Rothbury, but still hadn't found herself wanting to celebrate in the usual way at all. It had been the toughest of years.

But here she was, eleven months later with her new catering venture up and running … and today looking very much the seasonal part. Helper Abby's bright-green jumper was fittingly sporting an elf, and Lucy had to smile as they both set to work behind the counter. Abby then went off in search of a couple of coffees to fire them up, whilst Lucy cracked on with organising the catering. Warmed with cappuccinos, they were soon busy prepping the fresh pizza bases.

A few minutes later, Lucy looked up to find Abby grinning at her goofily and wearing a pair of bright-red antlers.

'Hah, brilliant,' she spluttered into her cup. 'Where did you get those from?'

'The stall over there, it's great fun.'

'I need a pair!' Lucy smiled, then paused. 'Hmm, though maybe not for when I'm working at the oven, come to think of it. Might set them on fire as I lean in! And end up frazzled at my first ever Christmas pizza event. So, perhaps not. Hmm, I wonder if they do mini ones for Dachshunds, though? How cute would that be. I could take a pair for Daisy. Did you spot anything like that?'

'Nah, don't think so. But I did notice a pet stall setting up across the way.'

'Ooh, well I'll certainly have to visit that before the day is out.'

Daisy, who was in the back of the Jeep today, deserved a new Christmas outfit at the very least.

The quaint town of Corbridge had gone all out with its festive decorations. There were beautiful little real-fir Christmas trees hoisted and angled high on the old stone walls of the many independent shops and cottages. Lights of all colours and sizes glowed and twinkled. It was still late morning as yet. How gorgeous would the little town look later in the afternoon when dusk settled. Lucy began to feel a flutter of excitement, along with a nip of anxiety to make today a real success. Already, there were several locals and visitors mooching about, no doubt keen to get in and find the best gifts and goodies early. A couple dressed in warm coats and woolly hats slowed beside the horsebox and perused the pizza menu.

'Hello there. We'll just be another half hour until the pizzas are ready to serve,' Lucy explained. 'I'm just waiting for the oven to get up to temperature.'

'No worries, pet. I was just checking it out for lunchtime,' the balding middle-aged chap answered with a smile.

'They are *so* good,' added Abby, 'I can absolutely vouch for them. Lucy's pizzas are legendary. All made to her Italian grandad's recipe, you know.'

'They sound great. The real deal, then. I look forward to trying them,' answered the bobble-hatted lady who was stood close beside him.

'Hah, Abby, you're a star,' Lucy laughed as the couple

wandered away, arm-in-arm. 'Who needs advertising, when I've got you?'

In fact, Lucy couldn't wait to start serving her new 'Turkey and Trimmings' pizza. A bit of a festive experiment, to be honest. But who knew, it could well turn into the new pizza craze for Christmas. With tasty bite-sized slices of turkey, mini pigs-in-blankets (chipolata sausages wrapped in streaky bacon), little sage-and-onion stuffing balls, a sprinkling of cheddar and mozzarella cheeses, and with, of course, for those who wanted it, a drizzle of cranberry sauce. It was a real festive feast. (She'd drawn the line at sprouts, feeling it was a topping too far!)

She'd experimented on Jack a few days ago, back at her cottage kitchen, and this was the combination that stole the show – all the right components and the tastiest of flavours. It had come out of the oven looking delicious too, and had smelled roast-Christmas-dinner pizza divine. She couldn't wait to see how the market-goers would take to it. Eek – the proof of the pizza and all that!

There were other tasty options, of course, including her classic margherita with the sweetest of cherry tomatoes and mini balls of mozzarella, a roasted Mediterranean veg-and-feta combo, a spicy Italian nduja sausage, chicken with pesto and rocket, plus her Northumberland ham and portobello mushroom – always a crowd pleaser. Pizza paradise.

Soon, the logs were glowing in the oven and they were ready to go. Her first order came in for … a Turkey and Trimmings Christmas Special. Yay!

Abby prepped the festive toppings just as Lucy had shown her, and into the wood-fired oven on the big paddle it went. Forty-five seconds and one half turn later, it was pulled out, golden and crispy and meltingly cheesy on the top. It slid tantalisingly into the All Fired Up cardboard takeaway box. And the couple who had ordered smiled broadly as the piece de resistance was handed across.

'Wow.'

'Looks amazing, thank you.'

'Cranberry sauce drizzle to finish?' Abby asked with a smile.

'Oh absolutely, why not. Let's go the whole hog.'

And with a flourish, Abby trailed some arty cranberry lines in zig-zags over the top. 'There you go. Enjoy, folks.'

Lucy held her breath as the couple stood to one side, then took up a slice each and … bit down.

'So, what's the verdict?' Abby called across chirpily.

They stood munching for a heart-stopping second or two longer, then gave big smiles. 'Really tasty.' 'Delicious.'

Phew.

'In fact,' the woman took up, 'I think I might just forget about spending hours slaving over cooking roast turkey dinner this year. Let's get a few of these in instead.' She grinned.

They all laughed. And, as the couple moved off with their pizza box to hand, Lucy and Abby gave them a big thumbs up and a wave. The girls then turned to give each other a high-five.

As more pizzas were made, yet more customers were drawn to find where those delish-looking pizzas had come from. A queue began to form. It was going to be a busy lunch shift, and Lucy didn't mind at all. She was always happy to work hard if it meant her clients were happy and her new venture was taking big steps forward. She set about her work, humming away to the tune of 'Jingle Bells'.

The early afternoon went by in a whirl, with pizza after pizza going out, resulting in Lucy getting a bit of a sweat on beneath her woollen Christmas jumper. At last, there was a bit of a lull around 3:30 p.m., and after letting Daisy out of the Jeep for a quick toilet stop, she let Abby take a break. She was more than happy to continue prepping and cooking by herself for the next twenty minutes.

Abby came back with several bags, looking pleased with herself. 'You need to take a look around, Luce, there's loads of lovely bits for Christmas. Look, I got a gorgeous scarf for my mum, and some scrummy mince pie fudge for Nanna and Grandad. I even got to have a taste test. The salted caramel one was lush, so I got us a little bag to share on the way home.'

'Oh, that sounds scrumptious.' With that, Lucy's tummy started rumbling. In all the pizza-making rush, she hadn't managed to have any lunch herself. 'Well, it's pretty quiet just now, Abs, so I'll nip out now and take a look around while I've got the chance, if you don't mind. Just for ten minutes or so, so you can let anyone wanting pizza know I'll be back very soon. Keep an eye on the oven, but that's all you need to do. Enjoy a bit of a breather while you can. I have a feeling the supper-time shift will come around all too soon.'

'No worries.' There was an art to baking the pizzas, and Abby was more than happy to leave the oven as Lucy's domain for now.

Lucy took Daisy with her, and they wandered off into a twinkling paradise of stalls and shops, finding, firstly, the pet stand just over the road. Unfortunately, there were no mini antlers, but there was a gorgeous red-and-white Fair Isle-style jumper perfectly sized for her Dachshund, and a cute holly-patterned dog neckerchief which she couldn't resist buying.

'What do you think, Dais? Could this be your Christmas look this year? Like it?'

The dog wagged her tail excitedly.

'I'll take these, please. I just love that jumper.' Lucy handed over the goods to the friendly-looking lady behind the trestle-table, who was sporting her own red Christmas jumper with a white West Highland terrier on it.

'Oh, we've a wonderful local lady who knits for us.' She popped the items into a crisp white paper bag. 'Is she a short-haired?' She nodded in the direction of Daisy's lead, craning to see.

'Yes, black and tan. Dachshund. A real character. Aren't you, Daisy?'

'Aren't they all. My sister has a Dachshund, lovely, but for a small dog they certainly rule the roost. Great with the family, though; the kids all love her,' she smiled.

'Yeah, Daisy's brilliant with my three-year-old nephew.'

'Well, have a good day, my lovelies,' and the woman turned, ready to serve the next customer.

'Thanks, and you.'

With her hunger pangs still in force, Lucy was pleased to spot a familiar venue, Carrie's Coffee and Cupcakes trailer – perfect. She'd go say hello, and fetch her and Abby another brew and a much-needed snack.

She made a beeline towards the rich fresh-coffee aromas,

'Hey, Carrie, good to see you here. How's it going? Been busy?'

Carrie was dressed in a sage-green chunky knit, jeans and Doc Martens, her hair a mass of dark-auburn curls. 'Ah hi, Lucy. Yeah, very much so. Always a great event, this one. Been coming here for years. I love doing the Christmas markets, there's such a wonderful feel about them.'

'Yeah, it's so pretty, isn't it? The market, the village, everything. And today is my first Christmas market *ever*, actually,' Lucy confessed.

'Oh, that's exciting. So, are your pizzas going well? I did spot your horsebox earlier. But it's been all go, so I've never had the chance to come across and say hello as yet. Sorry, hun.'

A sparkling flash caught Lucy's eye, distracting her. At her feet was a whirl of tinsel, going around in circles. 'Oh … Daisy!'

The mischievous Dachshund had managed to drag a strand of tinsel from goodness knows where, and was now growling at it, twirling it about and thrashing it from side to side, like it was some kind of sparkly stranded prey. Carrie looked out and started laughing, as well as several of the passers-by.

'Oh my goodness, you're having a right game with that. Sorry Dais, but it's getting taken away. You'll end up choking on it, else.' Lucy was shaking her head with a smile at the little dog's antics. She spotted Abby chuckling away, watching from the horsebox too. 'What are you like?'

'Having fun down there, is she?'

'Getting too much into the Christmas spirit, I think,' Lucy laughed. 'Sorry, I'll just pop her back in the Jeep, minus the tinsel trail, and I'll be right back. I was coming over for a couple of coffees, actually …'

'No problem, I'll get them brewing and see you in a minute.'

'You little tinker,' Lucy chided the dog, who was giving her angelic 'Who, me?' eyes, as they headed back over to her vehicle. She looked about, still not sure where the now-dishevelled strand had come from, but nobody seemed to be missing it.

Lucy arrived back a few minutes later. 'So, where were we …?'

Carrie was still chuckling about Daisy. 'She's a little character, that one.'

'She sure is – fancy picking a fight with a strand of tinsel! Wouldn't be without her, mind.' Daisy had been her best friend, through the ups and downs of the past year. And the little dog's naughty antics had brought a smile back to Lucy's face, when at times it had been hard to find one.

Lucy glanced over to the horsebox, *her* horsebox, recognising all she had achieved since that low, and was so thankful that things were beginning to turn around for her.

'So, I was after a couple of coffees, and I'm going to have to have some of these gorgeous cakes too.' Lucy started browsing the flavours: red velvet, double chocolate, cookies and cream, lemon drizzle …

'Oh, and how's Jack?' Carrie asked, with a knowing smile. 'I've heard you two have become a bit of an item?'

'Ah, yes … we have been seeing each other,' Lucy felt herself flush for some reason, she wasn't quite sure why, as it wasn't exactly a secret.

'Ah well, he's a nice lad. Often stops by for a coffee and a chat when we're working at the same events. Likes to tell me all about his travels and adventures. Been to so many amazing places, makes my life seem a bit dull … In fact, I wonder where he'll be setting off next? Every year he seems to take some time out and head off somewhere new …'

Lucy suddenly felt uncomfortable. So, it was well known about his worldwide wanderings. And it didn't sound like they were just in his backpacking past. Was he already making more plans? The open laptop and the New Zealand page surfaced in her mind once more.

Why did her romantic relationships always seem to be fraught? Liam's affair … The thought of Jack leaving … heading off for foreign shores … It all made her heart feel heavy. But she resolved, whatever would be, would be. She wasn't going to worry herself back to a low point. She'd turned her life around this past year, she was heading *up* that hill, and she was going to bloody well keep on going.

She ordered two cappuccinos, and unable to resist a cupcake each for her and Abby, plumped for a toffee-drizzled banoffee and a cinnamon-frosted red velvet. She also spotted some delightful-looking festive gift boxes: four cupcakes with swirls of creamy-white frosting, and cute sugar-paste toppers of Santa, Rudolph, a snowman and an angel, with pretty stars and snowflakes sprinkled over. Beautiful festive works of sugary-baked art. And she knew just who would love them …

'Oh, and I'll take a box of these too. They look delightful.'

Yes, she'd call in to see her brother Olly and family on the way back home. It would be a great reason to stop by, and the perfect token of appreciation to thank them for all the times they'd looked out for her and Daisy. If her romantic relationships were rocking and rolling, and her friendship with Becky was now on troubled waters, at least her family were always her anchor.

❄

The dark of a starry winter's evening settled over the quaint market town. Carollers began to sing their last round of songs, gathered around the steps of the Market Cross in the square, and magic and frost filled the air. Smells of cinnamon and spice, pine and mulled wine drifted by. Lights glowed from the big Christmas tree that took pride of place beside the cross and from all the shops and stalls with their seasonal finery.

The day had been hectic, but rather lovely. She and Abby began to pack up, and as Lucy took down a strand of silver tinsel from the hatch, she realised that today had made her feel rather festive too. Like a bit of that Christmas magic was in the air. Whatever was to come, she was determined to make this festive season a special one.

And as she stood beside the horsebox, closing down the shutters, she overheard a couple of teenage lads (who she'd served not long before) talking about her pizzas. They'd had the nduja sausage with extra chillies.

'Mate, that pizza was brill.'

'Yeah, spicy and, like, really lush. Best I've had in ages.'

Lucy stood there feeling quietly proud, a warm smile spreading across her face. She gazed up at All Fired Up. Papa would have been proud of her, for sure. She reminded herself what she'd already achieved; this really was one dream that had become a reality. She shored herself up with that realisation. And the fire in her belly to make sure her business continued to go from strength to strength was as sure as the fire in that pizza oven.

Chapter Thirteen

Waking up in her cosy cottage bedroom the next morning, Lucy stretched contentedly and gave a yawn. Daisy came to at the same time, snuffling her way higher up on top of the duvet and pushing her nose into Lucy's hand in greeting.

'Morning, Dais.'

Lucy received a happy lick in reply. She still felt a little tired after her full-on day at the Christmas market, but finally getting a good night's sleep had done her the world of good.

Looking around her cottage boudoir, with its off-white shabby-chic furniture and curtains and cushions in cool-linen shades of blue, grey and white, Lucy very much felt that this was now home, in the warmest sense of the word.

'Well little lady, breakfast and then a walk on the beach? How does that sound?'

The word 'breakfast' worked its magic, with Daisy's tail wagging merrily in anticipation. Lucy sat up in bed, swept her legs around, and scooped up her little dog. They were soon downstairs in the kitchen, dog kibble poured and coffee on the go.

With their toast-and-butter stack swiftly licked clean by owner (and dog), and coats on, they then set off, the white wooden front door of the cottage opening onto a dazzle of autumn sunlight.

All Fired Up was there where she'd parked her beside the cottage last night, and Lucy was just about to trip on by for her wander on the beach, when she took a closer look. The vintage horsebox looked wrong somehow. Strangely sunken …

Lucy walked on over, trying to see what might have happened … when it dawned on her. *Oh*, the tyres, well the two she could see from this angle, were well and truly flat. How odd! Surely it would have felt all wrong towing it home last night like that? She moved closer, crouching down to inspect, with Daisy sniffing curiously at her side. Not just two tyres, but all four were down. Totally empty. The metal wheel hubs almost touching the ground. Oh no, there was no way her poor old horsebox would be going anywhere like that. Blimey, she'd have to get it sorted out before her Alnwick market session this week.

Something just didn't add up: if she'd driven over some glass or debris on the road on the way back yesterday, surely she'd have felt it, noticed a change? At the least, a wibbly-wobbly feeling as she towed, or worse, making her swerve … possibly going off the road. She couldn't countenance it at first, but perhaps it had been done last night … deliberately?

No. Not here, in her safe haven of a village, where everyone was so friendly?

She knelt down by each tyre to take a closer look, discovering a nail still in one – ah, okay, she might have run that over. Then, another nail was lying on the gravel driveway by the second tyre, which had a small hole pierced in it, and then there was a *slash* in the third. She felt a bit sick. This was no accident …

Who might have done such a thing? Bored youths, someone with a grudge? But she couldn't think who might possibly feel like that. Other than hosting the street party, she was a quiet soul at home, and she hoped she came across as friendly and approachable in the village. This made her skin prickle … it was just so hard to get her head around.

Should she call the police? Ring Jack, for some comfort or advice? Her mum or Olly? But she didn't want to worry anyone unnecessarily. She just needed time to think. She sat on the low wall of her back courtyard for a few moments gathering her thoughts.

Pragmatically, she realised she needed to get some help to get her horsebox back up and running and on the road again. It was her livelihood, after all. Most likely she'd need a new set of tyres – damn, yet more expense. And, as Cathy at the village shop was seemingly the fount of all knowledge, Lucy headed off in that direction with Daisy trotting by her side. It wasn't quite the walk they'd had in mind for this morning, but things needed sorting out.

There was a customer waiting at the till when they arrived, so Lucy bided her time and picked up some milk and bread. She then ventured forward to pay.

'Hey Luce, hi.' Cathy, as usual, was smiling, her tone bright and breezy.

'Hello, Cathy,' she replied, noting the subdued tone to her own voice.

'You okay, pet?'

'Ah no, not really,' she confessed. 'I've just had a bit of a shock, to be honest.'

'Oh … you do look a bit pale. Why not take a seat?' The shopkeeper gestured to the small plastic chair she kept near the till for the elderly to have a rest if needed – and of course a little chat – before their walk back home with their shopping. 'What's happened, lovely?'

Lucy took up the seat, realising that yes, she did feel slightly wobbly with all that had gone on, and began: 'Well, when I went out this morning with Daisy, I noticed the horsebox, my pizza business … well … it looks like someone's let the tyres down. There's a slash mark and a couple of nails left there. I've been wracking my brains wondering if it might have happened on the way home yesterday. It was dark, I might not have spotted something in the road I suppose, but well, I'd never have been able to manoeuvre it to park it up. That's one tight gap. The box would have been all over the place. No, it *must* have happened last night in the driveway.'

'Oh goodness. How dreadful. So, it seems like sabotage?'

'As much as I can tell. Has anything like that happened before around here?'

'No … of course not,' Cathy seemed rather affronted. 'Never heard of anything like it in our little village. And if any of our younger lads and lassies got involved in anything like that, they'd be grounded for weeks.'

'Sorry, I didn't mean to suggest they might …' Lucy hadn't meant to cause offence or to imply anything. 'I'm just at a loss …'

'Ah, it's alright pet. You're upset, I can see that. It is very unusual, mind. The village is safe as houses normally, no wonder you're worried.'

With that, Paul, one of the members of the Book Club, turned up, evidently hearing the word 'worried'. 'Hello there, ladies. So, is something up?' News clearly carried fast around here.

Lucy explained the scenario, suddenly feeling a bit tearful. The reality of it hitting home.

'Oh, I'm so sorry to hear that, petal.' Paul gave her shoulder a friendly rub. 'Well, we can help get you straight. Don't you go fretting.'

'Yes,' Cathy took up, 'first, you need to get in touch with Will at the garage on the main road. Nice chap. In fact, why not go and call in now, tell him all about it? He'll be able to put you right, for sure.'

'Oh yes, I used him when my Mini had a puncture. Got it sorted out in no time. And far cheaper than the quotes I'd had from the big-name companies over in Alnwick.'

After a few more minutes chatting with them both, and then reassuring Cathy that she felt fine, Lucy set off along with Daisy, who'd been waiting patiently tied to the dog loop outside.

They walked the hundred metres or so along to the old-fashioned garage – which looked very much like it was back in the '70s – where two big doors of the shed-like building were swung open.

'Hello?' Lucy called out, eventually finding Will, who was sporting an oil-stained red boiler suit and trundling out from under a vehicle on some kind of wheeled wooden board. He sat up, with a spanner to hand and a welcoming smile. 'Good morning, and how can I help?'

After telling him all about her problems, she was met with a concerned shaking of his head and several loud tuts.

'Aye, that's right unusual, that. We don't often get bother around here. Very strange for it to happen on our doorstep.'

Lucy's concern was heightened again, and a weary sigh escaped her lips.

'Now then, don't you worry, lass. I'll come take a look this morning and we'll get your horsebox moved over to the garage here first thing on Monday, ready for the new tyres – which I'll most likely have to get ordered in.'

After a back rub for Daisy, Will stood with Lucy sharing a bit more chitchat, finishing with a promise to keep the prices fair and saying he'd give her an estimate as soon as he'd seen the damage. Lucy then set off home.

With all the drama of the morning, her emotions were feeling a bit frayed. A warming cup of coffee and a friendly ear was needed, so rather than go back to the cottage just yet, knowing that the sight of the damaged All Fired Up would make her heart feel even sorer, she decided to head for the Driftwood Café. She'd spotted the window seat was empty, and she and Daisy might be able to sit and watch the world go by for a while.

As it turned out, the village grapevine had swung into

action and the news had already reached the café owner, Louise. She came straight out from behind the counter, making a beeline for Lucy and Daisy. 'Oh pet, what a terrible thing to have happened. Here, sit down and I'll fetch you a nice warm drink. What do you fancy?'

'Ah, a coffee would be great, Lou.'

'Of course, coming right up, and it'll be on the house, my lovely.'

'Aw, thank you.' She felt a bit choked at the small but heartfelt gesture of kindness.

After she'd brought over the coffee, Lou sat down beside Lucy. 'Well, what a carry-on. How are you feeling? Gutted, I bet?'

'Not too bad,' Lucy sighed, trying her best to rally. 'Just a little shook up.'

'And you really think someone's done it on purpose?'

Lucy gave a small nod.

'Why, that's terrible! Any ideas who it might be?'

'No, none at all.' Lucy paused, wracking her brain. 'Maybe someone jealous or upset by my business? But I've no idea who.' The catering community seemed completely supportive, not bitter. Becky? No, she hated that that thought had even come to mind, but no, she would never be that nasty. Whatever was going on between them, she knew for a fact that her friend wouldn't look to purposely hurt Lucy or her business. Someone in the village, perhaps? No, it was more likely a chance act of hooliganism, someone who didn't know her at all. A one-off. Hopefully.

'Are you going to report it to the police?' Lou continued.

'No, I don't think so, Lou.'

What chance did they have of catching anyone now?

No-one had been hurt, well, apart from a few emotional bruises. Lucy just wanted to get All Fired Up back on its feet and move on.

'Well, we've got the whole of the village on Neighbourhood Watch alert now. So, if anything else should happen, we'll be on the case, for sure. We'll catch the blighters if they dare decide to come back, I'm telling you.'

She suddenly pictured Lou and the café gang out in force with rolling pins and wooden spoons as weapons, and she had to give a smile. 'Thank you.' It was good to feel the village had her back. It helped make her feel that bit more secure again.

Walking back to the cottage a while later, however, she felt the anger stirring in her belly. How *dare* someone threaten her life at the cottage! Not to mention all the hard work she'd put into making All Fired Up a success. It was bloody annoying and, she had to admit, it had cast a real shadow.

And despite the community's warm and genuine support, Lucy's newfound foundations here in the village suddenly began to feel a bit shaky.

Chapter Fourteen

Monday morning, and Will's tow truck arrived outside of Cove Cottage.

After Lucy had called Jack and told him everything that had happened, he'd come right over, staying with her for supper and overnight; keeping her company and making sure she was safe. The pair of them listened out for any unusual noises or signs of bother through the early hours, but, thankfully, there was nothing. Jack had left fairly early, having an appointment to keep with his bank, but made her promise to ring him straight away if she was worried about anything.

Seeing All Fired Up getting winched onto the low loader made her heart contract. Yes, it was just some tyres that were damaged, and they'd get fixed fairly easily, but she still felt hurt and disturbed that someone could do something like that.

She needed a friend, but the person she usually turned to in times like these wasn't exactly speaking to her ... Once again the thought struck her: this was silly, this distance with Becky – they'd been the closest of friends for years, they needed to have this out once and for all. It was time to clear the air.

Lucy took out her phone, bit the bullet and dialled. The tone rang on … and on.

She sighed, hung up, and then punched in a hasty text.

Oh, Becks, am feeling rotten. Something's happened. She paused, then added: *Miss you. x*

After making herself a coffee, finally, her mobile rang. Her friend's voice came through with a tentative, 'Lucy … h-hi.' A beat of anxiety was apparent. 'What's up? Is everything okay? You're worrying me.'

'Hi Becks, hey …' It was a relief to hear her friend's voice at last. Lucy ploughed on, 'How are you?'

'Ah, yeah, pretty good.' Becky's tone stayed fairly cool, however. 'But what about you? What's going on?'

This was so hard over a phone. Not being able to see her friend's face or gauge her body language left Lucy feeling even more confused. 'Look, I know things haven't been easy between us lately,' she ventured, 'but … I've had a shitty couple of days, and to be honest, I could do with a friendly ear. Can we get together? Talk things over a bit. I hate that we've been so distant.' Lucy's voice broke a little, and there was a horrid tight knot in her throat.

'So, it's happened then, has it …?' Becky ventured.

'What?'

'You and Jack … it's not all so rosy, then.'

'Becky, it's nothing to do with Jack. It's something else …' Lucy was getting frustrated now. 'Jack's been great, actually. Really supportive ...' That was a lot more than could be said of her so-called best friend of late.

'Okay, sorry ...' Becky's tone softened.

'Anyway, it's to do with my business, the horsebox ... and well ... look, can we meet up? I'd like to see you, not have some stilted conversation over the phone ...'

'Okay, sure. How does a walk on the beach sound?'

This was progress, Lucy felt a beat of hope. 'This morning? You mean right now?'

'Yeah, why not.'

'But ... shouldn't you be at work?'

'Hah, well, that's another story.'

'Oh, right. Well, we'll catch up then ... about everything.' There were many gaps to fill in, by the sounds of it. 'So, Beadnell? We could grab a takeaway coffee and stroll the sands. Daisy would like that too.'

'That sounds a plan.'

Lucy gave a mental air punch. At last, a breakthrough between them. Small steps, but it was progress.

❄

Grey clouds massed ominously and there was a chill wind coming off the sea. Wrapped up in her thick winter coat, woolly hat and gloves, Lucy stepped down out of the Jeep and then scanned the car park whilst letting Daisy out of the back – no sign of Becky yet. She wandered across to the Beach Shack, tucked by the edges of the dunes. A warming cup of coffee was in order, and it might just help settle her nerves. It was the first time the friends had met in weeks.

And as well as the gloomy sky above, there were still clouds hovering over their friendship.

The Beach Shack was a quirky converted container that made the most delicious barista coffees and hot chocolates. There was usually a tempting bake or two to choose from too – today's were gooey chocolate brownies. The seating area was outside and consisted of weathered wooden benches. It was casual, yet perfect in a beachside way. Ideal for sandy toes, damp dogs and friendly (or at least she hoped so) chats.

'Hi there …' Lucy smiled at the girl behind the counter. 'Umm …' Should she order for Becky? She was pretty certain her friend would be having her favourite cappuccino, and she fancied a flat white herself; feeling more than ready for a coffee hit after another restless night.

Just as she ordered, she spotted Becky's red saloon pulling into the parking area. She felt a lift of relief, swiftly followed by a pang of nerves.

She paid for their drinks, and headed over to a bench. Daisy spotted Becky heading their way and her tail began to wag effusively.

'Hey …'

'Hi.' Lucy took a steadying breath. 'You okay?'

'Yeah. You?'

'Yeah, I think so …' Lucy stopped herself. 'Honestly, no. It's been a crap couple of days.'

It was awkward and lovely to be together again. The salty air seemed filled with so much that had yet to be said.

'What's happened, Luce?' There was genuine concern in her friend's tone.

'Ah, someone's only gone and let down all the tyres on

my horsebox ... some time on Saturday night. Slashed one, put nails in the others. It was on purpose, Becks. And that makes me feel so uneasy.'

'Oh shit, that's awful, Luce. Do you have any idea who?'

'No. It was right outside my house. My new cottage, where I was rebuilding my life ... and the horsebox, it's my business, I've put everything into that ... I'm still finding it hard to get my head around it, to be honest.'

'No wonder. That's so mean.'

Lucy took a sip of coffee. 'Going to cost me a couple of hundred quid in new tyres too. That's the last bit of savings I've got right now.'

'That really sucks ... I'm sorry, Luce.'

'Yeah, I'm hoping it's just been some yobs, a one-off.'

'Hopefully. Well, it's getting a bit chilly just sat here, shall we head off for that walk?' Becky asked.

'Yeah, good idea.' They set off down the slipway and strolled the sands with their cardboard coffee cups to hand. The occasional dog walker passed, with a brief hello, plus a sniff and tail wag between the canines. Despite the cold wind and the broken-cloud grey-blue sky, the view was stunning. An expansive arc of blond beach stretched before them, with shimmering drifts of sand blowing. The sea was frothy and turbulent. There was a moodiness to the peachy-gold colours that hung in the gaps between smoky-pewter clouds. The scene was set in sultry washes like a watercolour painting.

Their footsteps padded in the damp sand.

'So, are you still with him?' Becky asked quietly.

'Yes,' Lucy answered simply. She knew the question was coming.

'Uh-huh. And, how are things going then?'

'Good, yeah.'

'So, he must still be at the charming the pants off you stage?'

'Look Becky, I know you're finding this hard, me having a relationship with Jack, but … well, everything with you and Jack, it was all such a long time ago. I don't get why you are still het up about it all … so bitter?' It was time to get everything out into the open, no holds barred. It was the only way they were going to forge through to the other side.

Becky's brow creased, 'It's not Jack I'm worried about. That's so in the past, honestly. It's *you* Lucy, I really don't want to see you get hurt. You've only just got out from Loser Liam's clutches. You deserve better … Someone who'll be there for you, who'll look after you.'

Lucy sighed. Yes, things with Jack were a bit complicated, but he still made her heart sing. 'But Jack *is* my better … he makes me happy, Becky.'

'Okay, so he might do for now, but what about when he's used you up, when he's ready to move on to someone else, somewhere else?'

Ooh, with New Zealand hovering on Jack's laptop and possibly his horizons, it was like Becky was prodding at a sore wound. She really knew how to hit the spot. Lucy faltered; did she dare open up?

Lucy gave a sigh, and tried to find the words she needed. 'Okay, so I don't know totally where we're going yet, me and Jack, but what I do know is that we get on really well, that there's a caring side to him, a gentler side, and I've fallen for him … big time.'

Becky rolled her eyes dramatically.

'Just hear me out, okay.' Lucy found some inner strength and now she'd started, she needed to say her piece. 'There's like this extra layer to him that he keeps from the world, but every now and again, *I* get to see it … and it's lovely, *he's* lovely. And he's made me take stock of my life,' she continued. 'With Liam, well, we were just shuffling along a lot of the time, I suppose.' Lucy paused; she still wasn't quite sure how she was feeling about her relationship with her ex. She took a breath and refocused on Jack. 'With Jack I feel I can run and have fun, and yeah, maybe we'll trip and fall at some point. He might well bugger off to the other side of the world, for all I know. But you know what … it's worth the risk.' She was on a roll now.

'And if it all finishes tomorrow, I'll be glad that I knew him … that we had this time together.' She felt a lump in her throat at the thought of it all being over. She paused, thinking … is that how it would be? Just a passing phase, that they'd fade and falter?

'Jeez, you've got it bad.' Becky pulled a face. 'Bloody hell.'

All went quiet between them as they strolled on. Lucy had said her bit, she'd even surprised herself at the strength of feeling she held for Jack, the way it had all spilled out. And, Becky was no doubt digesting that.

They'd reached the old harbour by now, with its ancient lime kilns and stacks of lobster pots. They paused to sit on the wall; a small gap between the two girls with Daisy huddled close by at their feet, the wind and the waves rolling in against the solid stone outer harbour wall. The salty smell of the whipped-up sea filled the turbulent air, along with the haunting cry of a gull as it battled the elements.

'Becky, is everything okay with you? You and Darren doing alright? Your family? You've just been so closed off … and well, a bit *angry* …'

'Yeah, yeah,' her friend batted the question away. But her response sounded a bit too flippant. Not really an answer at all.

'Look, however you feel about me and Jack, I'm still here for you too, Becky. If ever there's anything …'

'Yeah, yeah, I'm fine.'

It was one of those 'fines' that didn't sound fine at all.

'Well … just so you know that.' That was all she could do, offer that branch of friendship. And keep on offering it.

'I'll still see *you*, Luce. But don't you go getting any ideas that it's all going to be cosy couples from now. Alright?' Becky clarified.

'Umm, alright.' It wasn't ideal, but it was at least a step in the right direction. Lucy nodded, feeling a bite of disappointment, but perhaps all her friend needed was time. 'Anyhow, why aren't you at work today?' she took up.

Becky looked awkward. 'We're down to a four-day week just now.' She worked in sales and admin for a bespoke kitchen manufacturer. 'And, well …' Her voice dipped, 'they're looking to make redundancies. Last in, first out and all that. Yep, I'm one of the ones likely to be in the firing line …' She was trying to sound upbeat, but Lucy could see through it.

'But you only just started there last year?' It was beginning to fall into place; Becky's withdrawal, her reticence. 'Oh Becky, why didn't you say anything? You must be feeling awful.'

'Hah, well you and me both, by the sounds of it.'

Without their friendship crash mat to fall back on recently, their problems had hit even harder.

'Oh Becky, you love that job and you're really good at it. And I'm sorry that you didn't feel you could talk to me, that we've been so bloody distant these past few weeks.'

'It wasn't just you, Luce. I'm sorry too.' She gave a sigh. 'And I suppose I've been a bit stubborn about Jack … he'd still better not do anything to bloody hurt you, mind! And, well … I think I might have been sticking my head in the sand about work. Hoping all this job stuff will go away. But it's not looking that hopeful, to be honest. Might be back at square one, hunting for a new job, and we have the mortgage to pay, the bills … Darren's wage will never cover all that.'

'Ah, that's such a worry. I wish I could help you financially, but I'm just about all out myself since I've put everything into the pizza venture.'

'I know, and I wouldn't expect you to, anyhow. Let's just be there for each other from now on. I need my friendship air supply back.'

'Me too.'

Lucy breathed a huge sigh of relief as they gave each other a hug.

The wind then grew stronger and spit-spots of rain started. Daisy was shivering, so Lucy scooped her up, cradling her against her chest. 'Time to head back, hey?'

'Yep. Not the best day for a walk. We must be bloody nuts.'

They headed back along the sands.

The rain intensified and was actually stinging their cheeks now. 'Well, this wasn't quite the coffee and beach stroll I'd imagined, I must say,' shouted Becky over the roar of the wind, pulling her puffer-coat hood tighter around her head.

Within seconds, the heavens opened. The two girls made a run for it, but by the time they reached the car park they were drenched to the skin. Jeans sticking to cold wet legs, hair dripping, and one very damp Dachshund.

'Quick, get in!' Lucy gestured to her Jeep, fumbling with the key fob.

'Bloody hell! Where did that come from?'

'Whose idea was a bloody beach walk, anyway?'

They looked at each other, both of them sopping wet, yet weirdly they were grinning.

Despite the rain, Lucy's determination to fight for their friendship had thankfully managed to knit it back into something warm and protective. The thread of their friendship might well be a little frailer than usual, but it was absolutely still there.

Chapter Fifteen

'One, two, three and … up.'

Prickles and pine scents blasted Jack's face as he and the chap from the garden centre hoisted the tree up onto Ruby's roof. All he had to do now was strap the trunk down securely on the campervan and off they'd tootle to deliver this beauty of a festive fir to Lucy's cottage. After that awful carry-on with her horsebox being vandalised, he'd wanted to do something to cheer her up, and this seemed the perfect plan.

He hadn't been to buy a Christmas tree for donkey's years, he realised. Not since he was a lad with his dad … oh, and of course, Daniel. Images flooded in of them wedging a bushy Nordmann pine into the rear of Dad's Ford Escort Estate. It was always too long, of course, and the tall spiky tip ended up rather precariously above the gearstick, somewhere near Dad's shoulder, where it poked through the front seats. Daniel sat up front – he always seemed to 'shotgun' the passenger seat as the elder sibling –

and Jack squeezed into the single seat space beside the tremendous tree, with bits of branches poking through the mesh wrapper, prickling him. But that didn't stop that festive joy, the excitement they felt as kids, heady with the knowledge that Christmas would soon arrive.

He felt his throat tighten. Memories of Christmas pasts … when the world once seemed so magical.

Jack pulled himself back to the present. 'Ah, cheers, mate.' Trying to hoist the pine on top of the campervan would have been really tricky by himself, but the lad here had seemed happy to help. Mind you, he was now sixty quid down, he mused wryly. Oh yes, Jack had gone 'large' with the tree, and seeing it almost filling the length of Ruby's roof, he now wondered if it would actually fit into Lucy's cottage living room. It wasn't the biggest of spaces, after all. Hmm, there might have to be some serious furniture shifting to accommodate it! But hey-ho, or ho ho ho … it was Christmas.

And, for the first time in years, Jack began to feel a tingle of excitement about Christmas coming. Thoughts of going back to Lucy's cosy cottage, setting up the tree with her. The log fire burning in the hearth. She'd promised to cook him supper too, so he had no reason to rush away. The afternoon and evening were theirs to enjoy.

❄

After a steady drive along winding still-frosty country roads, Jack pulled to a stop outside Cove Cottage.

Lucy must have been watching from the front window, as she was out on the pavement in seconds to greet him …

and the rather large tree. Daisy was at her heels barking furiously at the strange bushy item on the roof.

'Shush, Daisy, it's fine. It's just a tree.' Lucy looked closer, 'So, you went for a real one then?'

'Yeah, you can't beat it.' They'd always had a real tree at home. Well, until Daniel had passed away, that was, when a smaller, sadder-looking fake fir had been bought at John Lewis, and was pulled down from the loft every year in a pretence that life was anywhere near normal. 'And before you say anything, it's okay, I got it from the place that plants at least as many new trees as it cuts down. Sustainable and all that …'

'Right, well that's good. It'll be lovely, I'm sure,' she paused, looking up at it thoughtfully.

'What?' Jack could tell something was up.

'It's great, thank you, but … you do know we're still in November, and it may well be bald by the time Christmas actually gets here,' Lucy added cheekily.

'Ah well, I'll have to take a chance.' In his enthusiasm to recapture some Christmas joy, he hadn't actually considered that. 'Plenty of watering, and … we can make the most of it *fir* now, can't we,' he quipped as he gave a rakish grin.

Lucy had to shake her head and smile at his lame pun. She couldn't help but get caught up in his enthusiasm. After all, it was going to be great fun putting the tree up and decorating it together. It was brilliant to have a special someone to share the build-up to Christmas with this year.

'Yeah, absolutely,' she agreed. 'Come on then, let's get this festive beauty inside.'

❄

'Left a bit … no, right a bit. Argh, steady!'

Lucy felt like she was about to topple off, much like the silver wooden star that she was trying, precariously, to place on top of the humungous Christmas tree (the tip of which was slightly bent over and brushing the cottage lounge ceiling). It had to be an eight-footer, at least. Jack certainly didn't do anything by halves! She'd been perched on Jack's shoulders for the past ten minutes, trying to reach the top tiers. They'd had to move the armchair out from beside the hearth to wedge the beast of a fir into the corner.

Wham's 'Last Christmas' was beating away from her iPhone, and wafts of supper drifted tantalisingly through from the kitchen; a casserole of beef in ale with a seasonal pinch of spice and a sprinkling of grated orange peel was slowly cooking away. She'd light the log fire soon, ready for them to settle down on the sofa. Hah, Daisy was already there snoozing, after tiring herself out chasing strands of tinsel about. Oh yes, a lovely evening together looked to be panning out nicely.

The star at last slid down to rest securely on a knobbly bit of the slightly bent-over tip. And hey presto! 'O-kay, that's it. I'm done,' she called out.

'Thank heavens for that,' a voice groaned from below. 'My shoulders are about to give out.'

'Hey, you, don't be so cheeky … Anyway, a strong young man like you, with all that hard-earned muscle, should find it easy,' she teased back.

Jack was laughing as he crouched to set her down, giving Lucy a tickle under the ribs where his hands spanned her waist, which made her giggle.

They then stood back to look at their handiwork. The

tree glistened and twinkled with loops of fairy lights, some silver and gold baubles, and a few strands of silver and tinsel.

'It's very pretty ...' Lucy started, but then her voice trailed.

'Yeah, it is ...' Jack didn't sound totally convinced either.

'Hmmm ...' Lucy pondered.

'Bit bare,' they both declared together.

'It's because it's so big.'

'One should never complain about a big one,' Jack said formally, whilst grinning away.

Lucy burst out laughing.

'Well, I do happen to know where we can get a few additions. There are some gorgeous decorations for sale at the Driftwood Café. I spotted them when I called in last week. They've got all their Christmas stuff in now.' She glanced at her watch. Though it was almost dark outside, it was still only four o'clock. 'They'll still be open, if we hurry.'

'Sounds like a plan.'

Shoes on, coats grabbed, and they dashed out.

❄

The café door's tinkly bell went with a welcoming chime. Aromas of coffee and baking filled the air. A couple of tables were occupied, with some hushed chatter going on, but the Driftwood Café had that end-of-day feel. Abby was wiping down the empty tables, whilst Louise was carefully covering over the cakes behind the counter.

'Oh hello, my loves. Great to see you. How are you both?' Lou asked.

'Hi, Lou. Hello, Abby. Yeah, good thanks.'

'So, how can I help you?' asked Louise. 'Coffee? Hot chocolates? It's certainly that time of year. Marshmallows, cream?'

'Well, we're actually here to get some new tree decorations. I saw your gorgeous new festive crafts were in the other day. We've just put up the Christmas tree at mine ...'

'Oh, lovely.'

'But well, it's on the large side and my measly old decs look a bit lost on it, to be honest.'

'I see. Well, go ahead and browse to your hearts' content. Our very talented local craftswoman, Eve, has been working with driftwood and sea glass. She's made some beautiful festive pieces.'

Indeed, the wooden shelves were laden with hand-crafted treats: little hearts and stars made from silvered driftwood, scattered with tiny beads of sea glass in reds, greys and blues, and a delicate drift of glitter over them. There were snowmen ornaments, cute felt puffins sporting festive scarves, wooden Father Christmases, festive plaques, and gorgeous hand-stitched animal toys finished with festive holly and tartan-patterned bow ties.

'Freddie would love one of these,' commented Lucy as she spotted them. 'Oh my goodness, look, there's even a Dachshund with a snowflake scarf on. That's it, I'll have to get this one to go in with his parcel. His very own Dachshund toy, how brilliant.'

'Yeah, he'd love that ... he adores Daisy,' agreed Jack.

A tree-shaped stand on the table was hung with a further assortment of decorations. Lucy was delighted by some of the driftwood hearts that glittered delicately in the lights, and Jack was drawn to the stars. So, they chose three of each, then Lucy picked up a box of globe-shaped glass baubles with a unique sea-swirl pattern in silvery blues and greys.

'These are wonderful, Jack, see how the patterns look just like the sea. Perfect for my seaside cottage. I'll have to take these.'

'Yeah, they are really cool. Unique.'

Lucy headed for the till with her festive assortment, including of course, the soft-toy Dachshund.

'Aren't they just fabulous,' commented Louise, as she began to bubble wrap the decorations, popping them one-by-one into a crisp white paper gift bag.

'Yes, perfect.'

And she thought how lovely it was to have new decorations that she and Jack had chosen together for their first Christmas tree, not just the leftovers from her and Liam's last dire Christmas. New steps forward.

'So, can I interest you in anything else, folks? Some cake? I have a little Rum and Raisin Bread and Butter Pudding left? Or my famous Driftwood marshmallow-and-flake topped hot chocolate, perhaps?' Louise was ever the charming host.

Now that did sound good. And, well, it was still a while until supper time.

'Well, it'd be rude not to,' Jack took up, evidently thinking the same thing.

'Yeah, go on then, Lou. Two of your finest hot chocs, please.'

They took up seats at the nearest table and chatted away as they listened to the backdrop of frothing and stirring sound effects. The café soon filling with the cosy aromas of cocoa and warm milk. Two large white mugs then appeared before them, sporting a thick froth of whipped cream and a scattering of mini marshmallows, with a chocolate flake to dip in. 'Here you go, guys. Enjoy!' beamed Abby.

'Oh, delish!'

'Thanks, Abby.'

The hot chocolate was indeed delicious, and without realising it, Lucy ended up with a creamy moustache.

Jack looked at her with a wry grin, and then moved a gentle fingertip above her top lip to wipe it off for her. Giving her *that* look, the one that often appeared in the bedroom. Hmm, once they'd finished drinking this blissful cocoa concoction, it was absolutely time to get home and nestle down beside that tree and cosy fire.

❄

The pair of them held back long enough to enjoy the melt-in-the-mouth, slow-cooked beef supper, served with a caramelised onion mash, all made by Lucy herself. She was very proud of her culinary efforts, and Jack was suitably impressed.

'That was absolutely fantastic, Luce.' He patted his contented stomach.

After quickly clearing away the dishes, and jointly

washing and drying up, they made their way back to the lounge, where the tree with its new decorations glimmered.

'So, it's not just pizzas I'm good at,' beamed Lucy as she sat down beside him.

'Oh, I *know* that.'

And with those words, he took her face between his hands, tilted her chin, and gave her the most sexy, toe-tingling kiss ever. As their lips finally and reluctantly parted, he pulled away to look deep into her eyes, giving a heartfelt smile.

Wow.

They slid down to the rug in front of the fire. Removing each other's clothes, in a tantalisingly sensual dance, they were soon skin-on-skin, fingertips tracing, and hearts racing. And then they took their time, making love slowly, beautifully, with the crackling of the flames and the heat of the log fire warming their bare flesh, not quite a match for the strong and urgent fire of desire within them.

❄

Later, settled on the sofa with a glass of red wine in hand and most of her clothes back on, Lucy leaned against Jack's T-shirted chest, with her feet curled up beside her. The fire had settled to a gold-orange glow, flickering gently in the hearth. A gingerbread-spiced candle filled the room with its warming scent, making a dance of patterns on the wall.

'It's been such a lovely day,' she half spoke, half sighed.

Sitting there, gazing at the tree they'd decorated together, made her think about family times; Mum, Nonna, Olly and Alice, little Freddie, her dad and his partner Jo. It was a little fractured, Lucy's family, but now the dust had settled on her parents' break-up and the years had passed, they all rubbed along fine. And she loved seeing them all over the festive season. She wondered what Jack's family was like? They'd had to cope with so much, losing a son, a brother ... Lucy knew that Jack visited regularly and was obviously very fond of his family.

'You know, I'd loved to meet them, your parents ...' The words just spilled out. It was an honest declaration after this special day they'd had together. She was beginning to feel comfortable and homely with Jack. And well, Christmas was always about family time for Lucy.

But she felt Jack's body freeze beside her. Sensing that something had changed, she shifted to face him, and the look on Jack's face made her stall. He seemed taken aback.

'Oh ... right ...' he stuttered, his gaze dipping down to his lap.

Dammit, she'd said the wrong thing. Had she overstepped the mark? Moved forward too fast?

She quickly tried to defuse the situation. 'You know, I don't mean I have to see them just yet, your parents. It was just a thought. No pressure.' But still, there was a feeling of static in the air, and though the pair of them sat close with Daisy curled between them, the frostiness continued.

Lucy picked up a magazine that was lying on the coffee table, and idly flicked through.

Jack began flicking through the channels with the remote. 'Anything you fancy watching?'

'Not really. You choose.'

He settled on some reality TV; a bunch of celebrities holed up in a castle, a series that they'd often enjoyed. Lucy abandoned the magazine and stared at the screen but found she couldn't concentrate on the programme at all. She sipped her wine, with a headful of worries and doubts. Could Becky have been right after all? Was he inevitably always going to up and leave at some point? Was meeting the parents a no-go zone? Was her gorgeous Jack just the perpetual commitment-phobe, the wanderer?

Lucy found herself feeling awkward for the rest of the evening, and then later on, strangely lonely, with her thoughts buzzing about in her head as she lay in bed with Jack beside her. She could hear the rhythmic sound of his sleeping breath and feel the steady beat of his heart. But her own heart now seemed to be hammering out warning signs.

She might have told herself that she'd go with the flow, let him swan off to those foreign shores if he so wished. But tonight Lucy just wanted to hold onto him – and never let go.

Chapter Sixteen

S at on an old rug beside his pitched tent, high up on a moorland hillside, thoughts rolled through Jack's troubled mind. The air was clear and crisp and it was no doubt going to be a frosty night, but he didn't mind. He had good hiking and camping gear, and he certainly needed a bit of head space.

Last night ... the thought of Lucy meeting his parents, doing the whole family thing. He'd never done that with a girl – well, not since his high-school sweetheart fourteen years ago. As an adult, he'd always kept that bit of distance, and well, if things seemed like they were getting a bit too heavy, he'd know it was time to just move on. Letting himself fall for someone, letting his heart loose, putting it out there to take that inevitable bashing, this was all *way* out of his comfort zone.

God, he knew he loved her, spending time with Lucy was amazing, but it also felt like falling ... and not like some little trip on a pavement, oh no, more like he'd just leaped out of a plane without a bloody parachute.

He gazed out across the valley.

Dusk was beginning to fall, deepening the shadows on the moorland slopes beneath him, and above him, painting ridges that edged the Cheviot skyline with dark indigo contours. He loved space and freedom, reflected here in these hills and the wilder parts of the coast. Outside of his cocktail events, he could get up and go whenever he wanted. Be on his own whenever he needed. Was he really ready to be tied down?

But her face filled his mind, that glossy dark hair, those intense brown eyes, the smell of her perfume, her skin … memories of last night by that fireside, and the many nights before, arose within him. Bloody hell, he felt so torn.

He drew out the old notepad from his rucksack, and began jotting down a few words. Jack often turned to his writing in times of doubt or pain, when he was struggling with his emotions. Doodling 'Lucy', 'in too deep', 'lost', until the words began to weave like threads in his mind, into a poem. Fragments of his heart on paper:

> *A lock of your hair brushes my cheek and*
>   *wakes me.*
> *And I feel alive,*
> *As if every sense in my body is popping, like the*
>   *bubbles in a glass of champagne.*
> *And I feel in love. There, I've said it.*
> *It both lifts me and pulls me down*
> *Into a well of vulnerability, where*
> *I'm in too deep … lost to you.*

Am I lost to myself?
Do I stay? Or is it time to softly walk away?

He was annoyed with himself for acting so coolly with Lucy yesterday. He'd never meant to hurt her, but the look on her face told him otherwise. He found it hard, voicing his feelings face-to-face, it was hard to be vulnerable. And he'd learned over the years to avoid the hurt of losing someone you loved.

He remembered all too well the ominous date that was drawing near. Another year that his brother hadn't had, would never have. This was always an extra-difficult time for Jack and his family.

He gave a heavy sigh. Perhaps this night in the hills might help him make some sense of it all … or, he mused wryly, give him hypothermia.

Where did he and Lucy go from here? He really wasn't sure how to handle this one … this intriguing and gorgeous Northumbrian–Italian dark-haired woman had taken him quite by storm. But was it getting too complicated?

Whatever he decided, he needed to let Lucy know, and soon. Perhaps they were at a crossroads, and he had to decide which way to turn.

Chapter Seventeen

Lucy had struggled to sleep. Daisy had been most put out by her bed companion's constant tossing and turning. In the dark of a late November night, with the wind rolling around outside, Lucy's world felt unstable.

Just thinking that she and Jack might be in trouble made her heart feel so sore. Yesterday – the day after that Christmas tree scenario – she and Jack had shared a couple of brief, sharp texts, both of them skirting the elephant in the room and the 'meet the parents' clanger. And since then he'd been ominously quiet. She'd been through so much with Liam, it couldn't all go wrong with Jack too ... And if it *did* fail, then bloody hell ... she'd miss him ... their trips down the country lanes in the campervan, walks on the beach holding hands ... his touch, his chat, his smile. She'd rather got used to curling up beside him in the cottage's double bed, nestled beside his bare chest, and bare limbs, feeling those taut muscles as she trailed her fingertips over his warm skin.

Thoughts whirled like the last of the autumn leaves outside. Lucy had slipped in and out of a restless sleep through the early hours, waking finally at seven to find the room still dark, the cottage central heating creaking awake with her.

She got up and pushed her feet into cosy sheepskin slippers and wrapped herself up in her warm fleece dressing gown, heading downstairs to make a mug of strong tea. She needed reviving. And she needed some fresh air.

Walking Daisy on the beach soon afterwards, as the sun broke out over the North Sea, she told herself to pull her big girl's socks up and crack on. She was worrying herself sick, without getting to the bottom of things with Jack. She'd find a way through. She and Jack needed to talk, to be honest with each other. For one thing, she needed to find out the truth about his travelling plans. And okay, so maybe Jack wasn't ready for the 'meet the parents' moment as yet, but that didn't mean that he didn't think a lot of her, perhaps even love her … *did it?*

❄

One bit of good news, and today's silver lining, was that the horsebox was now 'All Tyred Up!' as Will at the garage had quipped merrily over the phone, telling her that her pride and joy was ready for her to come and collect any time. And so, by the afternoon, her dove-grey horsebox was back at home and on the driveway. It had looked so bare there these past couple of days. Well, at least that part of her life was getting back on track. And she'd be up and running again in time for her regular market slot on Thursday.

On that note, Lucy realised she better get some more pizza dough made up and ready. It would give her something else to focus on too. Mixer out, music on, she set herself away. She usually had quite a light touch when she kneaded the mix, but this evening the sounds of her thwacking filled the kitchen, taking all her pent-up emotions out on the dough. Hah, kneading could be therapy, after all.

❄

Settled on the sofa an hour later with a cup of tea and a much-needed cuddle with Daisy, her phone buzzed to life on the coffee table.

Caller ID: *Jack* … Aw, phew … *eek.*

Lucy's fingertips trembled as she answered, 'Hi, Jack …'

'Hey, Luce … uhm, can I come over?' There was a hollow note to his voice which chilled Lucy, stirring up her doubts and fears all over again.

'Ah, yeah, of course. You alright?'

'Yeah.'

'So, you mean like *now*?' Lucy checked. It was past 9 p.m.

'Please … yeah.' There was something undeniably sad in his tone.

Oh God, was this it? Lucy felt her stomach drop like a stone. He'd decided they were getting in far too deep, with all her talk of meeting the parents. Was he now ready to up and leave … move on? She felt herself slip into a cold sweat.

'Okay, well, I'll see you soon.' She tried to still the panic that was flooding her veins, and her voice. 'So, a-are you coming across from your place?' She was trying to gauge where he was, what might be going on.

'Yes, so I'll see you soon, okay?'

And with the briefest of goodbyes, that was that. Bloody hell, she had another fifteen minutes or so to fret – that was as long as it would take him to drive over.

By the time she heard the putter and clunk of Ruby pulling up outside, Lucy was pacing the living-room floor; her heart swirling and plummeting with a foreboding fear.

There was a rap at the door, and then Jack walked on in. Lucy went to greet him, with her heart feeling like it was lodged somewhere in her throat. There he was, his face pale and drawn, but still looking strikingly handsome.

Oh God. Well, she may as well face this head on. Get it over with. Steeling herself, and trying her best not to let her eyes mist, she asked, 'Jack, is everything okay?'

He stood facing her, looking lost, as her stomach churned.

There were two long beats of silence before he answered. 'Not really. God, this is difficult, Luce.'

She wasn't sure if she could breathe at this point, swallowing down a knot in her throat. She longed to dive into his arms, but they were down by his sides, his body language so closed. Might she never feel those arms around her again?

Jack held her gaze, gave a sad, heavy smile, 'It's, it's just … it's his birthday today …'

'Whose?' Lucy was confused.

'Daniel's.'

Lucy exhaled. Though it was awful to see his grief, so raw … she couldn't help but feel a sense of relief. There was evidently more to Jack's coolness these past few days than what had been happening between the two of them.

'Oh Jack …' Her arms were outstretched.

He stood … for a few seconds, then moved into that supportive space.

And she held him, oh so close, right there in the narrow hallway, with Daisy – tail wagging at their feet – ready to join in the group hug at ankle height. Gradually, Lucy felt his body begin to give, folding into her warmth. Their breathing slowed, steadied. When Jack finally pulled away, there were tears in his eyes.

There she'd been for the past two nights, worrying herself sick about having said the wrong thing, imagining all sorts of commitment-phobe break-up scenarios. But all the while Jack had been hurting, grieving. Lucy dissed herself. She could have been there for him last night. If only he'd opened up earlier. But she wasn't a mind reader, they were still new to all this, as a couple. It was hard when Jack closed down, shut himself off in his grief, but … he was here now. He'd come to her, in all his raw vulnerability. And that in itself was a huge step. Her arms were still gently holding him as they stood facing each other.

'I'm so sorry, Jack. It must be such a hard time for you and your family. Tell me how I can help? Cup of tea? Glass of wine? More holding you close?' She offered with a caring smile.

'Well, more of *that* would definitely help,' he responded, with a glint of the old sparkle coming back to his eyes. 'But for now, a glass of wine would be good.'

They headed for the cottage kitchen, where Lucy uncorked a bottle of red. Taking up the two stools, they began to settle down, the heaving emotions beginning to calm as they quietly chatted.

'It must so difficult. Every year, every occasion … birthdays, Christmas,' Lucy prompted gently.

'Yeah,' Jack nodded, his eyes still a little misty. He took a gulp of wine.

Lucy didn't want to probe too soon, too far. For all his bravado, and cocktail barman antics, Jack was a deep soul. If he wanted to talk about losing his brother, it needed to be in his own time. There was still so much to iron out between the two of them, of course there was. But all she needed to do right now was to support him.

✳

Lucy had hit the nail on the head, Jack reflected. Today had been a struggle. Birthdays, Christmas, family occasions, that's when memories and feelings resurfaced like shards of glass from an old wound. It wasn't that you ever forgot; not one day went by when he didn't think of his brother in some way, a fleeting glimpse of his face, an echo of his laugh, a saying he might have used, a kick of a football, an unexpected waft of the Lynx Africa body spray Daniel used to pile on as a teenager – especially when Dan's crush for Lily Douglas at Middle School hit hard – but these anniversary days, they were like little daggers, ready to give you a stinging prod.

He and Lucy were now in the lounge, having moved from the kitchen to seek out the comfy sofa. The red wine was slipping down nicely and it was beginning to loosen his tongue. 'We went up to the dune today,' Jack started, his voice soft, bruised. 'The one where we scattered his ashes ...' He'd taken Lucy there several weeks ago, showed her the place.

Lucy looked up and held his gaze with the tenderest of smiles.

'Me, Mum and Dad. Mum took a flask and some cake she'd made specially, and we just sat for a while up at the top, chatting. Remembering stuff, you know ...'

'Oh ...' Lucy placed her hand tenderly over his, and stayed quiet, leaving him the space to talk. They were shoulder to shoulder, with Daisy wedged snoring in the slim gap between them.

'He'd have been thirty-one today.'

So young. Just a year older than Lucy, and two older than Jack.

Jack took a slow breath, then sighed, 'Didn't even get to see his twenty-first.'

Dachshund Daisy then reached a snoozy paw out to touch his hand. It was probably accidental, but it looked like she was supporting him too, bless. Lucy couldn't help but give a sad smile.

'I had a message today,' he continued, 'from Emily, his old girlfriend. She keeps in touch now and again ... said she was thinking of us all and sending love. And then, I foolishly looked up her page – we're friends on Facebook – and there she was, all smiley-faced with her husband and their three-year-old son ... and shit, it just floored me ...

'Daniel never got to have that. To get married. Be a dad. *Will never* get to have that. It's such a bastard. And I know I can't change anything, and I know it's been a long time … but it still hurts, Luce. It still bloody well hurts.'

'Of course it will, my love. It's just so unfair.' Lucy couldn't begin to imagine losing Olly that young, for him never to have met Alice, or have had little Freddie.

'Hah, death doesn't do fair,' Jack's tone was steely, full of hurt. 'It's arbitrary … some bolt out of the blue when you're twenty, some old guy of ninety-nine withering slowly away. Who knows why or when …? Probably just as well …

'You do learn to carry on, you have to, there's not a lot of choice,' he continued, 'but it's tough sometimes. Catches up on you, you know.' He paused.

'I can't pretend to know exactly how you feel. What that grief must be like for someone so young, so close … But I know it must be really tough.' Lucy squeezed his hand.

Jack saw the Christmas tree there, twinkling away before them. It had been so nice that afternoon putting the tree up together, until he'd snapped and then clammed right up.

'I'm sorry, Luce, about closing down on you … about the parent thing. Sat there on Dan's dune with Mum and Dad today, well it made me think. I don't want you to feel shut out. But I've got to be honest with you, it's just too soon … *for me.* You seeing them, meeting up, playing happy families. It's still early days, Luce.' He really didn't want to be hurting her, dashing her dreams, but he had to be honest. And he couldn't change who he was overnight.

'Yeah, okay.' What else could Lucy say? She didn't want to lose him by pushing him too far, too fast. She leaned her head against his chest, so he couldn't see the unbidden tear that had trailed down her cheek.

'That's cool. Thank you.'

Lucy tried to gather her emotions. Tonight couldn't be about her; Jack was struggling, anyone could see that, but she was left with more questions than answers about their relationship. At least he had come to her … he had been honest … but it left her wondering again … giving his heart, letting her into his life fully, would he ever be ready?

Chapter Eighteen

J ack stayed over that night. They made love; their closeness physical. Their bodies still in tune at least.

The next morning, Jack was up and made his way down to the kitchen, freshly showered, with merely a towel draped around his hips. He'd nipped out to get a couple of coffees to take back to bed for the two of them. Lucy was still up there, making the most of a rare lie-in. There was no rush this morning, no event bookings to prepare for, and the whole day ahead. Another hour in bed maybe, then a stroll on the beach, a casual bite of lunch perhaps … After all the mixed emotions of yesterday, a chilled-out day was needed.

Jack had let Daisy out for her morning pee in the back yard a few minutes ago, and she was still there sniffing about as he poured the coffees. He heard her barking excitedly, and turned his head. It was probably just a blackbird or something setting her off.

With that, the glass-partitioned back door to the cottage

rattled. There was a knock at the same time as the door blasted open.

'Coo-eee!'

And there, wrapped in a thick black woollen coat and sensible weather-proof bootees, was Nonna. A blast of chill air and a happy Dachshund came in with her. Jack felt distinctly and dangerously underdressed. His cheeks were no doubt blasting an embarrassed pink too. After all, it was more than evident that he hadn't just arrived at the cottage himself.

'Oh …!' There was a second where the elderly lady seemed slightly flustered. She pursed her lips, taking in the view before her with wide eyes before saying, 'Oh, *morning* Jack. Nice to see you!' She gave a cheeky grin.

'Ah … yes … morning, Nonna,' Jack bumbled out, tightening his grip on the towel around his waist.

'I imagine my granddaughter is still upstairs,' she added, smooth as you like. 'I am a bit sharp.'

'Oh, is she expecting you?'

Bloody hell, there he'd been, wanting to avoid getting involved with family commitments. And here he was, face to face with Lucy's grandmother. To be fair, he had turned up rather out of the blue last evening. But Lucy hadn't mentioned anything about an impending visit. He glanced at the kitchen clock; it was only 8:45 a.m. Perhaps it had slipped Lucy's mind. Jack held onto the towel even tighter, hoping nothing else might *slip*.

'Oh no, pet. It was all a bit last minute. Marjorie next door mentioned she was popping over to run an errand Seahouses way, and well, I thought I may as well take the opportunity of a free lift, seeing as we were virtually passing the door. Thought it'd be a nice surprise.'

'Well, it's certainly a surprise.' Jack managed a wry smile. 'Well then, I was just about to take up a coffee for Lucy. I'll go do that now ...' He had to get away, get some clothes on. He wished he'd picked up the big bath towel now, not the bloody hand towel. 'And then we can pop back down, make you a cup of tea or something. I-I'll let her know you're here.'

'You do that, pet.' Nonna's face was beaming with a knowing smile. She looked to be suppressing laughter, in fact.

'Well, make yourself at home.' Jack couldn't get out of that kitchen quick enough, leaving the drinks on the side. He trotted up the narrow stairway gingerly, clinging to the towel, just in case the old lady had decided to follow him. But there was no sign of her as he reached the top, phew. 'Lucy, ah, Luce ...' he hissed urgently as he stepped inside the bedroom door, 'your nonna's here.'

Lucy lay sprawled in their crumpled sheets.

'What? Seriously?' She bolted upright. 'At this time of day? Are you sure?'

''Course I'm bloody sure. I haven't just seen a ghost. She's sat in the kitchen waiting for a cup of tea.'

Oh good Lord, just when Jack hadn't wanted to get all 'family fussy'. Nonna's timing was really out. But then Lucy took in the image of Jack before her and couldn't help but grin. 'And you were dressed like that ...?'

Jack had to smile too, shaking his head at the craziness of it all. 'Didn't have a lot of options. The tea towel on the side was even smaller.'

❄

Lucy dressed hastily and headed down to the kitchen, blushing furiously as she opened the white wooden door.

'Morning, Nonna. Well, this *is* a surprise.'

'Good morning, Lucy. Nice to see your young man just now. Going well, is it …?' Nonna raised an amused eyebrow. She knew how the world worked these days. The young ones being a bit freer and easier. It was all certainly different from her own courting times.

Lucy squirmed with embarrassment; she really didn't want to discuss her budding and slightly complex relationship with her grandmother.

'Hmmm … cup of tea?' she offered, moving the conversation swiftly on, as she discovered her own cup of coffee which Jack had made earlier, cooling on the side.

Nonna continued undeterred: 'Well, I hope he's taking all this seriously. You don't need to be wasting time on someone who'll mess you about. It's about time you found yourself a good man, Lucy. Someone to be there by your side.'

'I know, Nonna, but it's not the Middle Ages, times have changed. Relationships don't have to be all wedding rings and promises of forever. And I can manage quite well enough on my own …'

'I know you can *manage*, pet. You're successful, ambitious, hard-working, you've got your own home, and I'm so proud of you for that. You've turned your life around with your new pizza venture. But I'm not talking about that, I'm talking about having some love and laughter in your life. Having that special someone to share things with, someone who'll stick around … it all makes the world seem that bit brighter. I wouldn't have been without your papa all those years.'

Lucy nodded, feeling strangely emotional. Nonna's words picking at her recent wounds.

'Now you've turned things around after that horrid business with Liam,' Nonna added, on a roll, 'maybe you can see you need to be with someone who really cares for you. Someone you can share your hopes and dreams … your life with. And Jack, *well*,' the old lady continued with a wise smile, 'now he's a different laddie to Liam altogether.'

A smile crept over Lucy's face at that observation. They were indeed polar opposites. Liam, so bloody staid and boring.

'He's charming, for sure, Lucy. And he seems a nice enough, lad,' she said, lowering her voice. 'But I do worry that he'll end up being a bit of a fly-by-night … a bit of a heartbreaker. Anyhow, that's for you to make your own mind up on, I suppose.'

Lucy stayed quiet on the matter, her own doubts still lingering silently even after last night's heart-to-heart. Yes, Jack was adventurous and romantic, caring and passionate, and he certainly made her soul *and* her body sing, but was their relationship enough to make him stay, to commit to anything longer term?

With that, the man himself reappeared in the kitchen, this time fully clothed.

'Morning, Jack,' Nonna chanted.

Lucy felt herself flush after Nonna's candid conversation.

'Nice to see you dressed,' the old lady added, cool as a cucumber.

❄

With another hour before Marjorie was due back to pick Nonna up again, they decided to take her across to the Driftwood Café for a bite of brunch. She'd already had her porridge this morning, apparently, but admitted with a twinkle in her eye that a toasted teacake and a nice cuppa might not go amiss.

Whilst Jack and Lucy tucked into sausage baps, made with the famous Bamburgh Bangers from the butcher along the coast, Nonna told them all about Rothbury life, including the latest gossip from the bowling green, with the pompous Vice Chair found to be cheating, surreptitiously shifting his opponent's ball with his foot – scandalously hilarious amongst the older generation of the village. And Mrs Devlin, a mere snippet of a thing in her forties, had left her admittedly grumpy and rather lazy husband and moved in with recently widowed Mr Clark, who was well into his sixties, and a keen member of the tennis club. With the village verdict undecided as to whether they might have already been seeing each other for some time beforehand, or whether it was mere cuckoo-style opportunism.

'So.' Nonna moved the conversation on. 'What have you two got on? Any plans for the day?'

Jack mused wryly at that point that his intended plan for a long and leisurely lie-in with her granddaughter had had to be curtailed, but he found he couldn't be annoyed with the old lady. He had to admit it was nice that she'd wanted to see Lucy, and had made the trip over. Jack's own grandparents lived further away, one set were based in Yorkshire, where his father had been brought up, and he had a granny in Devon, so their visits were less frequent. He was very fond of them, however.

'Well,' Lucy answered, 'just a quiet one really. We've both had a lot on lately ...' Her voice trailed. Wary of looking too clingy, she didn't want to commit Jack to have to do anything in particular.

'Ah, we'll probably walk the beach at some point. Maybe go for a little drive in Ruby,' Jack mooted.

Nonna raised her eyebrows inquisitively, 'Ruby?'

'Oh, that's my campervan,' Jack explained. 'She's a real character, and she's ruby red. Hence the name.'

'Ah, yes, I remember seeing her at Lucy's party now. Lovely looking camper, she is. A Westfalia, by any chance?'

'Yeah, how do you know?'

'The left-hand drive and the layout of the front screen were a bit of a giveaway. Oh yes, me and Lucy's papa had a few adventures back in the day. Our friends, Stan and Lorna, had a campervan very similar to that. We had some wonderful weekends away with them. It was compact, to say the least, so me and Papa would be tucked up on blow-up lilos in the awning overnight.'

'Really?' *Who knew?* Nonna's antics never ceased to amaze Lucy. She had certainly lived a full and interesting life.

'Oh yes,' the old lady began to chuckle, 'it was all great fun until the time your papa's lilo punctured in the middle of the night. We used to line two single ones up together. Woke up on the floor, he did. Said it was like sleeping on a bed of rocks. Oh, and his back … He could hardly move that next morning.' She smiled nostalgically. 'I remember it like it was yesterday. Could hardly walk … looked like John Wayne, just off a horse. Well, me and Lorna had to stifle our giggles. It was unlike your Papa, but he was *so* grumpy that next day. Like a bear with a sore head. Ah, those were the days …'

The two younger ones smiled at her fond memories.

'In fact, I'm thinking of planning another little adventure,' announced Nonna. 'Yes, something for next year. Well, me and Marjorie, that is. She seemed quite up for it when I mentioned it the other evening.'

'Ooh, what's that then, Nonna?' Lucy was curious.

'Spring in Sorrento. A bit of a final fling.'

'Oh …' The words *final fling* stuck awkwardly in Lucy's mind. The thought of Nonna jetting off to Italy set off huge alarm bells. 'Well, I hope you're not thinking of popping your clogs while you're over there?' Lucy was joking, but her words suddenly felt foreboding. All of a sudden it hit her that Nonna wasn't getting any younger. She was no spring chicken, after all. What if anything should happen to her beloved grandmother whilst they were away? It was only last year she'd been a bit poorly. 'Have you thought it through, Nonna? You'd need proper insurance in place, and that could be expensive.' Lucy's sensible streak was coming to the fore.

'Well, I think it sounds amazing,' Jack chipped in. 'I've spent some brilliant times in Italy. Such a cool place. All that history … Had a real memorable night drinking Negronis down by the Coliseum.'

Jack was encouraging her now too. Crikey, it was all a

bit different from Nonna's usual organised coach trips to Scarborough. In fact, the furthest her grandmother had travelled in the past ten years was the Lake District. She wondered if her mum knew about any of this. Or had Nonna been planning to launch it on them as a done deal, flights booked and everything? She wouldn't put it past the wily old girl.

'Well, I've looked into insurance, yes,' Nonna answered pragmatically, 'and Saga do a good one. It's a bit expensive, but it'll be worth it.'

'Ri-ght,' Lucy was still a bit dumbfounded. She wasn't quite sure why all this was worrying her so much, it wasn't like they were heading off somewhere really dangerous, but she just felt suddenly protective of her precious grandmother.

'I want to go while I'm still able,' Nonna explained. 'I want to go back and visit all the old places me and Papa were so fond of. See some of his relatives too, there are a few still remaining. We still send each other Christmas cards. I might even get to meet their grandchildren, the next generation.' She was smiling wistfully.

'Well, that sounds a great idea, Nonna,' Jack said, clearly backing the plan. The world adventurer that he was ... Lucy found herself feeling irked. They'd all be bloody well setting off now ...

'Any top-ups, folks?' Louise appeared with a fresh cafetière of coffee, and offered to make Nonna another pot of tea.

'Oh, that'd be lovely, dear. Thank you.' Nonna lifted her cup with a smile.

'Now then Lucy,' Lou took up, 'don't forget it's

Christmas Book Club this week. Followed next week by the grand Christmas Tree Light Up on the village green.'

'Ah, okay, thanks. Yes, I've been catching up on my festive reading. Looking forward to it. And the Christmas tree in the village, that sounds good, too.' Lucy gave a weak smile, her mind still fizzing about Nonna's possible foreign trip, as she accepted a top-up of coffee.

'Don't know where the time is going, November is whizzing by … Christmas'll be here before we know it,' Lou said with a happy tut.

'It will indeed,' agreed Nonna.

With that, Jack excused himself for a moment, heading off for the café's bathroom.

'Yes, you need to go and have some adventures too, Lucy,' Nonna took up, going back to her earlier theme. 'You're working hard, I know that, but sometimes you need to take a little time out too. It doesn't have to be expensive. It's the simple things that are often the most fun. A sunny afternoon and we'd pack up a picnic when Sofia was little, head off to the beach, sometimes even go for supper once Papa had finished his shift on the buses. You need to go and live life, Lucy. Find someone special to live it with …'

Well, that was easier said than done.

'Maybe … I've a lot on my plate just now, though,' Lucy's response was purposely vague. 'With the business just finding its feet and all that … And I do think you need to think carefully about your trip,' Lucy continued, now Jack the Go-For-It-Guy was out of earshot. 'Consider all the issues of foreign travel, medical care … I – well, I just wouldn't want you to get caught out.' Lucy didn't want to be the party-pooper but someone had to spell out the facts here. Her wonderful grandmother could end up stuck in a hospital, miles from home, without the right cover. No family at her side, nothing.

'It's something I really want to do, Lucy,' Nonna said, a determined glint in her eye. Lucy knew to let it rest, for now at least.

Adventures, taking life by the balls … Why did that still scare Lucy so much? Yes, she'd gone in all guns blazing for her new pizza venture, but relationships, leisure, travel … maybe it was time to take a leaf out of Nonna's book and lighten up a little. See where life took her?

And Jack, well, her heart dipped again at the thought; whether he had any intention of including her in his next adventures, or even in the next few weeks of his life, she couldn't be sure of that at all.

❄

Invitation to

The Christmas Book Club

The Driftwood Café

7 p.m. Thursday 25th November

❄

Chapter Nineteen

Christmas was gearing up in Lucy's village. First up was Book Club night at Driftwood and with it being late November, this week's theme was 'Best Christmas Books'. They had been asked to bring along their favourite festive reads and were going to tell each other why they loved them so much.

After a frosty early-evening stroll from the cottage, Lucy entered the Driftwood Café – its jingly bell announcing her arrival – and as well as everyone bringing a festive bake themselves, it was apparent that Louise had gone all out with festive foodie treats for them all too. The table was laden with cinnamon-and-spice-scented mince pies, filo-and-marzipan melting stollen slices, and a yule log covered in thick chocolate frosting. The smells – ah, divine – bringing back memories of Christmases past. Lucy's mouth was already watering.

'Hello, hello, come on in,' Lou greeted her, coming out from behind the counter.

'Hi, Lucy.' 'Evening, Luce.' Helen and Sarah were already there, with warm, welcoming smiles.

'Hello, pet,' Glynis added, 'pull up a seat, come and join the gang.'

'Don't hold back, help yourselves to the spread, my lovelies,' said Louise. 'Abby's just warming the mulled wine, or there's the usual tea and coffee, if you prefer.'

'Ooh, mulled wine, that sounds delicious. And look at this scrumptious lot. You've really pushed the festive boat out here, Lou. How fantastic.' Lucy had a big smile plastered over her face as she added her offering of homemade Christmas-tree-shaped buttery shortbread. They were certainly in for a feast this evening.

What a warm welcome too. Books and baking, and a big dollop of friendship. It was enough to brighten any day, however chilly it was outside.

'Well, it's only Christmas once a year. I have my friends gathered, and 'tis the season to be jolly.' Louise brought over yet another plate filled with treats. This time a stack of gooey-looking brownies.

'More? Blimey, Lou, there's enough to feed an army here,' exclaimed Paul.

'Hah, yeah an army of elves,' added Cathy.

'Look you lot, you'd be moaning soon enough if I didn't put out a good display. Anything left over can be used tomorrow in the café; I'm not that daft. And these happen to have a festive touch of Baileys in them.'

'Oh, well in that case …' Helen's eyes had lit up.

'Anyhow, have you all brought along your favourite festive reads?' Louise set down her baking platter. 'Anyone want to set the ball … or should I say *bauble* … rolling?'

A happy groan broke out amongst the group.

Abby popped her hand up. 'Well, I absolutely adore *The Christmasaurus* by Tom Fletcher. Mum started us off on it a few years ago; she'd bought it for my younger sister, Freya. Now I have to read it every year. It's like part of my Christmas preparations. December hits, I fetch it out from the bookcase, curl up with a mug of hot chocolate and I'm all set up.'

'Yeah, I love all the Christmas children's books,' chipped in Cathy, 'I remember reading them with my little ones every year. *'Twas the Night before Christmas* and *The Jolly Christmas Postman*, such magical books. Always kept them back, special like, so they didn't get read any other time of the year. There's that wonderful sense of anticipation and excitement to the story, even pulling them off the shelf makes you feel instantly festive.'

'Well, it's *A Christmas Carol* for me,' pronounced Glynis, after helping herself to a slice of stollen. 'Dickens was such a clever writer. Still so relevant today, too. And who'd have thought … a ghost story for Christmas, and a warning with it. His characters like Scrooge are just brilliant, aren't they?'

'Yep. And you get so wrapped up in that Victorian dark winter world,' commented Paul.

'It wasn't all doom and gloom though, remember the Cratchit family and the warmth of that home over the festive season. It's a reminder to be caring, to think of others,' continued Glynis.

'Yeah,' Lucy agreed. She'd enjoyed that Dickens story, though she had to confess it was the *Muppet Christmas Carol* version that stuck in her mind.

'Cosy, heart-warming Christmas books are what I

adore.' It was Sarah's turn next. 'I have a few faves such as Milly Johnson – loved her book *The Mother of all Christmases*. It was happy, a little sad in parts, and it gave me all the festive feels. And then Sarah Morgan, she always creates a gorgeous Christmas story. Heidi Swain, Trisha Ashley … I could go on and on with different authors …' Sarah raved, evidently an avid fan of a Christmas tale.

'Oh, plenty for my Christmas list there. I'll have to jot those authors down. I like a bit of a festive escape at this time of year,' said Abby. 'Curling up with a book when it's all cold and miserable outside, bliss.'

'Yeah, I enjoyed Trisha Ashley's *The Twelve Dates of Christmas*,' it was Lucy's turn to add to the bookish Christmas list, 'and I'm halfway through *Christmas Under a Cranberry Sky*. That's lovely so far, it's by Holly Martin. Her books always lift me up.'

'Well, sorry to put a spanner in the works, but I'd much rather something gripping,' Helen spoke up. 'I'm all for "A Very Murderous Christmas". And that's exactly how I'll be feeling when the kids are squabbling, when me ex turns up with his new arm-candy, and I'm betting the bloody turkey dinner turns out all dry.'

'Bah humbug, Helen!' Paul exclaimed with a wry smile. 'Hey, are you alright though, pet?' he followed up caringly. 'Christmas can be a tough time when things aren't so good at home, can't it.'

'I'm okay, guys … well, I'm getting there.' Helen was putting her brave face back on. It had been a difficult year, with her divorce recently come through, and a young family to try and stick back together.

'Well, if you need somewhere to escape to over the

Christmas season, you know where me and Martin are?' added Paul. 'The Baileys is always on ice, there'll be prosecco in the fridge and we've plenty of festive fodder.'

'Yeah, and I'm always here for you too, Helen,' Louise offered kindly. 'The door here at Driftwood and at home is always open.'

There were nods of support from around the table.

'Where are you for Christmas, pet?' Lou continued.

'Over at my mam's. We'll be fine, thank you, and well looked after. Dean is having the kids Boxing Day. That'll be me, all set up with a movie on and a family tin of Quality Street all to myself.'

'My door's always open too, Helen. And you're welcome to bring the kids along,' Lucy offered, remembering that lonely feeling all too well.

'Aw, thanks everyone.' Helen took a swift dab at her eyes with her hanky.

Plates loaded with brownies and mince pies then did the rounds.

'Top-ups anyone?' Abby had the jug of mulled wine to hand.

'Gosh, these are delicious. Did you make them, Lou?' Cathy asked.

'Yeah, you've got to love a brownie.'

'But what's in them again? They taste amazing!'

'A dash of Baileys, or you could use brandy or rum, whatever you fancy really …'

'Boozy Brownies. Bloody brilliant.' Paul was sat licking his lips. 'That's another one for my baking to-dos. Martin would be in heaven with these.'

'Well, talking of food, my favourite book at this time of

year has to be Nigel Slater's *The Christmas Chronicles*,' Lou smiled. 'Full of festive anecdotes, stories about Christmas traditions and recipes too. My Christmas go-to, that one is. It's just fabulous. And you can dip in and out. I like that when it's such a busy time of year.'

The conversation then turned to Christmas in the village. Embleton had already started putting its lights up.

'Oh, and don't forget to come along to the Christmas Tree and Carols night, Lucy.'

'Ooh, yes, when is that again? Sounds lovely.'

'Next week … Friday, 3rd of December.'

'Oh yes, it's a gorgeous event,' Cathy added. 'All the village gets together for the lighting up of the Christmas tree. And then there's mince pies and tea and coffee over in the village hall.'

'The children from the village primary school come along and sing for us too.'

'Great. Can I do anything to help at all? Maybe I could make some panforte to go with the mince pies.'

'What's that then?' Paul quirked an eyebrow.

'It's an Italian-style fruit-and-nut cake,' Louise chipped in, knowledgeably.

'Yeah, my nonna has a great recipe for that. It's a family favourite at Christmas time. Filled with almonds, fruit, honey and spice.'

'That sounds delicious. I'm sure it will be very welcome. I'll let Brenda on the committee know,' Cathy replied.

The chat continued for a while, all calm and leisurely, until the mulled wine ran out and the teapot was drained. With tummies pleasantly filled, festive plans afoot, plenty of new Christmas book recommendations to check out, and just a few weeks left until the big day itself, the last Driftwood Book Club of the year came to a very jolly close.

❄

Lucy headed home with a festive spring in her step. But as she turned the corner onto her street, something seemed amiss. At first, she thought it was ice glinting, but as she neared, she saw a smattering of glass was lying on the pavement near to her cottage, glimmering in the light of the old-fashioned street lamp.

Lucy's heart started to beat double-time, she quickened her pace to find that her Jeep's passenger window had been shattered. A circular hole glaring at her as if a stone had hit it. She felt her heart sink – her good mood immediately shattered too.

Not again! This couldn't be coincidence, surely? Was somebody actually targeting her? But who, *why?* Or was she just putting two and two together after the tyre incident, and scaring herself needlessly, when it could well be just some freak accident?

She moved around the Jeep, her palms all clammy with nerves, and looked at the horsebox; might that have been sabotaged again too? But checking it out up close, that vehicle, at least, seemed unscathed. Finally, she turned to scan the front of her little house. The door, the windows, they were all intact. Thank heavens for that, as little Daisy had been home alone while she'd been out at the Book Club.

Oh … did they know she was out? Had someone been watching her? Her blood ran cold. She glanced over her shoulder, felt a prickle of anxiety, then grabbed her keys from her purse and bolted in through the front door, locking it firmly behind her. Telling herself all the while that there was probably a simple explanation, some accident, or perhaps tomfoolery gone a bit too far with the local kids. But despite her reasoning and the flood of warmth from her cosy cottage haven, her new life here suddenly felt threatened. Her bolt-hole violated.

She was overreacting, she repeated to herself, trying to stop the flow of anxious thoughts. But as she found Daisy, with her tail wagging away in the kitchen, Lucy couldn't yet still the hammering of her heart.

❄

Invitation to

Christmas Tree Light Up and Carols

Embleton Village

Friday 3rd December, 6 p.m.

❄

Chapter Twenty

Tonight was the 'Christmas Tree and Carols Celebration'. And just about every cottage, shop, pub and hotel was doing its part with window displays, fairy lights and even a flashing Santa Claus and reindeer swinging between the rooftops at the far end of the village – the real Santa would certainly know to stop here.

There was a real buzz about the place with villagers, young and old, watching and helping to decorate the massive Christmas tree (yes, it was even bigger than Lucy's, haha!) which had been hoisted up on the grassy area at the end of Front Street, just down from Cathy's shop and next to the Dunstanburgh Castle Hotel. There was even a cherry picker in situ, with a chap reaching for the top branches, trying to secure the last loop of multicoloured lights.

Caught up in the festivities, Lucy had placed a row of pretty fairy-lit wooden stars along her front windowsill and had added a fir wreath to her mantelpiece. She'd also bought new Christmas stockings for her and Daisy to hang up by the fire. She'd even considered getting one for Jack, but then wondered if that might be yet another step too far and give him the wobbles once again.

She wondered what they might in fact both do over Christmas? It was still early days in their relationship, so they'd most likely be spending Christmas Day with their own families, but aside from that, could she dare to hope that they might get some special time together too? After a rather lonely last Christmas, that would certainly be rather lovely.

The sound of hammering brought her back to the village activities. The lighting-up ceremony was to take place later on at 6 p.m., once it had got dark. Lucy had already baked her panforte, ready to help out with the village hall catering. Her cottage kitchen was still filled with the aromas of toasted nuts, cinnamon, fruit and spice. She'd just stepped out to take a look at proceedings and to show off Daisy, who was trotting along beside her sporting her latest Nonna creation – an Argyle-style cream-and-green winter knit.

Walking the village loop, Lucy came across Cathy stood by the massive pine, giving instructions to the heavens. Well, actually to her husband Kev, who was the chap up the cherry picker stringing out loops of coloured bulbs and dangling very big baubles.

'Hey, Cathy, the tree's looking great.' Lucy smiled.

'Oh hi, Lucy. Well, it'll be even better tonight with all the lights on. That's when the village starts to look really magical.'

'You all ready for Christmas, then?'

'Hmm, getting there. Mind you, with the village shop

open right up until five o'clock Christmas Eve, I certainly have to be organised.'

'Oh, I bet. It'll be all go.'

'It is indeed. Luckily my mother-in-law doesn't mind cooking the Christmas dinner, so we all pile around there for a big family get-together.'

'Ah, that sounds perfect ... Looking forward to this evening?' Lucy added.

'Yes, it's always a lovely do, and it seems to mark the beginning of Christmas in the village. It's when my kids start to get excited – the levels dial up a notch here on in.' She gave a weary smile.

Brenda, from the Parish Council, appeared, looking flustered and bustling forward with a supersized, rather gaudy golden star ready to top the tree. 'Found it at last, right at the back of the bloody village hall cupboard.'

'Oh, I've just dropped the panforte cake I promised at the village hall. I left it on one of the trestle tables. I hope that was okay. The door was open ...' Lucy explained.

'Marvellous. And how very kind of your young man to offer to serve mulled wine this evening too. What a super idea.'

'It's our pleasure,' replied Lucy. 'Well, everyone's made me feel so welcome since I arrived here.' It really was lovely to feel a part of this village that she could now call home, and Lucy was more than happy to do her bit to help. The only shadows that had been cast here were those of the horsebox tyres and the incident of the car window the other night, but she'd gathered her nerve, told herself it was most likely an unfortunate fluke. With the glass now fixed at the local garage, Lucy had decided to draw a line under it – otherwise she'd only spiral into a pit of anxiety.

A sudden 'Toot! Toot!' announced the timely arrival of Ruby, swinging in from the main road and pulling up beside them. Hearing about the village event, Jack had also come up trumps, offering to help out that evening by serving complimentary mulled wine. He figured it'd be a nice gesture, and as a bonus, it might just let a few more people know about his Cocktail Campervan. VW Ruby would be sitting pretty, parked up beside the festive tree in line for any camera shots by the local press too. Oh yes, that might just be a smooth marketing ploy – Jack was ever the entrepreneur, spotting an opportunity a mile off.

'Hello, you,' said Jack, who was looking rather dashing in a dark-blue-checked flannel shirt and indigo jeans. He gave Lucy a warm smile.

'Hey …' She jumped into the passenger seat, popping Daisy on her lap.

And that was followed by a brief but cute kiss that made Lucy's cheeks glow. The Christmas spirit was evidently infectious.

❄

Fragrant aromas of cinnamon and spice wafted through Ruby's cabin; the mulled wine was ready and keeping warm in a large tea urn that Jack had borrowed for the occasion from his mum's WI group. Jack hadn't strictly declared what he'd be using it for. (Blimey, he'd have to give it a damn good wash before returning it, lol, or the next coffee morning in the Alnwick Hall would be full of sniffy comments about the rather peculiar taste.)

He had another huge back-up pan prepared, plus more bottles of red wine, oranges and spices to add to the mix ongoing, if need be. Who knew how much a gaggle of festive, thirsty villagers might get through?

He'd also made sure to cater for the children, bringing cartons of cranberry juice and bottles of soda to make fizzy cranberry mocktails in festive cardboard cups, including the little ones in the fun. Lucy had had a bit of a soppy look on her face when he'd mentioned that to her. He had a brief moment of panic, but told himself it was likely because he'd come across as sweet and thoughtful, and not because she was yearning for kids herself any time soon.

With Ruby organised and ready to move the short distance from one street to the next, Jack, Lucy and Daisy – who, of course, had to be part of the village celebrations – leaped back in. Parked up alongside *the* Festive Fir soon after, where a few last-minute tweaks were being made by the committee to its lights, tinsel trails and baubles, they set up. A few early birds from the village were gathering already, for front-row viewing.

The camper's chrome counter also glittered with tinsel, mini baubles, plus some sprigs of holly. Jack and Lucy quickly put the final touches to a seasonally smart Ruby, and after setting out neat rows of holly-patterned cardboard cups, they were soon ready to pour. Lucy offered to do the children's drinks so Jack could concentrate on serving the warm spiced wine – teamwork was key.

Daisy was sat in the passenger seat, having had an outfit change into the new red jumper from the Corbridge

Christmas market along with a sparkly collar, more than happy to watch the world go by, with just the odd bark for good measure to remind everyone she was there.

'Right Luce, ready for action?' Jack asked with a grin.

'Absolutely, and I'm looking forward to this evening. It's great to be in my home village, there's bound to be loads of people I know …'

Soon voices could be heard from along the street, with people gathering from all sides. Cars began to park up, with excited chatter filling the air as families spilled out, with two-year-olds and eighty-two-year-olds holding hands. It was a cold clear night, the sky now dark with a smattering of stars, and a mist of chilly breath filling the still evening air.

As Jack began to pour out the first fragrant cups, the scented steam from the ruby-coloured liquid wafted out.

'Ooh, that smells delicious. Mulled wine, is it? Lovely. How much do I owe you, pet?' their first customer, a grey-haired lady, asked as she stepped up to take one.

'Oh no, it's all complimentary,' explained Jack. 'A gesture of goodwill, and the start of a merry Christmas for us all, hopefully.'

'Oh, that's wonderful. You sure?' She sounded most surprised to be getting something for nothing.

'Absolutely. Lucy here has just moved into the village, and well, we wanted to do something to help out this evening.'

'Well, welcome to the village, both of you.'

Jack raised his eyebrows at the assumption that they lived together, but stayed quiet. Lucy felt herself blush beside him.

The lady continued, unaware of her faux pas that had left the pair of them feeling awkward, 'And in that case, I might just pop something in the charity box back at the village hall later, in lieu.'

'That sounds a lovely idea,' agreed Lucy, relieved to move the conversation on. 'A kind gesture that keeps giving, how nice.'

'Coo-ee, Val, over here! We can see the lights better from up the hill, I reckon …' beckoned a sixty-something lady who was all wrapped up in a shawl and a grey woolly hat.

'Well, thank you very much. Wonderful to see you young things doing some good in the world. Much appreciated … and I'll just take another for my friend there, if I may. Toodle-loo!' And with that she bustled off, sporting a big smile.

Word soon spread that The Cocktail Campervan's refreshments were for free, and a merry queue began snaking its way along the street – and after a sip or two of the potent wine, it was likely they were going to be even merrier.

❅

Jack was enjoying the buzz as the villagers and visitors gathered. His mulled wine was going down a treat, with some back for second helpings already. He recognised a few friendly faces from Lucy's autumn street party, and had a quick chat with Kev, Cathy's husband, who'd been the chap dangling precariously from the cherry picker earlier. Jack knew a few people to say 'hello' to in his own small village, but tended to think of his lodgings with Matt as more of a temporary base. But here in Embleton, well, there seemed to be a huge heart to this village of Lucy's.

He glanced across as she served out cranberry crushes for the kids, taking the time to chat with them and their parents too. She wasn't just beautiful outside, he realised, with a tug within; she was beautiful inside too. But could he really be the one to give her what she needed in life? Was it time to make the break before things got more complicated, or messy, between them? She caught him staring, quirking an eyebrow as if to say, 'What's up?' then giving a warm smile. He'd always bolted before there was any chance of getting attached. But with Lucy ... damn it, he was still torn and standing at the crossroads.

With the queue still long, and more arrivals by the minute, Jack went back to his pouring and serving. The village tree light-up was evidently thirsty work!

'Any more of that there spicy wine left?' asked a burly middle-aged chap with a mass of greying-brown curls poking out from beneath his woolly hat. He leaned on the chrome countertop. 'Good stuff, that is. Warms the cockles.' He gave a chuckle.

'Of course,' Jack said, ever courteous, though he was a bit anxious at this point about supplies drying up. He'd already used the back-up pan, and was now on a top-up mix of wine, orange and spices. He hoped the lighting-the-tree part of the proceedings would come around soon, or they'd be running dry.

❄

A few minutes later, the primary school children began to gather around the tree, looking adorable with their winter coats on over their school uniforms, along with a couple of teachers and some parent-helpers.

After a request for a little hush and a lead-in of, 'And a one, two, three …' – with the crowd now expectant – they began to sing, quietly at first and then gaining in confidence. The voices were sweet and joyous, if a little wonky. The lyrics of 'Away in a Manger' rang out into the still of the evening. There was a hint of frost in the air, and the rendition of 'Silent Night' that followed was so beautiful that Lucy found herself with a tear in her eye, with those innocent lilting voices not always quite in tune.

And then, after 'O Little Town of Bethlehem' had finished, it was time for the lighting up. The parish's lady vicar taking centre stage, thanking everyone for coming, and for all their help today.

'So, without further ado,' she called out, 'I ask our councillor David Nesbitt to flick the switch.' There was a big black-painted cardboard box set beside her with what looked to be a cardboard lever. Lucy did wonder if that could possibly do anything or if it was just for effect, but somehow, somewhere, a switch was actually flicked in tandem and phew, on came the bulbs, strings of bold multicoloured lights pinged into life, with the gaudy-bright star lit up at the top.

The crowd cheered, someone shouted 'Merry Christmas!' and there were a couple of 'woops', before the children re-grouped and came back into song for a rousing rendition of 'Rudolph the Red-Nosed Reindeer', which the already merry crowd began to join in with.

Yet more mulled wine was partaken – Jack was sweating at this point. Then the vicar and the local councillor stepped up to say another round of 'thank-yous', and to invite everyone back to the village hall, where there were mince pies and treats and teas and coffees at the ready.

The gathering seemed happy to stand chatting with their festive drinks to hand for a little longer, with several children scampering about under the tree, probably on a sugar-fizz high by now. A couple of frazzled parents were on their heels telling them to calm down, no doubt fearing the festive fir might come down at any minute. But hey-ho, that seemed to be all part of the fun. Ten minutes or so later, small groups began to drift away, most of them heading down the road towards the village hall where the celebrations would continue.

As the crowd thinned, Jack noticed there was someone lurking in the shadows over the way, staring across at the campervan ... and more directly, at Lucy. The chap seemed vaguely familiar, and Jack felt a prickle run over his skin. It was him. The bloke who had been pestering Lucy at the wedding.

Lucy must have picked up on it at the same time. She looked over towards the figure, blurting out, 'Oh, what the hell is *he* doing here?'

Jack pulled up. 'So, you do know this guy, after all?' His tone was accusatory. She'd obviously been hiding something all along. 'So, who is it, Luce? And, what's he got to do with you?'

Lucy had gone bright red. But she found she couldn't answer, suddenly mute, stood wondering what was about to unfold. How did Liam have anything to do with her village of Embleton? Why was he even here? It was odd enough him appearing at that wedding ... but here, in her own village, that felt strange. As far as she knew, he was still living down in Morpeth, so this wouldn't be his neck of the woods at all ...

'Luce ...?' Jack was worried now.

'It's ... it's Liam, my ex ...'

Liam was coming across now. He was on his own. No new girlfriend on his arm or parents in tow. *Odd*, thought Lucy.

She leaped down from the campervan. Whatever was about to unfold with her ex, she didn't want Jack to get embroiled with it.

'Hi, Luce.' Liam was smiling at her.

'Ah, hi.' Lucy felt all kinds of wobbly inside. All those memories of old bubbled up to the surface, and at the same time seeing Liam here on her new home turf was really unsettling. She could almost feel Jack's eyes boring into her back at this point. 'So, were you here for the tree?' Her brow furrowed; it did seem a strange thing for a thirty-something male to be doing on his own. 'Umm, I didn't think you had any links with this village ...' Her voice trailed off.

'Only you,' he said. And again, that smile that she remembered so well.

'Oh.'

'Look, Luce,' Liam began, putting out an arm and leading her away from the festive stragglers, away from the campervan ...

Lucy felt frozen, her body somehow following on autopilot. She still couldn't believe it. *Liam: what the hell is he doing here?*

❄

'I've been a bit of an idiot,' Liam said, immediately laying it all on the table, it seemed. 'And I'm sorry – for everything that happened between us, for how it all ended …'

Lucy looked up sharply. *Well, that was the understatement of the year.*

'And well,' he continued, giving his best puppy-dog eyes, 'you know … if you ever change your mind. Miss the life we had …'

This was all completely unexpected, taking Lucy aback. Yes, she missed the early days, the getting-to-know-yous, the excitement of buying their house together … it hadn't all been bad, had it? But her brain clicked into gear just in time before she admitted to anything stupid. She didn't miss his boring bloody dictates – and she certainly didn't miss his cheating. Where the hell was this all coming from?

'What are you talking about, Liam? We can't just go back to where we were … pretend you never cheated on me. That hurt, *real* bad … We were meant to be getting married …' She found her hands were trembling and swiftly hid them behind her back. 'Look, I can't have this conversation now.' She couldn't listen to any more of this madness. Her cheeks blazing pink as she prickled with emotion.

She turned, ready to head back to Jack, but … the campervan had gone. She saw a flash of chianti red turn out onto the main road, heard the low chug of its engine motoring off. Oh no, had Jack taken this the wrong way too? She just needed a chance to explain. Bloody men. She let out a long slow sigh.

Oh, and where was Daisy? She'd been in the van too. In a whirl Lucy looked around, and there was Abby waiting patiently, if a tad awkwardly, at the street corner, holding her Dachshund's lead and giving Daisy a treat by the looks of it.

'See you around then Liam, I need to go …' said Lucy, but she didn't move immediately.

There were a few uneasy moments where Liam remained fixed to the spot as Lucy stood her ground too. Both struggling for words. And in the end, nothing seemed to fit. They'd already said their goodbyes, after all.

'So that's it … after everything …?' Liam finally bit, still trying to catch her gaze, daring her to change her mind. 'See you then, Luce,' he muttered, turning on his heel and striding away.

Lucy finally allowed herself to look up at him. Knowing so well the square set of his shoulders, the gait of his walk, and the stinging hurt of his betrayal.

Chapter Twenty-One

Lucy trundled up the path which led to the main doors of Nonna's little sheltered accommodation flat, walking past well-tended winter borders, a wooden painted snowman and a 'Santa stops here' sign, which she knew Nonna had put out herself (for the passing children). Her grandmother had lived here for the past ten years since the passing of her husband, Lucy's papa. Having her daughter nearby, her Rothbury community and a view of the Simonside Hills was her comfort.

After the antics of last night and the village Christmas tree dramas, Lucy found she needed a little comfort too this morning. And with a cheery bunch of red-and-white carnations to hand, she pressed the intercom buzzer, with an, 'It's only me, Nonna.'

'Hello, Lucy love. Come on up. Well, this is a nice surprise.'

Lucy soon entered the small living room, with its green floral-patterned sofa, matching armchair, dark-wood knickknack-filled dresser and nest of tables. There was always something so homely and comforting about Nonna's abode; it immediately helped to alleviate Lucy's jangling nerves. 'How are you doing, Nonna?'

'Oh, not so bad, not so bad. Well then, I bet you'll be ready for a nice cup of coffee and a bit of cake after your journey, pet?'

It sounded like Lucy had been on some kind of trek. It was only a twenty-five-minute drive from her cottage, but coffee sounded good nevertheless. Coffee, cake and comfort – Nonna's specialities.

'Yes, please, Nonna, but let me go and put the kettle on for you.'

'Well, I'll sort the cake, then. There's some of my Clementine and Limoncello in the tin. Me and Marjorie had a slice or two yesterday.' Nonna bustled up out of her armchair to help. She was sprightly for her late seventies, and liked to be kept busy, with her house always spotless and her baking tins and pantry well stocked – well, you never knew who might just decide to call by.

In the compact kitchen, Nonna started telling her granddaughter about the latest step in her scheme. 'Yes, Marjorie called by yesterday, and plans are afoot.' There was a cheerful tinkle to her voice.

'Oh yes, what are you two up to now?' Lucy asked, whilst spooning espresso-style granules into cups.

'There're some good deals on just now if we book early … Sorrento in the spring. Flights from Newcastle with coaches and everything all laid on.'

So she *was* still serious about this trip.

'Oh yes, it'll be beautiful at that time of year,' Nonna

continued animatedly, 'early April … before it gets too hot, and when the lemon trees are in bloom. Ah, it'll put a spring in our step for sure,' she said wistfully.

Lucy was still a bit worried about all the practicalities and the vulnerability of her beloved Nonna, but seeing her grandmother's face light up just chatting about her trip, well it was quite infectious … maybe she should just be supportive? Perhaps Nonna was right; she *should* go and have some fun whilst she was still able, rediscover some special memories and make some new ones with her friend.

'Ah, I give in, I suppose it sounds good, Nonna.' Lucy took a breath. 'Yeah, I remember our trip to Sorrento all those years ago. Me and Olly, Mum and Dad …' Back when they were still a four, it had been so special, with a trip to Pompeii, ice creams and fizzy Orangina down on the harbour-front overlooking a sparkling azure sea. An Italian adventure and a glimpse of her Mediterranean roots.

'You could always come along …' Nonna ventured, as generous as ever.

'Oh, April, you say … I'll be getting busy again with the pizza van bookings by then.' Well, hopefully, she mused. 'Remember, I'm still getting established, and I need to build on the good start All Fired Up has made this year.' Her business still needed a lot of work and energy to really find its feet and become a viable success. And, Lucy had to admit she couldn't quite imagine her thirty-year-old self holidaying with two late-septuagenarians – well, not for a whole week. 'And I don't want to be cramping your style, Nonna!'

Nonna smiled, 'Oh, I wonder if Papa has any attractive cousins out there?'

'Now, what are you scheming? I have Jack …' she said, her voice a little squeaky as she remembered the way things had ended, with him disappearing off last night.

'Not for you. I'm thinking of me and Marj …'

Really? Lucy raised her dark eyebrows. Nonna was teasing, surely. There was in fact a telling cheeky twinkle in her blue eyes. And Lucy knew that no-one had, or would ever, come near to Nonna's dearest Papa.

'Well, I might find a dashing consort for Marjorie, at least.' She was grinning mischievously as she plated up thick slices of golden, zesty clementine cake.

'Crikey, it's not only holiday insurance I've got to worry about for you, Nonna. I think you pair might well need a chaperone to keep you out of mischief.' Lucy couldn't help but grin.

'Well, like I say, the offer's there. You can't always be working, Lucia.'

'Thanks, but not this time. I really do have too much on.'

They wandered back through to the snug sitting room, where winter sunlight flooded in through the window.

'So, how are things with you, pet?'

'Okay. Busy, busy, with lots of Christmas bookings just now.'

'Oh, I'm so glad your new venture is doing well. You deserve that. Papa would be so proud.'

'Thank you.' Memories of Papa flooded back. Her pizza-making big-hearted hero.

'And how's your young man?'

'Ahm … fine.'

Her grandmother arched an eyebrow. 'What's up, pet?

You sound a little troubled?' Nonna could spot a heavy heart from a mile off.

'Ah, it's complicated,' Lucy said with a deep sigh.

'Try me. You don't get to my age in life without living a little ...' Nonna gave a smile of encouragement.

Lucy took a sip of strong coffee before beginning. 'Well, firstly Liam turned up out of the blue last night ... at an event in my village.'

'Liam?' Nonna frowned.

'And Nonna, it couldn't have been by chance, he lives miles away ... he was on his own ... he wanted to see me, to talk. He was trying to apologise, to smooth things over. He seemed ... different.'

'Well, I hope you haven't forgotten how badly he treated you.'

'No, of course not.' Lucy had had more than two years of disillusionment and then hurt and heartbreak to cope with.

'Let him say his "sorry"s, but don't go getting yourself reeled in again, pet ... He was always a bit wily, that one.' Nonna had never much warmed to the lad.

'I know, and I'm not that daft. But I didn't realise how much it would affect me, seeing him again like that. I think I'd been hiding a lot, burying old hurts. I just feel really unsettled right now. Maybe we do just need to have it out properly. Talk things over, then we can let everything lie and move on.'

'Perhaps, Lucia, but be careful. Look out for yourself in all this.'

Lucy nodded, before taking another slow breath. There

was something else bearing heavy on her heart. 'And then, there's Jack …'

'Jack, the charming cocktail man, yes? Well, I hope he has been treating you right? Don't go jumping from the frying pan into the fire.'

'Hah, I won't. And yes, he has been.' Lucy's heart stirred with feelings for Jack. Feelings that were intrinsically deep, but felt slightly dangerous too. 'He didn't exactly take it well when I slipped off to talk with Liam last night. But how could I not? I didn't want to have some heart to heart, raking over old ground, in front of Jack. It was too personal. Anyway, Jack then whizzed off without even saying goodbye.'

'Hmm, it sounds like you two need to talk. And well, if he saw you go off chatting with this old flame, maybe there's a flash of jealousy going on …'

'Maybe …'

'Think about it, how would you feel if he slipped off to chat with an ex-girlfriend in front of you? Wouldn't be easy, would it?' Nonna turned it around, helping Lucy see another side. Perhaps the old lady did have some fondness for Jack, after all, she mused.

And for Lucy, whoa, just the thought of Jack with someone else made her feel horridly queasy.

'No … I suppose it wouldn't. But he ought to be able to trust me, Nonna. We need to be able to trust each other. Surely, I can talk to my ex without him flipping out?'

'Trust is something you need to build in a relationship, Lucia. So just keep talking, keep being honest with each other. Keep building on that. Then one day … if it's the right relationship … you might find yourselves tightly holding hands and then reaching for the stars together.'

Lucy looked out of the window into the flower-filled garden below, as if trying to gaze into the future. She hoped her dear old Nonna was right – perhaps age did bring great wisdom after all.

❄

Come along to

The Claverham Castle Christmas Fayre

Saturday 11th December

From 1 p.m.

Crafts, Baking, Gifts, Santa's Grotto and so much more

❄

Chapter Twenty-Two

L ucy was up with the lark and bustling away in her cottage kitchen. Even though she'd had a bit of an unsettled night, she found herself singing 'Jingle Bells', substituting 'bells' for 'balls' as she went to check on her pizza dough balls, which had proven nicely overnight. Next, she chopped turkey and sliced mushrooms and onions for toppings, ready to fill the cool boxes to transport later. If today at the Claverham Castle Christmas fayre was to be as busy as she hoped – with Emma from The Chocolate Shop suggesting it was her favourite and busiest festive booking – she'd be glad to be more than a few steps ahead with her prep.

Ellie, the castle events organiser, had filled her in with more details of the extravaganza and the event sounded bustling and eclectic. Ellie had come across as lovely on the phone too, proudly explaining how they'd built up the Christmas Fayre over the past few years, encouraging local businesses to get involved. It had apparently become a bit of an annual attraction in the Northumberland area, and a highlight in the festive calendar. After all, what wasn't to like … crafts, foods, carols and cocktails, all set in the grounds and hall of an ancient castle? It sounded like the perfect Christmas setting.

Lucy gave a sigh, thoughts of her relationship woes bursting her festive bubble. Even though Jack had eventually responded to her calls after all the drama with Liam, he'd still been frosty this week. They'd been keeping in touch with messages, mostly thrown out by Lucy, but there was definitely a new layer of unease. An elastic band of tension stretched between them. But … didn't all relationships have their ebbs and flows? And as Nonna wisely said, 'trust had to be built'.

So, after weighing it all up carefully, Lucy had decided to meet Liam for a coffee, to get this all out in the open and to draw a line under everything. She'd received a text message from him the day after the village tree event.

Hi, it was good to see you again, Luce. x

She'd floundered a bit before eventually replying with a polite:

It was nice to see you too.

There was no point being all bitter and chewed up over something that was now in the past. But he'd completely blindsided her and she hated how it was casting a shadow over everything with Jack. In the shock of it all, she hadn't managed to say everything she'd have liked, she worried she hadn't made her position crystal clear – so now she needed that airtime.

Look, do you want to meet for a quick coffee? she'd texted as a follow-up, purposely using the word 'quick' to give her ex no illusion that this was some cosy reunion.

They'd been all set to meet at a neutral venue in the local town of Alnwick yesterday late afternoon, when Liam phoned to say he was held up at work but had to pass by her village on his way to meet a client the next morning, so could he pop by hers instead? This had felt a little uncomfortable, to be honest. She hadn't wanted Liam here in her new private space – it was bad enough that he'd landed in her village the other night. This was her bolt-hole, after all. But hey, these things happened. So, she'd found herself saying yes, whilst telling herself it'd be fine.

Now Liam was due in about ten minutes, so Lucy quickly downed tools in the kitchen and went to spruce herself up – nothing glamorous mind; she wasn't out to impress. But she still found herself feeling nervous as she brushed her hair and changed into a casual cardigan and jeans.

Then came the sound of a vehicle pulling up outside. So he was here then. But hang on, thought Lucy, how did he know exactly where she was? It suddenly occurred to her that she'd never given him her address ... had she?

'Hey, Luce, thanks for this.' Dressed smartly in navy chinos and a stripy shirt, he was all chummy-toned niceness at the cottage threshold. 'Sorry if it's put you out at all.'

'Ah, no worries,' she said, a little flustered. 'Come on in.' Lucy led him through to her kitchen.

'Hey, nice place you've got here.' Liam looked about him as he took up a stool. 'Compact, yeah … but neat.'

Compact? How had she forgotten the way he could make little digs yet wrap them up to sound like compliments?

'So, it sounds pretty hectic for you at work?' Lucy started with small talk as she clicked the coffee machine on.

'Yep, all go.'

'So, where's your client meeting today?'

'Oh, ah … yeah, just along at Seahouses. Small business property sale, a few land issues … yeah, they need a bit of advice … thought I'd do an onsite visit.' He sounded a little uneasy.

'Right …' Lucy stirred. 'No sugar?'

'Nope. Sweet enough.'

The words irked. One thing Liam had never been was sweet. Sensible, hard-working, steady, professional, dedicated – well, to Arnott & Co., perhaps not so much to *her*, judging by the messed-up end of it all. And suddenly, making conversation seemed like hard work. The turmoil of it all was brewing inside her once more.

'So, the cocktail bar guy … You two an item, or what?' he continued, with a slight twist to his lips.

'Yeah, we are, actually.'

Liam began to shake his head slowly, like a disappointed parent. 'You know, you really don't need to be hanging about with someone like that, Luce. Trailing around in a campervan like a nomad.'

'*What?*' Lucy turned sharply to face him, beginning to realise that inviting him round might have been a mistake after all. What had she been thinking? Imagining he needed to get stuff off his chest, perhaps offer an explanation for his hurtful behaviour, seemed like a pipe dream just now. For all his talk, the leopard that was Liam didn't seem to have changed his spots at all. 'Liam, you have no right to be telling me who I can or cannot "hang about" with. What a bloody cheek. You well and truly lost that right when you pissed off with your office fling,' Lucy said, getting all fired up now.

'That was a mistake ... I've explained that, Luce. A misjudgement.'

'So that makes it alright, then?' Her tone was terse.

'Of course not. But I've already made my apologies. Can't you see fair to let it drop? It's time to move on, Luce. If there's any chance of a new beginning for the two of us, then ...'

He was annoying her now. 'Can't you see, Liam, there is no "the two of us" anymore, that ship has long sailed!' It was clear they were both on *very* different pages. She needed to get him out of her cottage *right now* and out of her life. She gulped down her coffee, ready to make a move, and stood up. 'I think you just need to leave, Liam ...'

'So, how's the horsebox?' he chipped in, staying on his seat.

'How do you mean?' Lucy turned to him, feeling on edge.

There was a menacing glint in his eyes, just a flicker.

She felt herself grow cold. Alert.

'Old thing like that, well the tyres can go flat easily and all sorts ...' he continued coolly.

Bloody hell, her heart began to pummel, it must have been him ... the flat tyres, the nails... maybe even the Jeep's window? It all began to stack up.

There was a beat or two of silence, as they stared at each other. Lucy's heart going ten to the dozen.

'Was … was it *you* …? Who let the tyres down on my horsebox?' She continued to stare him down, cold prickling down her spine.

''Course not. You're getting paranoid.' His smile was wonky. He took a sip of coffee, hiding his eyes. But a second later, he couldn't resist adding, 'Got your attention then, did it?'

'Christ, it *was* you … And what about the Jeep? The smashed window? Was that your doing too?' She was incredulous, yet somehow it all began to fit. 'Liam, how is any of that going to get us anywhere? How could you be so *bloody* vindictive!'

'Okay, okay … let me explain … so after seeing you and Jack at the wedding like that, yeah, I was a bit jealous. It hurt, Luce, seeing you with another guy. Look, I'm sorry about the tyres. I'll pay you whatever it cost to replace them. All water under the bridge, hey?'

Did he think she'd be happy with that? Throw a bit of money at her to put it right?

'And ah … the window … well, that shouldn't have happened. I just wanted the chance to speak with you. I was trying to catch your attention … there was no answer at the door and well, I was throwing small stones at your bedroom window pane, just in case. One went a bit off track.'

He'd come to find her? He knew which was her bedroom window? This was getting weirder by the minute.

'What?'

A low growl emanated from Daisy's kitchen bedspace. The little dog having picked up on Lucy's stressed tone.

'You know what, Liam, boy am I glad I've finally found you out. Oh yes, I've really got to see what a little toad you really are. The office affair, well that's just the tip of the iceberg, isn't it? Thank God we never had the chance to get married. What a bloody disaster that would have been.'

'You're making a mistake here, Luce. Campervan boy, he'll never come to anything. Listen to me, I know you … What we had was good. We had a lovely home. Nice cars.'

'No, Liam. You never really knew me. It was all a sham. You were just looking out for yourself. Just like you are now. And Jack, that's his name, not campervan boy. Jack is bloody lovely, and worth a million of you … And if you don't get out of here in the next five seconds … you'll have the police on your case. Oh yes, damage to property, harassment … And, if you dare to come back here, to *my* village again … well, I'll catch you by the bloody scrote and hang you up by it.'

Suddenly a frenzy of barking rang out and Daisy started a furious nipping of Liam's trouser legs.

'Jesus,' Liam cursed, flailing about. 'Get that mutt off of me!'

Daisy had leaped forwards, and was in full defence mode, loyally protecting her owner. Liam now hopping from foot to foot, yelping.

Lucy waited a good thirty seconds before calling her off: 'That's enough Daisy.'

The little dog finally backed down; Lucy scooping her up before Liam, foot poised, had a chance to give her a kick. If he'd done that, well, she really would have hung him up by the scrote! Perhaps out in the street, and left him dangling from the top of the village Christmas tree. The biggest, ugliest Christmas bauble ever!

Liam stood defiantly staring the duo down. Lucy was suddenly fearful how she'd be able to physically remove this strong and now angry bloke from her property.

Then, as if knowing he was beaten, all flustered and red in the face, Liam turned, and scuttled out of the kitchen and away. Lucy's heart was still pounding as she heard the front door slam and his saloon car rev up and go. Good bloody riddance. With feisty heroine Daisy safely in her arms, giving a farewell see-you-off bark, she had a feeling Liam wouldn't be showing his face around here any time soon … and that suited them both just fine.

The air wasn't just cleared, a huge storm had broken and thundered her ex out.

Chapter Twenty-Three

With no time to waste after that crazy meet-up, the horsebox was all loaded and ready an hour later. She managed to switch into Christmas mode, and yes, the only thing needed to set the festive scene now was snow, Lucy mused, as she set off on that chilly December morning. The radio news had in fact mentioned flurries over the hills, but often at this time of year the snow was something and nothing, a mere dusting. You might not see any at all down in the valleys.

After dropping Daisy off at her brother's for the day, Lucy wound her way carefully through the country lanes, heading inland towards the Cheviot Hills. A patchwork of farmland, dotted with sheep and cattle, and fields showing hints of winter barley shoots and cabbage-like sugar-beet tops, rolled away either side of the route. The horsebox bumped along an uneven stretch of tarmac as the road narrowed. Lucy slowed as an old-fashioned road sign indicated the castle was just a mile away.

Turning in through the majestic stone pillars and cast-iron gates of the castle entrance, Lucy drove the horsebox carefully along a grand avenue lined with huge old gnarled-branched beech trees. The castle itself then appeared, all aged-cream stone walls and crenellations, fairytale-like. Stone steps led up to a big old wooden door, where two small Christmas trees stood prettily either side of the ancient portal, adorned with twinkling white lights. Oh yes, this beautiful historic place certainly looked the part and was already more than living up to her expectations.

Just as she was wondering where she was meant to be parking, out came a tall gentleman wrapped up in a long navy woollen coat, sporting – in the place of a scarf – a very jolly red bow-tie with a holly pattern on. He skipped down the steps, calling out, 'Over here, my lovely. We've got you positioned here to this side of the front entrance. That's it, you'll be next to …' He checked his clipboard, 'Yes, that's it, The Cocktail Campervan.'

Ah, so not only would Jack be here all day with her, she'd be parked up right beside him too. Oh well, maybe being placed so close might mean they'd get chance to chat, perhaps help each other out. And maybe, she'd get chance to explain the latest Liam saga too, and put paid to any of his unfounded fears of rivalry. Hopefully they'd finally be able to bridge that awkward gap that had started to develop between them. 'Okay, thank you.' She began to manoeuvre the horsebox into place, with various hand signals going on from the chap in the bow-tie, as though he were landing a plane. She had to give a smile; she was an ace at parking this now, but it was nice that he was trying to be helpful.

Once she'd pulled up into position, the gentleman was

stood beside her window. 'We have electric hook-ups ready for you, and for anything else you might need, just shout. Myself and Derek will be bobbing about all day. Oh, I'm Malcolm, by the way.' He put out a hand for her to shake through her Jeep window.

'Lovely to meet you, Malcolm, and thank you.'

'Oh, and Ellie and Joe will be on hand too, of course. I expect one of them'll pop out to see you soon. I'll let them know you're here. Well then, I'll let you get yourself sorted.'

'Thanks.'

Lucy was looking forward to meeting Ellie in person; she'd sounded so friendly on the phone. Also, she couldn't wait to have a sneaky peek at the main hall of the castle and take a look at the other stalls. She might even manage to get some extra presents sorted for Christmas for her family and friends, with it now being the festive countdown. With assistant Abby due to turn up in an hour or so to help with the pizza production, she hoped she'd get chance to have a mooch about at some point.

First things first, though. Lucy was here to work, and she needed to get her pizza oven lit and ready as soon as possible. There were logs to burn, and perfect pizzas to prepare.

'Let's get this show on the road,' she called out to herself as she stepped down, ready to open up the horsebox and create her most festive ever version of All Fired Up. Oh yes, she was going all out with the Christmas theming. As well as selling her pizzas, some prettily-boxed mini panettone had caught her eye at the Italian wholesalers. She was going to stack them for sale on the countertop, alongside slices of homemade clementine and limoncello cake made to Nonna's recipe. Pizza and puddings, why not?!

Lucy, sporting her festive Rudolph jumper, carefully set out a fir-and-pine-cone garland above the open hatch. She had extra fairy lights, silver and red baubles in bunches, a selection of pretty wooden-crafted stars, and her usual Italian bunting had been replaced by a *Merry Christmas* sign with each flag bearing a letter.

Within twenty minutes, the logs were burning nicely; they'd still need more time to get up to temperature, but they gave such a cosy glow in these winter months. It was so much more pleasant working at the oven now than it had been sweltering away back in the summer.

Looking up, she spotted a striking vintage campervan making its way along the driveway. Ah, Ruby was here. And, of course, along with Ruby came Jack. Lucy's stomach gave a flip as she saw him there at the wheel.

He pulled up alongside the horsebox and Lucy gave a tentative wave and a smile, but she was met by a stormy-faced Jack.

'Hi,' she said meekly, walking over to Ruby to welcome him. 'All okay? Ready for a busy day?'

'Ah-hah,' was his brief reply, as his eyes darted away from her. 'Right then, I'd better get sorted. Time's of the essence. We've only got an hour until it officially starts.' It wasn't just the air that was chilly, Jack's tone seemed very frosty too. One o'clock was lift-off, so Lucy conceded she'd better get on with her pizza preparations. It certainly wasn't quite the reunion she'd hoped for.

Bow-tied Malcom appeared once again, clipboard to

hand. 'Good morning, wonderful to see you here at Claverham Castle. You must be Jack, yes?'

Jack gave a brief smile and nodded.

'You're the only campervan we've got, so lucky guess.' Malcolm let out a ripple of laughter. 'Okay then, Jack, you're just here.' He gestured to the space next to All Fired Up.

Was it Lucy's imagination or did Jack's smile totally drop just then?

'Wonderful. Have a successful day.' And with that, Malcom turned with a spin of his black leather heels, with another vehicle arriving tout suite.

❄

Jack raised Ruby's hatch to reveal the stage-lit bulb blackboard, which he'd chalked up with today's specials – a Cranberry Fizz (he'd found the most amazing cranberry liqueur to add to chilled prosecco), Spiced Mulled Wine (of course!), hot chocolates served with whipped cream and all the works (with Bailey's and rum versions too), Irish coffee, a Dark and Stormy cocktail, Toffee Apple cocktails, mocktails and more … He couldn't help but glance over at Lucy, her hair swept up in a dark glossy knot, concentrating on stacking a pile of boxed cakes. His heart gave an involuntary squeeze.

He pulled his focus back; he'd better get on with his work. He started to twine fresh holly, fir and ivy – gathered from his parents' garden – along the front of Ruby's chrome counter. He also had a big red velvet bow to drape over her front windscreen, tinsel aplenty, and silver and gold baubles to decorate his garnish stand.

And, even though it was chilly working outside at this time of year, he was looking the part too, sporting his black-tie tuxedo outfit with a dashing red-velvet bow-tie. He loved to give his all to the whole Cocktail Campervan experience. Ruby was gleaming and polished, being a fabulous festive red herself. Standing back proudly from his handiwork, he gave a nod; Ruby did look rather splendid, he had to admit.

As they were the only two catering units positioned here at the entrance of the castle – the ones who'd make the first impression – The Cocktail Campervan and All Fired Up absolutely needed to be spot on, giving a warm, festive welcome. Even if their respective owners were feeling a little disgruntled with each other at this moment in time. Smiles were laid on, and emotions masked – for now at least.

❄

Eager to get some breathing space with fifteen minutes to spare before opening time, Jack was curious to take a quick look inside the castle. He headed up the well-worn stone steps. The ancient wooden door was left ajar, ready for the public invasion. It opened onto a small passageway, leading to heavy iron gates, and then into an open-air courtyard area. A perfect cobbled square inside the four walls of the castle. It was like he'd walked back in time … medieval, with a touch of Victorian, with several stallholders setting up their pitches: hand-crafted wooden gifts, candles, jams and preserves, and a chap with a real chestnut roaster – the smell was delicious, conjuring up days of old. There was something rather Dickensian about chestnuts roasting, Jack mused. He recognised the Jam Lady and gave a friendly hello.

There was noisy chatter and a general sense of hustle and bustle coming from inside. Jack stepped in, taking in tall mullioned windows, old tapestries hung on the walls, and two huge fireplaces with massive tree-trunk-style logs alight, giving the room a mellow glow and a wintry wood-smoke smell. Inside the Great Hall, it was all stations go, with boxes of goodies and gifts being unpacked and displays set out. A massive Christmas tree stood in one corner which almost touched the extremely high ceiling; it had to be twenty feet tall at least. Impressive. And looking about, there must have been at least thirty different stalls there. It was like a festive Aladdin's Cave.

'Oh, hello there.' A thirty-something woman, who was wearing a holly-patterned apron over a black dress and long boots, with dark-blonde hair piled messily on top of her head, approached. 'Can I help at all?'

'Oh, just having a quick look about before we start. And, I was hoping to find the loos, to be honest. I have The Cocktail Campervan out the front,' he explained.

'Ah yes, you must be Jack. I remember chatting with you. Hi, I'm Ellie, the organiser. So nice to meet you.'

He was impressed that she'd remembered his name from the booking.

'Wow, it looks great in here. What a stunning castle.' It was all a bit different to his semi-detached lodgings with Matt.

'Yeah, it is quite impressive, isn't it? Still find it pretty awe-inspiring myself, and I've been living here for eight years now.' She gave a warm smile, which lit up her face.

'Ellie, sorry to butt in, but we need you down in the tea rooms,' a gentleman dressed in smart tweeds called out. 'Doris is having a problem with the mince pies, apparently.'

Malcolm, who'd welcomed Jack and Lucy earlier, then stepped forward, adding, 'Oh Lord, don't say she's gone and burnt them again.'

'Well, nice to meet you, Jack. Sorry, got to dash. Malcolm will point you in the right direction for the bathrooms.'

It was all systems go in there. And it'd soon be time for him to go back to the campervan – he only hoped a busy afternoon of serving would distract him from his woes with Lucy.

❄

Lucy couldn't help but feel anxious. Jack seemed really determined not to engage with her, and her assistant, Abby, still hadn't arrived. With time rolling on – it was 12:20 already – they were going to have to hit the ground running. Hearing vehicles pulling in off the country lane, and trundling down the gravel driveway, Lucy nervously brushed down her apron. Taking up her hatch-side position, and forcing a smile on her face, she made herself ready to meet and greet the first arrivals. Car doors began slamming, releasing the first expectant, chatty customers, followed soon afterwards by a fresh convoy of vehicles coming through the castle gates. Christmas had landed at Claverham Castle. Lucy at last felt a ripple of anxious excitement. Another big event to put under her belt, another step forward for her business.

Then, thank God, Abby arrived in a flurry, dashing into the horsebox and pulling on her apron at lightning speed. 'Sorry Luce, didn't mean to cut it so fine. Mum needed the car today, so she had to drop me off here after our shopping trip. Took a while getting here, sorry. We got stuck behind a tractor in the lanes, and there's a huge queue we had to bypass at the gates.'

'No worries, you're here now,' Lucy said, mightily relieved she'd made it, 'and that's what matters.'

Across the way, she heard barman Jack lighting up with his festive bravado. 'Hello there, and welcome to the Claverham Castle Christmas Fayre. Can I interest you in a mulled wine, or a Bailey's hot chocolate? Some Cranberry Lemonade Fizz for the little ones?'

Lucy felt a pang. She wished he'd lit up like that when he'd seen her earlier.

'Turkey and Trimmings Pizza, anyone? Mozzarella-melting garlic bread?' Lucy called out, forcing a welcoming grin.

There was no time to dwell on their rocky relationship right now. The punters had landed, and the caterers needed to be on it like a car bonnet.

Chapter Twenty-Four

'It's a little ...'

'Slow ...?'

'Hmm ... yes, I suppose so.'

'A few nerves, boss?'

'Don't worry, Abby, I'm sure it'll get going for us soon.'

The first arrivals had smiled politely in the horsebox's direction, but had wandered right on by.

'All we need are our first customers of the day and then the rest will follow,' Lucy said with a tight smile, but sounding a little stressed.

'Absolutely,' said Abby, who was busy swirling their special tomato sauce onto a production line of bases, and looking on the bright side.

In the meantime, across the way, Jack was already on a roll, shaking and serving his cocktails, chatting away as he worked, and pouring out glass mugs of spice-scented mulled wine. Tinkling laughter rang out from a group of smartly dressed thirty-something women, which made customerless Lucy feel even worse. He was so damned charming, and made it all look so easy, strutting his stuff over there at his bar. And in her present state of unease, that irked her. Oh yes, he was all charm and chat at the bar, but when it came to real relationships, love, any hint of real commitment, well, he just seemed to duck and dive. Lucy longed to know where she actually stood.

At last, a young couple came up to the pizza counter, saying how pretty the horsebox looked, and ordered a slice of the Christmas Special, plus a Ham and Mushroom. What a welcome diversion that was.

Soon enough it all changed and they were suddenly full throttle, with pizza slices going out by the dozen.

Customers were eager to try her Turkey and Trimmings Pizza: tasty turkey meat with mini circles of pigs-in-blankets, and bite-sized nibbles of sage and onion stuffing sprinkled over. To Lucy's delight, there were many positive comments, though one small boy did pull a face, telling his mum there was no way he'd be having turkey dinner on his pizza, and certainly not with sprouts on it! Lucy had to laugh at that.

The castle was soon buzzing, the Christmas fayre in full swing, with visitors drifting in and out, tasting the goodies at the various food stalls, including All Fired Up and The Cocktail Campervan, whose mulled wine was warming the happy shoppers, whilst they hunted down the perfect Christmas gifts. Smells of cinnamon and spice, of pine trees and winter woods, wafted by on the chilly air.

❄

'Ho, ho, ho!'

Around an hour later, Lucy looked up from her pizza cooking station to see Santa Claus, traditionally dressed in his red-and-white suit with a huge swag bag of presents slung over his back, on … yes, a quad bike, brumming noisily down the driveway. A host of children and parents had gathered at the top of the castle steps, accompanied by Ellie, Malcolm and a short middle-aged woman with a rather severe bowl-like haircut. 'Wave to Father Christmas, boys and girls,' she called out.

The children did as they were told, though they hardly needed encouraging; waving wildly and shouting out their 'hellos' excitedly.

Ah yes, Lucy had seen on social media that there was to be a Santa's Grotto here, as well as traditional carols in the courtyard, and pony-and-trap rides organised throughout the afternoon. Oh, she wished she'd mentioned it to her brother now; little Freddie would have loved all this.

She watched. Santa Claus was tall, elderly and on the slim side, even though he had a fake belly under his red jacket that on closer inspection seemed to be drifting sideways. 'Right then, you lot, who's been good this year?' he called out rather gruffly, as he pulled up at the bottom of the steps. 'If so, follow me.'

He was certainly a rather quirky Father Christmas, but the kids didn't seem to mind. A crowd of them trooped after him into the main castle like he was the Pied Piper. The hessian swag bag filled with gifts was no doubt luring them in.

❄

Once the lunchtime queue had eased, Lucy took the opportunity to go exploring, leaving Abby in charge for a short while. She felt a ripple of excitement as she ventured up the steps and in through the heavy wooden gate of the castle entrance.

A cobbled stone courtyard greeted her, like something out of medieval times, where several stalls were set out, with colourful tarpaulin tops. Lucy browsed the cute wooden plaques and toys, handmade cushions, and gorgeously scented candles and crafts. The smell of chestnuts from the little cart warmed the air as she wandered by.

Up another flight of stone steps now, the handrails of which had been garlanded with swathes of fir and ivy, and she gave a small gasp as she stepped into the grand hall of the castle. With glowing fires, carols playing, candles lit, and festive food and craft stalls galore, it felt like a December dream. A huge Christmas tree twinkled with coloured lights in one corner, and oh look, the cutest Santa's Grotto was waiting to be discovered at the far end, with quad bike Santa in situ on a great big chair, a huddle of excited children gathered around his feet. Their expectant smiles seemed to be catching as Lucy found herself with a big grin in her face.

She spotted Emma, who she'd met at the seaside festival at Warkton-by-the-Sea, surrounded by a stall of gorgeous hand-crafted chocolates, looking like something from a festive Willy Wonka film. Her trestle table was piled high with cocoa delights in foil boxes and pretty cellophane bags tied with Christmas twirling ribbons. Now here were some great gifts for her mum, Nonna and her friends.

She manoeuvred there through the crowds. 'Hey, hi Emma.'

'Hey, good to see you. How have you been? Are you working? Did you manage to get a spot?' Emma's smile lit her friendly face.

'Yeah, I'm fine thanks. And yes, the pizza horsebox is out the front. Thanks so much for the tip.'

'That's great, I'm glad you got in, it's a brilliant event.'

'Beautiful here, and it's so busy, isn't it?'

'Yeah, makes you feel festive yourself, even when you're working.'

'Definitely. Oh, and I met Ellie before, she seems lovely.'

Ellie had popped out to the horsebox earlier to see how they were getting on.

'Yeah, she is, and oh, just two tables along, be sure to say hi to Rachel, tell her I sent you over … that you're new on the scene. Oh and treat yourself to a sticky toffee pudding while you're at it – you will thank me, I tell you. They are divine.'

'Yes, I'll do that,' Lucy beamed. It was such a close-knit community, the catering crowd, and it was lovely to find herself welcomed into it. 'Thanks, and it's Rachel, you say?'

'Yeah, and her mum's called Jill. They have the Pudding Pantry over at Primrose Farm.'

'Oh yes, I've heard good things. Been meaning to take my mum across one day.'

'You should. It's gorgeous there.'

A date for the springtime then, Lucy noted.

Lucy couldn't resist picking up some gift-boxed truffles, fudge and Bailey's chocolates (that she might well have to keep back for herself). She even discovered some fantastic reindeer- and Santa-shaped chocolates for little Freddie.

She waited her turn, and then paid Emma with a smile. 'These look gorgeous.'

'Thanks, and when I get a chance later, I'll pop on out to see you. Might well need a slice of pizza to keep me going.'

'Great, see you then.' Lucy felt warmed by their budding friendship.

After passing a pretty candle stall that smelled spicy and warm, just like Christmas, Lucy spotted a table piled high with 'award-winning' Christmas puddings; sticky toffee puddings, spiced ginger puddings, in fact there were puddings galore – ah-hah, this had to be the Pudding Pantry stall. A dark-haired young woman was busy serving, chatting away to a customer, and as Lucy browsed the mouth-watering selection, a slightly older lady with greying bobbed hair, wearing a spotted apron and a lovely smile, came across. 'Can I help? Would you like a taster?'

'Oh, hi, umm, yes please.'

'I've just put out some chocolate-orange pudding samples. Here.' She handed Lucy a small pot filled with a dollop of desert and a tiny wooden spoon.

Lucy's mouth exploded with the most delicious flavours. 'Wow, that's great. I'll take one of those, a Christmas pudding, oh, and I must have a sticky toffee pudding too. I've been recommended that by Emma.'

'Ah, Emma on the chocolate stall?'

'Yes … I'm Lucy, by the way,' she introduced herself. 'I'm working here today too. I have a pizza stand out the front.'

'Ah yes, we saw that as we came in. In a horsebox? It

looked so sweet. What a fabulous idea. Well, I hope you have a successful day.'

'Yeah, seems to be going really well so far. It's my first time here … My first year in business, actually.'

'Well, best of luck with it all. Lovely to meet you.'

The younger lady gave a friendly nod and smile, but was held up serving a flurry of customers.

'On that note, I'd better get back to it. Nice to meet you, too.'

Oh … As she stepped outside, the sky had changed to a hush of heavy grey, and soft flakes of snow had begun to drift down in gentle flurries. It was a beautiful sight, like something from a fairytale. But something in those brooding clouds also told Lucy that a new weather front was moving in, and as she caught sight of her wayward barman in The Cocktail Campervan, a chill settled in her heart too.

Chapter Twenty-Five

'Good afternoon, ladies, and what can I get for you? Something to warm you up perhaps?' Jack grinned cheekily as snowflakes began to dust his cheeks.

'You can say that again.' The plumper of the two middle-aged women nudged her friend's arm, as they giggled like a pair of teenagers.

'Well, I have just the thing. My Toffee Apple Cocktail.'

'Ooh, now what's in that then? Sounds right up my street.'

'Brandy, caramel, cinnamon, and apple juice, on ice or served warm if you like.' He arched an eyebrow.

'Well, that's me sold, young man. You can fix me one of those, please. Warmed would be lovely,' she added suggestively.

'Sounds bloody gorgeous, Susan. Shame I'm the driver, though.'

'Never fear, I can do a non-alcoholic version without the

brandy. It's not quite as naughty, but it's certainly as nice.' Jack gave a wink.

'Go on then, why not? Can you throw in a cuddle too?' she chuckled.

Jack grinned and started his mixology magic, giving them a great show of shaking and stirring, finishing with a flourish as he poured out the golden liquid into glass tumblers.

Next up were a couple wanting some festive fizz, so Jack served a sparkling cranberry and clementine prosecco cocktail. They took their flutes, saying 'Cheers' and clinking glasses, just as the snowflakes decided to flurry down a little heavier. The lights on Ruby twinkled and glowed around them, and they looked delighted.

'Fizz in a flurry,' pronounced Jack with a smile.

'Thanks, this is just brilliant, mate,' the chap was grinning, 'and I love your campervan so much. Hey, do you do other events?'

'Yeah, of course. Why?'

'Well, we're getting married next year, and … well, cocktails in a campervan would be brilliant. Yeah, we'd love for you to be there as part of the reception. That'd be fab, wouldn't it, Debs?'

'Yes, that'd be so cool.'

'Sounds great.' Jack handed over a business card. 'I've done lots of weddings. And I can personalise everything for you, too. Just contact me whenever you like.'

The couple wandered off merrily, and Jack couldn't help but glance over at Lucy then, who happened to be watching him too. Their eyes met for a moment and then quickly tore away.

Jack looked up at the brooding sky; it had turned a deep, cloudy grey. The snow was certainly getting heavier, and with the Fayre due to end in an hour or so anyhow, people were now beginning to drift off home.

Abby's mum had heard about the weather turning and given her a warning call. Boyfriend Callum had then offered to come and collect her, arriving – very sweetly – with a kiss on the cheek for Abby, and his warm winter coat to cover her less-than-adequate-for-snow All Fired Up uniform.

'Hey folks, all okay here?' He gave a broad grin. 'Ready for the off, Abs?'

Abby looked to Lucy, who smiled in agreement. The hardest of the work was done and she was more than happy to let her assistant get away.

'The roads are getting a bit dodgy out there, by the way,' Callum added. 'Alright if you take it slow, but you might want to think about getting away soon yourself, Lucy. Or maybe we can wait for you, if you'd like? Follow you back, just in case?'

'Ah, that's kind of you, Callum, but this stove takes an age to cool down, and I can't go anywhere 'til then. No, you two head off. I'll be fine.'

'You sure?' Abby checked.

'Certain. Go on, get yourselves away. There's plenty of people here to help, if need be,' she added reassuringly, and a little more confidently than she felt, watching the snowflakes continue to drift down.

'Okay, well you take care. Give me a text when you get back then, yeah?' Abby stressed.

'Yep, of course. You sound like my mum.' Lucy had to smile.

But as they walked away, Callum's arm slung protectively around Abby's shoulder, Lucy couldn't help but feel a wistful pang for how things had changed so much between her and Jack. With bloody Liam putting his spanner in the works, and Jack all Mr Frosty lately, she felt all out of kilter. Somehow vulnerable.

So, swiftly shaking herself out of her pensive mood, for the next half hour Lucy was serving and cooking solo, but that was okay, as she hadn't wanted to pack up too soon and disappoint any customers, and things were now beginning to quieten down anyhow. She'd had an enjoyable and profitable day workwise; that much she could tell from the bulging cash box. And it was lovely in many ways to be standing by a hot oven in the dark with snowflakes falling around her. She couldn't wait to get cleared up and get away home to cosy up. And maybe, just maybe, she could corner Jack and force him to hear her out about the Liam debacle before they went their separate ways into the cold night.

But it looked like the weather had other ideas. With just fifteen minutes to go until the official closing time of five o'clock, it started bleaching it down. Lucy quickly began clearing up, watching the visitors and the carol-singing schoolchildren and their families now leaving in droves. Lucy, however, would still have to wait a further hour before the oven would be cool enough to move back into the horsebox for transportation.

It wasn't long before the majority of the stallholders had packed up their goods in their vans, and were setting off steadily up the driveway too – which already had a two-inch layer of snow. Lucy began to feel anxious; she had never driven the horsebox in snowy conditions before.

Jack came across then, still seeming subdued. 'Do you think you'll be alright? Driving back?' he asked, not quite looking her in the eye.

'Ah, I'm not sure … I've never driven with the horsebox in snow before.' She couldn't hide her concern.

Snowflakes stuck on their eyelashes and clothes.

'Okay, don't worry.' He bit down on his lip. 'Look, I'll stay … until you're ready to go, that is. I'll follow you back some of the way at least. We can get to the main road together … see what the conditions are like there.' The words sounded stiff.

'Thank you.' Lucy gave a gentle smile. She longed to fold herself into his arms, but there was still that feeling of distance lurking between them.

They packed away as much as they could, and then headed inside the castle to take shelter while they waited for Lucy's oven to finally cool. The last of the stallholders were tidying up in the hall, but most had now left. The castle staff were busy clearing up too. Lucy gave a wry smile as she spotted a lady dressed as an elf hoovering the area under the huge Christmas tree.

Malcolm came dashing in the main door, the high-viz orange apron he wore over his coat covered in snow. He banged on a wooden table for attention, 'Sorry folks, but you'll just have to hold fire here for a while. No point setting off just now.'

'Oh, why? What's happened, Malcolm?' Ellie asked, as she helped to fold down one of the trestle tables.

'Joe's trying to sort things out, but a large transit van has skidded on the road, must be bad ice, and ended up across the lane and partly in the ditch. The road's shut for now. No-one can get past.'

'Oh, is everyone alright?' Ellie sounded concerned.

All ears around the room pricked up at the news.

'Yes, the driver's fine, just a bit shaken up. It was Alan with his wooden toys, bless him. Think the van's front end is a bit of a mess, though.'

There was a gasp and murmurings around the room of 'Poor Alan,' and 'What a shame.'

'Can I do anything to help?' Jack stood forward.

'Thanks, but there are already several people on hand. We're waiting for a breakdown vehicle to come from the local garage. Best stay dry and warm in here for now.'

'I'll stoke up the fires then.' Father Christmas appeared from out of the Grotto, looking rather dishevelled after an afternoon of herding children. 'Derek, you wouldn't mind fetching some more logs, would you?'

'On it, Lord Henry.'

So, Father Christmas also doubled as a lord. *How marvellous*, thought Lucy. This place really was full of surprises.

'I'll keep you all updated,' Malcom promised those remaining in the hall, as he lifted his collar and popped his woolly hat back on, ready to face the elements once more.

'Thanks, Malcolm. Well then, while we're waiting, can I get anyone a warm drink from the tea rooms?' Ellie called out to the remaining stallholders. 'I'll bring up a couple of trays of tea and coffee, shall I? I'm sure there'll be a few mince pies floating around too.'

'Thank you, that sounds lovely. Can I give you hand?' Lucy offered.

'Yes, that'd be great. Come on down with me.'

Lucy followed Ellie down a winding circular stone stairwell which led from the far corner of the hall, that looked like it might well suit the Rapunzel story. Brrr, it was chilly in there. They levelled out and then, stepping through a heavy wooden door, they entered the castle tea shop, its large roaring fire ablaze. The ceiling was high with cast-iron chandelier-style lights and there were many antiquities and curiosities adorning the walls: huge antlers, copper kettles, ancient kitchen utensils, and tapestries.

The short dark-haired lady who Lucy had seen earlier with the children on the steps was bustling about clearing the tables.

'Doris, we've got a bit of an issue,' Ellie announced. 'The road's blocked, so the last stallholders are stuck for the time being. So, let's get the kettle and the coffee machine back on, and we'll make hot drinks for everyone.'

'Oh, crikey. Have the snows come in that bad? No-one hurt, I hope?'

'No, thankfully nobody's been injured. But there's been a good covering of snow out there. A van's slid and got stuck across the lane, so it's blocked. And from the look of it outside, the white stuff keeps on coming down too.'

'Ooh, I wonder if my Clifford will be able to get through to pick me up?'

'Most likely not, Doris, not unless he's in Chitty Chitty Bang Bang with wings. I think you'd best give him a call to hold off for a while.'

'Righty-ho. Don't want him getting stuck out there too.'

'So, are there any mince pies or anything else left over? Help cheer up the troops.'

'Yes, we'd made plenty, so there's at least two dozen still there in the kitchen. There's some shortbread and a few brownies too.'

'That'll do nicely.'

As they made the drinks, with Lucy in charge of pouring milk into a jug and setting mugs onto a tray, Ellie chatted away, asking Lucy all about her pizza business.

'I know it can be a real challenge. I came here to the castle eight years ago, having lived all my life in Newcastle. Bit of a baptism of fire, but very soon I fell in love with the place. Oh, and … also the castle's manager.' She gave a wide grin. 'Can't imagine being anywhere else now.'

'Aw, that's lovely.' Lucy felt a pang within. She was happy for Ellie, but also, she couldn't help but think about her and Jack. Could they ever be settled like that? Or was she just setting herself up for a fall?

❄

Back at the Great Hall, there was a buzz of chatter as the castle clear-up continued. A tall, elderly chap, dressed in a faded-cream cashmere jumper and green chinos, was sweeping up with a massive broom, trailed by a four-year-old boy.

'Grandpa, where did Father Christmas go?'

'Ah, I bet his sleigh came to fetch him, Jack … Now that all the other children have gone home.'

'Oh … but he had a quad.'

'Well, yes, he did for the last bit. But I bet the reindeers dropped him off in the woods first. How else would he have got here?'

The little lad stood thinking for a few seconds. 'Oh, do you think Rudolph was here too, then?'

'More than likely.'

'I bet he was. He likes the snow.'

The boy stood quietly for a few moments, evidently thinking, before he added, 'I thought Father Christmas was fat.'

'Hmm, maybe he's thinned down a bit with all the work he's got on,' came the answer, drily. Lucy could see the tall chap giving a wry smile. He then continued, 'He might put it back on again once he can stop and sit by the fire, and eat lots of turkey dinners and mince pies.'

'Ah … yes.' The little lad seemed satisfied with that response, adding, 'And chocolate too.'

'Did anyone mention chocolate? Here, I'll add some of my choccies to the goodie selection to go with our drinks, seeing as we might be here a while. Would you like something, Jack?' Chocolatier Emma opened up a couple of boxes of truffles and a packet of fudge, setting them out on the big wooden table at the centre of the room, alongside the plate of warmed mince pies, shortbread and brownies.

The little boy dashed forward to have first pick, diving in for some fudge and a chocolate brownie square.

'Ah, that's plenty, Son,' Ellie gave a warning, as after wolfing down the huge piece of fudge, his hand was about to delve in again.

'But Mu-um.' He frowned as he crossed his arms grumpily.

'Give everyone else a chance first, and remember to

mind your manners. There might be a little something left for you at the end if you're lucky. Come and help yourselves, everybody. We might well be here for a little while yet,' Ellie called to the remaining stallholders. 'And thanks, Emma.'

They tucked in, chatting between themselves as they continued clearing away and, all the while, outside the mullioned windows, the snow fell.

❄

'Any news?' Ellie asked half an hour later, as Malcolm trailed into the hall, shivering, and with each step shaking off a heavy dusting of snow. 'My goodness, it's like the arctic out there.'

He was followed by a tall, dark-haired, rather handsome man.

'Daddy!' The little boy ran up to him.

He swept the lad up into his open arms, and gave him a snow-dusted twirl.

'Father Christmas has gone now,' the boy rushed the words out, mid-air, 'but there are sweeties and biscuits, so it's alright.'

'Well, that's good. And *I* could murder a hot cup of coffee.'

'F-freezing out th-there,' Malcolm's teeth were actually chattering. He grabbed a mince pie and moved to huddle next to the fire. Derek, his partner, swiftly supplying him with a cosy blanket.

'So,' Ellie asked, 'any luck with the road? We've got

several people here, who've had a really busy day, waiting to get homeward bound.'

Joe shook his head. 'Sorry, folks. We did manage to get the van out of the ditch, but it was hardly able to stay on the road, slipping and sliding everywhere. Anyway, it's been towed by Simon from the farm, who made sure to get Alan safely as far as the village. But it's lethal out there. The snow's been relentless. The wind's picking up now too, and it's beginning to drift. Those roads are treacherous, even with a four by four. The tractor's just about okay, but not a lot else. It's not worth the risk.'

'We absolutely couldn't let you go out in that,' Malcolm warned from his fireplace position.

'Really?'

'Oh, crikey.'

A swirl of wind-battered snow spattered the mullioned windows dramatically as if in confirmation.

The gathering stood taking it all in, seeming a bit shocked.

'Oh, but I really need to get back, I've got a six-year-old at home,' Rachel from the Pudding Pantry blurted out.

'Don't worry, love. She'll be fine with Tom and Granny Ruth,' Jill, her mother, soothed. 'They'll be spoiling her rotten, in fact. We can give them a call.'

'True.'

'And I'm sure they'd rather you got home safely later on, than risk an accident,' added Lord Henry wisely.

'Yes, I suggest we all sit tight and wait for the storm to pass,' advised Joe calmly. 'We wait until the morning when we can check on the road conditions, I'd say ...'

'The morning?' The chap from the candle stall sounded aghast. His wife's face had paled.

'Oh ...'

'But ...'

'Lord Henry and Joe are right,' confirmed Doris, folding her arms with authority. 'Looks like we're all staying put for now. So, another pot of tea, anyone?'

'Thank you, but what happens next? How can we help?' Jack asked.

Lucy's mind was spinning at this new turn of events. Well, at least Daisy was safe and warm with Olly. She'd have to give him and then her mum a quick call to explain what was going on, so they didn't get concerned.

'Okay folks, I have an idea.' Ellie went across to have a quick word with Joe, who gave an affirming nod. 'Look, we can open up the stable rooms for you to stay in overnight. We use them as accommodation for weddings, normally,' Ellie explained.

'But ... won't that be a lot of work for you? We don't want to put you to too much trouble,' Lucy said.

'It's no problem, honestly. Derek, would you mind going and getting the fires lit in all those rooms? Find Colin, he's about somewhere, he certainly won't be able to get much grounds work done today, and Joe'll give you a hand too. And Doris, you are welcome to stay in the spare room of our apartment tonight. I'm not having Clifford or any of you here risking those roads, trying to get back in a snowstorm,' Ellie said, taking control.

'Are you certain?' asked the candle-making couple. 'We don't want to put you out ...'

'Well, it's either that, or you'll be camping in the hall, and it can be awfully draughty in here,' Ellie smiled.

'Well, uhm … thank you,' replied Jack, silently cursing. He'd have to spend a whole night here with Lucy, when his head was already spinning …

'Yeah, that sounds great,' said Emma. 'Though I'd better give Max a ring and tell him to take that casserole he's made back out of the oven, if I'm not coming home.'

'It's no problem at all. And,' Ellie continued, 'me and Doris will fix you up with something for supper later.'

'At least let us help out with that,' Jill offered.

'Well, Doris has been busy here preparing festive Sunday lunches for the tea rooms tomorrow, *but* considering these snows, I have a feeling my customers won't be able to make it through. We may well have just started roasting two massive turkeys for nothing … they'll need eating. There'll be plenty to go around. It might just end up being a bit of a late supper.'

'Sounds a plan. Let us add some puddings for afterwards,' Rachel offered. 'Sticky toffee or Christmas pudding, anyone?'

'Oooh, yes, please,' Emma grinned, knowing just how good they were.

'Well, in that case, I'm sure I can make us all a pre-dinner cocktail and find a bottle or two of fizz. Perhaps an Irish coffee later on too?' Jack took up. If they were stuck, then he may as well help make it a more pleasant experience for everyone.

'Ah, my pizzas have all gone, but I can help peel some veggies to go with the turkey?' offered Lucy.

'And me,' the candle lady added, introducing herself as Karen. 'Whatever needs doing, just say.'

'Thanks folks, and you can leave the stuffing to me. I have my secret recipe ready to prepare.' Doris, who'd evidently been listening in, popped her head out from the corner stairwell, bringing up a fresh pot of tea.

'Sounds like a team effort, then. Cheers, everybody.' Ellie looked delighted. 'Right then, while the lads quickly go and set up the rooms, I'll fetch some bedding.'

'Oh, let me help with that,' Lucy was quick off the mark.

'And me,' Rachel and Emma said together. 'Snap!' They laughed.

They finished off their hot drinks and mince pies, and soon set to work. All hands were on deck, leaving Malcolm snug by the fire, thawing out, bless him. Emma and Lucy teamed to be 'housekeeping' with Ellie, whilst Jill, Karen and Doris set off on mission sprouts and stuffing, tackling a mound of carrots, potatoes and parsnips too down in the tea rooms. Jack joined Joe and the lads in lighting the accommodation fires, and carrying extra logs – that were more like tree trunks – back to the hall to keep the flames flickering there in the huge hearth.

That team spirit had helped turn a crisis into something far more pleasant. Yes, they were officially snowed in, but by the sounds of it, they were going to be very cosy at the castle. Thank heavens their hosts were so welcoming. Yes, it all sounded very jolly. The only problem now was that everything was a little *too* cosy in this snowy lock-in; Jack and Lucy faced many hours in each other's company. And that meant there was nowhere to hide.

Chapter Twenty-Six

I t was bitter out there as Lucy and Jack battened down the hatches on both the campervan and the horsebox for the night. The wind and snow was swirling around them in an icy blast. Even with gloves and hats on, it was freezing. Lucy's toes were like ice blocks in her leather boots by the time they got back to the safety of the castle; weirdly numb yet tingling, her thick socks no match at all for this severe weather.

Derek then directed them to their accommodation for the night, which was out through a covered walkway in the quarter that was once the old stables.

'So, this is you,' he opened the door onto a double-bedroom suite.

'Oh …' mumbled Lucy.

'Right,' stammered Jack.

Derek picked up their hesitancy immediately, looking from one to the other. 'I have got this right, haven't I? You are a couple, aren't you? It's just that Emma said …'

'Yes, it's fine,' replied Lucy.

'Well then, I'll leave you pair to it. The fire will get going in a minute. There're plenty more logs and some coal there too. There are radiators, but well, they can be a bit quirky.' He pulled a grimace, as if well used to the eccentricities of the castle. 'Takes about a day to get them going properly, when they've been off for a while,' he explained. 'See you around eight for supper down in the tea rooms. Okay?'

'Yes, thanks ever so much, Derek,' Lucy responded politely.

'Thank you.'

And that was it. Jack and Lucy were left to their own devices.

The air felt heavy, charged with tension.

'Oh my God, bloody f-freezing out there, isn't it?' Lucy stammered, moving closer to the open log fire.

'Yeah, Joe reckons it's gone down to minus two. I don't think anyone saw this coming.'

'Jeez, and with that w-wind ...' Lucy was still shivering.

She stared into the fire, she could sense that Jack was close. She had to say something to break this icy atmosphere.

She turned around, forced herself to look him in the eye. 'Jack, what's going on? What's wrong? You've been so distant all day ...'

'It's nothing.'

'Well, it doesn't seem like nothing. You're cutting me out. Look, I know how it might have looked at the Christmas tree light-up, with Liam ...'

'I don't want to talk about it,' he bit, his tone stone-cold.

He was closing down on her, shutting off.

'Jack ... please. Talk to me... If we don't communicate...'

He just shook his head sadly, this was too much, his mind suddenly felt so heavy. He couldn't forget what he'd seen.

'Please, Jack, come here.'

'I'm going for a walk,' he mumbled.

'But it's Baltic out there, you'll freeze, come by the fire ...'

'I'll be fine, I just ... I need some space. Look, I'll see you back at the castle for dinner, okay?'

And with that he turned on his heel, opened the door into the wintry evening, and left Lucy staring disbelievingly into the flickering flames of the fire.

An hour later, feeling a little more comfortable after a warm shower, Lucy made her way back over to the main castle building. Walking into the tea rooms, she caught her breath. *Oh my goodness!* From what she had seen earlier, the place had been transformed; Ellie, Joe, and the castle team must have gone all out. The long wooden table was laid with the festive table decorations that had been up in the hall, along with some gorgeous white-winter-scented candles that flickered gently, kindly donated by Karen and James. Wow, the whole group seemed intent on coming together to make this a special night. And, after taking a heart-panging glance at Jack who was stood – looking a little chilly – at the far end of the table, it all served to make the distance between the two of them more obvious.

Ellie came bustling out from the kitchen, apron on and wooden spoon to hand, announcing that dinner would be ready in fifteen minutes, and politely declining the several offers of help at this stage, saying there'd be too many cooks in the kitchen.

After making sloe gin cocktails for all, as everyone assembled, Jack was delighted to offer two bottles of champagne 'to help the proceedings flow'.

Doris and Ellie then joined the gathering, delivering scrumptious-looking piled-high plates of turkey dinner to all. The pair of them finally sitting down with a relieved and well-earned 'phew'.

'This looks amazing, thank you so much for all this: Ellie, Joe, Lord Henry and everyone,' Jack said earnestly. 'So, let's crack these open and toast our hosts.'

'Hear, hear,' called out Malcom, who, having thawed out and returned to his former glory with a change of clothes and a sparkly bow-tie, had been busy along with Derek, putting the finishing touches to the table, with cutlery, wine glasses and all.

'Ooh, you can't beat a bit of festive fizz,' added Derek with a grin.

'Absolutely …' Jack beamed.

The popping of corks sounded celebratory as it echoed around the ancient chamber, with Jack pouring out a glass for everyone. Around the table was Joe, sat next to little Jack – who already had his own special glass of lemonade and was determined not to miss out on a party by going to bed yet, *no way*, especially not a *Christmas* party – along with grandpa Lord Henry, Emma, Rachel and Jill, Karen and James, plus Colin, the castle gardener.

Jack raised his glass with a 'Thank you so much' and a 'Cheers', which was joined in by all the 'surprise' guests.

'Hear, hear,' added Malcolm again.

Then young Jack shouted out, 'Merry Christmas!' which made them all laugh.

'You're a little bit early, young man,' said his grandpa with a smile.

It might have been two weeks early, but it was indeed a Christmas dinner to remember! The snow swirled outside, making shadowy-lace patterns against the window panes, as the fire in the tea rooms roared in defiance and the cinnamon-scented candles flickered. The food was festive and fabulous – roast turkey with all the trimmings, followed by 'Granny Ruth's' Christmas pudding with lashings of cream. The guests were far too full to move after the heady feast, and sat chatting amongst themselves, with stories of Christmases past; snow storms up in the hills at Primrose Farm for Rachel and Jill, and the wedding at the castle that nearly got cancelled by heavy snow a few years ago, saved at the last by the local tractor getting through with the bride, the groom and guests. A dinner to remember and like no other, with newfound friends that were already beginning to feel like family.

The feast's finale was Irish coffees all round, with Jack doing his cocktail wizardry in the kitchen. Little Jack was now slumped fast asleep in his chair, with a blanket tucked over him, after his own dinner finale of Rudolph-shaped chocolates from Emma. With the warmth of the fire, and the warmth of their company, no-one was in any rush to head back to their rooms as yet.

❄

This was what Christmas was all about: goodwill, good food and friendship. Lucy sighed as she glanced around the last-minute gathering, forged from adversity and kindness. Them all sat together around the tea-room table, with the world white and a little wild outside, enjoying joyful banter and chat against the backdrop of the huge crackling fire, they could have all drifted back in time, and been sat feasting in another century. It felt surreal yet also comfortable, and rather magical. And such festivities didn't have to be *on* Christmas Day at all. It just had to be together, with friends old and new.

She chanced a glance once more at Jack sat beside her. Malcolm, oblivious to their rift, had placed them next to each other on his swiftly drawn-up table plan. His features handsome with that sandy hair, slate-blue eyes that glinted in the firelight, as he chatted away easily with the others. His generous spirit offering champagne and cocktails to them all. She briefly thought about reaching for Jack's hand under the table, giving a squeeze of reassurance, but his harsh words from earlier echoed around in her head. She gave a heavy sigh – how could her heart be so warmed by this lovely community, this gorgeously unexpected feast, and yet feel so chilled at the same time?

❄

The evening came to a pleasant end with the now very-relaxed gathering draining the last of their Irish coffees. Tummies were full and fabulously feasted. Now that it was time to head back to their room, with no choice but to face each other once again, Jack felt a strong sense of trepidation.

Outside, the snow had slowed to a dusting of white flakes, falling gently and catching the light. It was freezing out there, so Lucy and Jack walked towards their stable-block room as quickly, and as carefully, as they could manage on the icy ground.

Lucy quickly closed the stable-style door behind them, trying to retain as much warmth as possible, and blew warm air into her icy hands. She took a moment to glance around the room with its rustic wooden beams, tapestry-style rug, roaring fire, and beautiful four-poster bed.

'I suppose this *would* have been a romantic bolt-hole, wouldn't it ...' she said, wistfully.

'I suppose so, Luce ...' Jack looked at her, his eyes suddenly glistening with tears.

'Oh, Jack, what's wrong?' she said, taking a step towards him.

He took a step back. 'Look, Lucy ... I ... I can't do this anymore.'

'What? Jack, you can't just run away all the time. Talk to me. Tell me what's up? There's something more to this, I know it. Your distance ... And if you'd only let me explain rather than clamming up ...'

He could only stare at her.

'I ... I thought you loved me, Jack,' Lucy said, feeling herself crumbling, 'that we had something really good.'

'I can't ...' His words sounded strangled.

'At least tell me why. You owe me that ...' Emotion quaked through her voice.

'If you must know. I saw it ...'

'Yes I know, you saw Liam arrive at the Christmas tree

event, and I shouldn't have gone off without saying anyth—'

'No!' Jack continued, more forcefully now. 'I saw him yesterday morning, I was passing … I was going to call by … after picking up some bits at the supermarket in Seahouses.'

She stayed silent, trying to work out what he was saying.

'It was Liam …. leaving your cottage. It was ten o'clock in the morning, Luce …' He couldn't look at her then, it hurt too much, his glance dropping to the ground.

'Oh Jack,' Lucy said, her heart beating ten to the dozen, 'it's not what you think. Yes, he'd come by, but for a coffee. It was just a chance to talk … to clear the air.' *Oh, what a mess.* Lucy felt panicky. The air between the two of them now felt so damned polluted, it threatened to choke them. 'You've got to believe me, Jack,' she pleaded.

'I saw what I saw, Luce.' Jack's tone was cold.

How could she make him see sense? This was ridiculous, an awful misunderstanding. But Jack, well, he had to have some trust in her too.

'You really think I'm capable of that? You think I'd betray you with that dickhead? I'd *never* hurt you like that. We have to be able to trust each other.'

'Trust …?' Jack looked at her, incredulous.

'I know what it might have looked like, but that's just not true. Look, it was Liam who let down the tyres on the horsebox, smashed the Jeep's window …'

Lucy knew she sounded frantic now, it looked like she was scrabbling for excuses. 'It was horrible, Jack, I just had to see him …'

'Luce, please, I really don't know what to think,' Jack said, rubbing his hands over his face. He paused, looked at Lucy again. 'Only that I need to take some time out from all of this.'

Lucy was frozen, she couldn't even utter another word.

And with that Jack grabbed a blanket from the bed, stalked over to the sofa, and settled down with his back turned. Their cosy little bolt-hole feeling as frosty as an igloo right now.

Chapter Twenty-Seven

The next morning, Lucy stretched out an arm, gave a yawn, then opened her eyes, realising where she was: it wasn't all some crazy Christmas dream, after all. But then she reminded herself – despite being snowed in at this gorgeous romantic castle – how it had all ended last night as a bit of a nightmare. Jack's words haunting her, *I need to take some time out from all of this.* That sounded so much like a goodbye to her. She felt tears rising, unbidden. She snapped her eyelids shut for a few seconds, trying to trap those droplets.

From the bedroom window, Lucy could see that the snow was still thick on the ground with a hard yet stunning frost; the sky a clear, cold azure. A couple of icicles had formed, hanging as glassy shards from the external window top.

She then looked over at the sofa, saw only an empty seat and a rumpled blanket. Jack was evidently already awake, perhaps prowling the cold castle grounds.

Lucy edged slowly out of the bed. It was chilly in there. The radiator system must be from the Victorian age by the looks of it, and the log fire had gone out hours ago. But none of that was anywhere near as cold as the dreadful feeling inside her heart. After dressing quickly, she headed over to the main castle, discovering Joe and Ellie down in the tea rooms, with Rachel, Jill and Emma. Jack was still nowhere to be seen.

The scent of toast and coffee lured her in. She needed something warm and comforting. After coffee, with hot buttered toast and a catch-up with the breakfast gathering, Lucy offered to help with the washing up. She needed to keep busy, keep her mind off things.

Washing up completed, and with a little time to kill until they could be certain the lanes were passable, she decided to take a walk in the grounds. After the snow, it now looked like a frosty winter wonderland out there.

Wrapped up in her warm winter coat and gloves, finding herself in the formal garden of the castle, Lucy gazed around her with awe. A splintery brushwork of white hoar-frost and glassy ice was clinging to every plant, stone, hedge, glistening in the morning sunlight. Everything had changed since their arrival just twenty-four hours before. The stunning frost-tinged scenery, and her relationship with Jack.

She walked on between neat privet hedges, discovering rose bushes with their last autumn blooms now faded and frozen in ice. All was still, hushed, except for the crunch of frost under her feet. She couldn't help but be entranced by it all. At a fountain where the water had frozen mid-flow, which looked like the most stunning ice sculpture, Lucy heard the sound of feet crunching behind her on the gravel path. She turned: Jack.

'Hi.' Her voice was soft, fragile.

'Hey …'

'It's beautiful here, isn't it? The frost, the sky, the plants held in ice.'

'Yeah,' Jack had to concede, feeling an emotional knot in his throat.

It wasn't just the snow or the frost, nor the castle and its beautiful setting, it was how they'd felt about being together these past few months. And now it was all falling apart.

They stared at each other for a few heartfelt moments.

'I'm setting off shortly,' Jack announced simply, yet there was a sadness to his tone.

'Oh …' After everything he'd said last night, Lucy didn't know which words to use or how to begin to pull him back to her … or, if she'd ever be able to. All she did know right now was that Jack needed his space. She had to give him time.

But would time ever be enough?

'Will you be alright?'

Was he asking about the roads, the snow? But it felt like he was asking would she be okay without him.

She gave a brief nod. 'I'll wait a while. Let the roads settle.'

'Take care, Luce.'

As she watched him walk away, with her eyes now misting, she wondered if this was Jack's way of saying goodbye.

❄

As Lucy watched Jack drive off, flashbacks rose up unbidden: of that beautiful morning together in Dunstanburgh; meeting him that first time at the posh birthday bash – her first event booking – hah, where he'd got punched storming in to protect her; sunny days drinking cocktails in the dunes; and his unforgettable shoreline supper when he wore full dinner jacket attire, them laughing as they got drenched by the incoming tide … this all played through her mind. It couldn't end like this, not over some silly misunderstanding. Could it?

Or, she considered, was it some cover for deeper misgivings, this need in Jack to not be tied down? She felt heavy with fear. This gorgeous but exasperating man was far deeper than he first appeared, she mused, thinking back to his cocky cocktail barman persona when she'd first met him. He was as deep as an ocean, it seemed.

She tried her best to shake off this spiral of melancholy. It was time for her and All Fired Up to get away soon too. After giving her thanks to the castle team, and checking on the latest road update with Joe, steadily through snow-caked lanes, she began to find her way home. Yes, she'd give Jack the space he needed for now. But soon, if he was still being stubborn, closed off to her, she'd go and knock on his door, go and see him and try and put the record straight. She wasn't giving in that easily. Their relationship was worth far too much.

Chapter Twenty-Eight

'Jack, are you alright?'

He was sat at his parents' kitchen table, overlooking their now winter-bare garden. It was a couple of days after the castle lock-in.

'It's just … you've been awfully quiet and well, slightly grumpy, I have to say,' his mother continued.

'You mean *more* than normal,' he replied drily.

'Well, yes. You know you can always tell me anything … If you need to talk …?'

'I'm fine, Mum, honestly,' he brushed it off.

'Okay, well … anytime …' she let the words hang like an offering. 'Another cup? Your dad'll be a while yet, he's off playing golf with Tony.'

'Yeah, go on then, why not.' He wasn't in any particular rush, and had headed over there purposefully, feeling strangely in need of some company. Back home at his lodgings, with Matt out at work, it had been way too quiet.

His mum fiddled on with the kettle, while he watched a

lone robin hopping about on the bird table, which was always well stocked with crumbs.

'How was the Christmas event at the castle the other day, did it go well?'

'Yeah, it was fine, I got some good takings,' he said, non-committal.

'And, how's that new girlfriend of yours? Lucy, isn't it?'

Jack's brow furrowed. Just the thought of Lucy made him feel sore emotionally.

'So, how's it all going? You seem to have been spending quite a lot of time together,' Denise persevered.

'Yeah, it's fine, she's great, she's …' Jack stuttered, his blank tone hiding a torrent of feelings. All the while he was thinking, *She's beautiful, talented, witty, wise and … she makes my soul sing.* 'But, well …'

Jack looked around the room. His mother had put out her Christmas decorations. A muted festive effort, of silvers and cool whites, but stylish nonetheless. They hadn't gone large on Christmas for ten years now; just showed it their passing respects, muddled through, holding hands with their grief, and moved on to another year.

'Well, what? Jack, you're not thinking of bolting again … like you always do?' There was a pause. His mother knew him well. Jack said nothing. 'What are you so afraid of, Jack?'

'Nothing. It's just not working out like I thought …'

Denise refilled the teapot, then looked up. 'It doesn't mean you don't get hurt, Jack, shutting yourself away … not getting too close, it just means that you end up hurting *yourself*,' her voice softened. 'Missing out on the chance of it ever leading to something bigger. This girl means something to you, doesn't she?'

Jack bit the inside of his mouth. The lie that was forming, and on the tip of his tongue, not sitting easily.

Denise took the seat opposite him after passing him his mug. 'You know, it's not always easy … *love*, but if you never let it in, you'll miss out on so much, Son. I think you deserve more than that. In fact, I think you owe it to yourself to give it a try.' She gave a gentle smile. Her lines more apparent than usual in the pale winter sunlight that splayed through the French doors. She had lived, she had lost, she had loved … still loved.

'Me and your dad … well, it's been tough at times, as well you know … but we've muddled through, and we were always there for each other when it mattered. That's what got us through, that's what gave us strength.'

'Yeah …' Jack's mind, his heart, were too full to process all those feelings into words.

'Do you know,' Denise continued, 'we nearly didn't get together at all, way back then …'

Jack looked up sharply. 'Really?' His parents had always seemed like the dream team.

'Oh yes, your dad was all gung-ho about getting married and having a family quickly. And well, I … I hadn't done that much, I wanted to see a bit of the world. I had a good job back then, too. I was a PA in a successful family firm that made fly fishing rods here in Alnwick. I had a lot of responsibility, used to organise the boss's travel, meetings and events, here there and everywhere. I loved it.'

Wow, this was a whole new side to his mum. And the

news that they nearly hadn't made it ... 'So, what happened?'

'We compromised. Sounds such a boring word, but in relationships, well, that's the glue: the respect, the love. It's all about give and take. I stayed on at work, we made sure to take a few special holidays, some adventures. And we waited a few years before trying for a family. We worked it out. Life changed when you two came along, of course, but I was ready for that then, and I've never looked back. You and Daniel were the best things that ever happened to me.' She gave a wistful smile.

'And everything with Daniel, that's when I needed your dad the most. Having someone to hold my hand through all that grief, that pain. It's okay to be vulnerable sometimes, Jack.'

He stayed quiet, processing her words. His heart felt so full, it might crush him.

'Anyway ... lesson over. I've probably bored you by now. But hey, I'm just trying to look out for you. That's what mothers do.'

He reached a strong hand over the table and gave hers a rub.

'I know ... and ... ah ...' This was all so intense. He needed a bit of time out. 'I'll just nip to the bathroom.'

He headed for the upstairs loo, needing some space. As he reached the landing, he spotted the door open to his brother's old room. A few years ago, his parents had redecorated it, put on fresh bedding, given it a new look completely. But they'd kept a few knick-knacks: a photo of Daniel smiling on his eighteenth birthday, when blissfully none of them knew what was to come; his old much-loved teddy bear he'd had when he was little; and a football trophy from when his Alnwick team had won the junior league. A shelf full of memories that tugged at Jack's heart. He was drawn to go in. Daniel's presence was still very much there, even after all these years, even after the guestroom-style facelift.

'Oh, Dan …' The words sighed inside his head. He knew he'd feel his brother's loss all his life. All those milestones missed, the might-have-beens, the big-brother advice that he could no longer ask for.

On the same shelf there was a card with a big yellow smiley face on; Daniel must have sent it in his first year of uni. Jack picked it up. The excitement in Daniel's tone coming through:

Miss you folks but am enjoying the adventure. Joined the five-a-side footie team, made a few mates through that already, and got my name down for mountaineering club. There's a trip to the Lakes coming up with that. Sounds cool. Trying rowing out next week too. Full on here but great! Carpe Diem, hey!

Hah, yes, Dan loved rattling off that phrase. 'Seize the day' in Latin. He was always like that, Dan, living life to the full. Not in a big, showy way, just getting on with it. Squeezing the most out of it.

And what was Jack doing with his life right now? Yes, the campervan business was doing well, but the rest of his life … the personal stuff … His mother's words were still fresh in his mind. He brushed his fingertips over Daniel's writing, then carefully replaced the card. Daniel wouldn't have wanted him to hold back. But sometimes it was hard to know which road to take, and his heart and his head were having trouble reading the road signs just now.

❄

Back downstairs, soon afterwards, Denise tried to lighten the mood with a little local gossip. 'Oh gosh, I do hope Lucy's doing okay, by the way. I heard from Trish at the golf club, who knows Cathy at the shop in the village there, that there's been someone going around slashing people's tyres and causing all sorts of damage.'

Jack's ears pricked up. He remembered holding Lucy close the night after it had happened, making sure she was alright.

'And to think that Lucy's ex has been behind it all, it must have been a real shock.'

He went cold. That was what Lucy had been trying to tell him, to explain back there at the castle, and he was so full of his own version of what he'd seen, he hadn't listened. He'd cut her off, hadn't he? Shite, he'd gone and messed up big time.

The road ahead was suddenly very clear.

'Gotta go, Mum. Thanks for the tea ... the chat.' He was up and out of his chair like Usain Bolt.

❄

Driving back in Ruby, he knew.

Why the hell was he thinking of walking away, when he should be bloody running towards her? He needed to see Lucy and he needed to see her *now*.

Passing the junction to his own village, he headed on for her village of Embleton. His pulse racing and his mind set. Fields of sheep and crops flashed by behind stone walls, hedges of hawthorn flickered as he whizzed by. And as he got nearer, there were glimpses of the sea at each turn, bringing him closer to her.

He turned off, now on her street, pulled up. *No*, her Jeep wasn't outside. Undeterred, he leaped out of the camper and dashed to her door, rapping on the old metal knocker. Daisy must be there as he heard barking, but there was no answer from Lucy. He rapped again, peered in the living-room window, no-one there. Then went back to try the lock. The cottage was all shut up. *Dammit.*

'Lucy?!' One last ineffectual shout. Bloody hell, she couldn't be out, not now. This felt so important. He had to put things right between them. As he stood on the pavement, feeling thwarted, but still full of adrenaline, the fifty-something neighbour poked her head out of the cottage next door. 'Can I help at all? If it's Lucy you're after, I saw her head out about twenty minutes ago.'

Oh dear, he must have been making a right racket. 'Ah, right. Sorry about the noise, it's just … it's something important.'

'Okay, well can I give her a message? When she gets back?'

'Umm, thanks but no, it's something I need to tell her myself.'

His shoulders sagged, and he felt deflated. There wasn't much he could do right now … After all, how was Lucy to know he'd gone and had some kind of relationship epiphany?

He got back into Ruby and drummed his fingertips on the steering wheel. Lucy hadn't even mentioned where she might be … And this felt like a conversation they needed to have in person; he couldn't risk any crossed wires over a text message. He cursed himself, what a jerk he'd been.

Tomorrow, he'd put it all right tomorrow.

Chapter Twenty-Nine

L ucy and Becky were at Oscar's wine bar for a girlie afternoon, catching up over cake, coffee and no doubt very soon a little festive fizz. Just the one glass for Lucy, who was driving, having a busy day ahead tomorrow with a fortieth birthday bash event to cater for. This was the girls' annual last-minute Christmas 'shopping' trip – though in all honesty there was never very much shopping involved. It was more a chance to enjoy the Alnwick Christmas lights, soak up the small-town festive feels, and to unwind a little. Settled in a cosy corner booth, with a few last-minute stocking fillers at their feet, Becky asked, 'So, how's life been these past couple of weeks? How's it all going with the party pizza van? And with Jack …?'

'Ah …' Where on earth to begin? She hadn't even broached the latest saga with her and Jack to Becks, hoping he might yet come to his senses. 'It's been busy,' Lucy thought it best to stick with the work angle, being safer ground. 'Yeah, and I've loved doing all the Christmas markets and fayres these past few weeks.' She really had, but her voice dipped a little remembering the castle fayre and the horrid fall-out with Jack. The gaping chasm that was in fact still between them.

'Oh, I bet it's been fun. Much nicer than being stuck in an office …'

'Well, it's certainly very different. Has its challenges, but yeah, it's been a good move.'

'And hey, I can't believe it was Liam who did that to your tyres. What an idiot! How the hell did he think *that* would help worm his way back into your life?'

Lucy had phoned her friend, telling her all about it. 'I know, crazy isn't it. At least I can relax again back in my village.'

'Yeah. Who'd have thought, hey? Love, or more likely in Liam's case jealousy, can make you do crazy things.'

Lucy shrugged as Becky shook her head. Love really was a whole damned crazy ball game.

The two of them sipped their frothy cappuccinos, sprinkled with a touch of cinnamon, and munched on slices of moist chocolate-orange cake. They'd also lined up a crisp buttery-baked mince pie each. Well, it was the season for mince pies and merriment.

'Anyway, how about you, Becks? Any luck with finding a new job as yet?'

As Becky had guessed, the company she worked for had given her her notice, having had to make some redundancies and, unfortunately, she found herself back on the employment register just in time for Christmas. She was trying her best not to let it get her down. 'Been for a couple of interviews. Just got to keep on trying, keep ploughing on.'

'Oh, good luck.'

'Well, the one at the travel agents sounds really good, and the lady interviewing me was lovely. So, fingers crossed.'

'Aw, I hope it comes off for you, Becks. You never know, you might get some good news and a new dream job really soon. You might even get some holiday discounts. A new start for New Year, eh?' Lucy was determined to keep her friend's spirits up.

'Yeah, let's hope so. Anyway,' Becky changed tack, 'How's lover boy lately?'

'Ah, he's fine. It's all fine …' Lucy's tone was undeniably flat.

'*Fine* …? Uh-oh Luce, that sounds a bit dodgy. It should be happy days for you two … still in that first flush. He's not giving you grief already, is he?' Becky frowned exaggeratedly.

'Uhm …' Lucy floundered. Maybe it was time to open up. Time to share her feelings, voice her concerns. She'd been holding so much back. 'Ah, Becks, it's a bit of a nightmare, actually. He's been pretty closed off for a while now. And well, I'd told you about us getting snowed in at the castle … and it should have been lovely, it was such a romantic place … but ah, he'd seen Liam coming out of my house that morning – that day when I found out about the tyres and all that malarkey, but Jack's put two and two together and now he thinks there's something going on between us. I can't seem to get him to see sense. That Liam's the *last* person I want to be around right now.' Her voice went quiet as she confessed, 'He's actually mentioned having some space …'

Lucy paused, expecting the 'I told you so' from her friend, but it didn't come. Becky just looked at her with a concerned frown.

'It's not all bad. It's only this past couple of weeks things have started going wrong. We've had some amazing times together …' Lucy was desperate for her friend to know the positives. 'When it's good, we just click, like *really* click. And it's not just the sex, though that's been pretty fantastic …'

A middle-aged lady at the next table spluttered into her peppermint tea.

'Okay, enough,' Becky giggled.

'Yeah, just the other week, we watched the sun rise over the beach at Dunstanburgh, and it seemed so damned right … so perfect between us. But this week, and at the castle do …' It was all starting to spill out now. 'Well, he seems like a different person. It's like some kind of shutter comes down … every time we begin to get close. I just don't get it.'

Becky paused, thinking, before replying, 'Well, the Liam thing, seeing him leave your cottage, that'd hit anyone hard.'

'But there's nothing in that. I just need to convince Jack that he wangled his way in that day. I can't stand the bloody guy.'

'I know. And, it sounds to me like Jack's afraid of getting in too deep?'

'Yeah, I know that's at the root of it all. And I think he's got plans to go travelling ...'

Becky looked thoughtful. 'Well, what do *you* want, Lucy? Truthfully?'

Lucy was quiet, finding what was in her heart, then finding the words: 'I do want to be with him. I want him to stay. But he's such a free spirit, I'm afraid he'll just up and disappear. Maybe you were right, Becks. He'll never settle. Maybe this thing with Liam, it's just an excuse, a way out. And right now, honestly ... I'm afraid of being alone again. If Jack goes, this'll hurt far more than Liam leaving me, I know that much.'

'Ooh, he really means a lot to you, Luce, doesn't he?'

'Yeah, he does.'

'Well, I can only say "Go for it" then. Be open about how you feel. You two need to talk, to have it out. You've got nothing to lose by being honest.'

'I might lose *him* ...' Her voice sounded fragile.

'You might, but that won't be because you talked about it. Hey hun, it's a risk you've got to take ... You've got to find out the real truth. And hey, maybe Jack needs that reassurance from you too. He might be just as afraid of losing you ...'

Becky did always have the knack of putting a new perspective on things, of getting to the heart of an issue. Lucy had so missed their frank chats of late.

'Thanks ...' And maybe ... just maybe ... she and Jack could yet find a way through this. If they both wanted it enough, that was.

'Hey, my turn at the bar. I think it's time for a glass of prosecco, what do you reckon?' Becky stood up.

'That sounds perfect.'

It was so good to have her friend back on board.

As Becky returned shortly afterwards, holding a glass of fizz for them both, Lucy gave a smile. 'Aw, this is nice, just like old times.'

Becky settled onto the bench-seat beside Lucy, her face turned serious. 'Luce, I need to be honest with you too. Look, I'm really sorry … that I made things difficult for you. For you and Jack. I do hope you two can sort things out.' Her friend took a breath then gave a slow sigh, like she was trying to find the right words. 'I've been doing some thinking … trying to work out why it was bothering me so much … you two. I know it was ages ago, that brief fling I had with Jack, and well, it would never have got anywhere, realistically. But I've been feeling like such a teenager about it all … and, of course, I really didn't want him to hurt you, but I also think I might have been a teensy bit jealous.'

'Really?' Lucy was surprised.

'Yeah, well Jack's always been drop-dead gorgeous, hasn't he? … But hey, it was never going to work out with me and him back then, was it? But you two, well you just seemed like this dream couple.'

'Hah, you think? Well, it's maybe not quite so dreamy right now. But hey, what about you and Darren?' How could Becky even begin to feel jealous about Lucy and Jack, when she was settled and loved up with her own partner? Becky and Darren had always seemed well suited. They had their house together, had fun together – yeah, with the usual ups and downs that couples a few years in had – but they'd always seemed like a great match.

Becky didn't answer, just sat looking awkward, pulling at a hangnail on her thumb.

'What's up, Becks? What's been happening?' The two friends had been so out of touch until recently, it saddened Lucy to have to ask. 'You and Darren ... you're still alright, surely?'

'Most of the time, yeah. It's just lately ... I don't know, it all feels kind of stale, like we're stuck in a bit of a rut. It's been five years, Luce. We know each other so well, *too* bloody well. And then there's his work, which seems to be taking over everything. Late nights ... early starts. He says it's a big project they're on. But honestly, I'm beginning to wonder if he might be having some kind of an affair.' Becky gave a small laugh as if jesting, but her face fell, as though she half-doubted him, and her own judgement too.

'Oh, Becks ... Have you asked him about it?'

'No ... I've been too frightened to.'

'But why? You two were always so good at talking things through. When me and Liam were stuck, making a right mess of things.'

'Hmm, it's just far easier to ask what's for tea, or "For Christ's sake can you pick up those dirty socks off the floor," than to ask, "Are you seeing someone else?"' Becky conceded, as her face crumpled. 'I might just be making a mountain out of a molehill, but *something* just feels off with us right now, I hate it ...'

Lucy put a caring hand on her friend's shoulder.

'Well, seems like we're both in a bit of a mess with our men right now, aren't we? But I'm sure there'll be nothing sinister to it with Darren. He's a good guy. But hey, if there is something, if you need me at all, I'm here for you, Becks. Always have been …'

'I know … and I'm so sorry. For shutting you out, like I have. Making you feel awful. You have every right to be happy … you and Jack.' Becky took a sip of her fizz, and looked around the bar, with its coloured lights and festive sparkle. 'I've been an idiot, haven't I?'

'Hey, don't be so hard on yourself. You've been having a hard time too lately. With your job, at home … Look, chat with Darren, *soon*. Find out the truth … I'm sure it won't be anything as bad as you fear. And hey,' added Lucy, 'I'm sorry too, that you didn't feel you could lean on me, when you needed to. Maybe I've been a little too wrapped up with the new business, and with Jack.' They both had glistening eyes by this point.

Becky looked up. 'Well, Jack had better bloody well not hurt you. He'll have me to answer to if he does.'

Hah, the old feisty Becky was back, and it was good to hear that.

'Seriously, you deserve to be happy, Lucy. And Jack, well he needs to pull his finger out and realise what a star he's found in you.'

'Hah, of course,' Lucy chuckled, but there was a beat of anxiety within her too, wondering how things really would pan out for their relationship.

Lucy vowed there and then to talk with Jack. No more secrets, no more hidden fears. Maybe tomorrow, once they'd finished working this birthday event, she'd ask Jack back to her cottage, and they could clear the air once and for all.

'Looks like we've both got some talking to do then, haven't we?' said Lucy.

'Yep, no more hiding away behind our fears,' added Becky.

'Cheers, hun.'

'Cheers.'

And the clink of their glasses had a chink of hopefulness.

❄

Surprise!

Shush, can you keep a secret?!

You are invited to

Craig's Surprise 40th Birthday Party

From 7 p.m., Thursday 16th December

The Grange, Belsay

❄

Chapter Thirty

R uby might be bloody gorgeous, but being vintage (aka ancient), she could at times be temperamental, especially when the weather was a tad cold, and this afternoon was unfortunately one of those times. Heading out of the house, the air was fresh and chilly. Jack had thrown a thick coat on over his tuxedo workwear. Yeah, it was going to be another cold night to be working al fresco – in winter, his mobile catering job wasn't always quite as appealing, he had to admit. But he still loved the banter, the buzz, and making people's parties and celebrations extra special for them. Even with a touch of the shivers, it was still far better than most jobs he knew of. And, of course, he felt a tug inside. He couldn't wait to see Lucy again – everything felt so much clearer now. But would it be enough, would *he* be enough, to convince her to stay after all he'd put her through?

He sat down in Ruby's driving seat, muttering hopefully, 'Come on then babe, let's get this party started,' and turned the key, to which she answered with a sluggish whirr, then nothing. Uh-oh, the battery seemed to be flat – argh, just as he was hoping to leave. He'd have to go and ask his neighbour, Rob, to help rig up the jump leads, and then he'd have to wait for the VW to come back to life. He had a few spare minutes to hand, having given himself plenty of time to get set up there, but he really hated being tardy for any event, and with this delay he was definitely going to be pushing it.

After a quick knock next door, giving a hopeful smile and the promise of a couple of pints at the local, neighbour Rob moved his white van into place, whilst Jack found the rather well-used jump leads that he kept in Matt's garage. Within fifteen minutes, Ruby spluttered back to life and was finally up and running and ready to go. But damn it, he was running late now.

With all that no-start-up palaver, he just hoped he'd remembered everything he needed for this Birthday Bash. He set his SatNav on his phone for the country pad's address, somewhere near Morpeth, and was at last on his way. Bottles and glasses clinking behind him, and a bit of a headache unfortunately now furrowing in his brow. It was dark outside already, being early evening in December, and once he'd turned off from the A1 the roads were narrow and winding. In his headlights he could see a sheeny glint to the tarmac. He slowed down, it looked to be a bit frosty out there; better to err on the side of caution, even if he was running slightly late.

From out of nowhere, a pheasant darted across the road in front of him. He couldn't help it; sheer instinct caused him to swerve to try and avoid hitting it. That was when

Ruby went into a slide … *Shit!* They'd hit ice. Suddenly, he could see the looming shape of a large tree ahead, and began to pump the VW's brakes frantically. Still it was coming at him.

Jesus, no! Time seemed to freeze … yet everything was hurtling towards him. There was nothing he could do but brace. No time for fear. Just a, *Fuck, no, is this it? Is this how it ends?*

Images of his mum, dad, Daniel … Lucy. Sounds of smashing glass, along with the crunch of metal, an acrid diesel smell … A massive jolt tremored through his body.

❄

The party was due to start in twenty minutes. *Where was he?*

Lucy had tried Jack's mobile – three times now. And no answer at all. This was so unlike him. He'd have let her, and of course, the organiser, know, if he'd been delayed for some reason. He was *always* on time with The Cocktail Campervan, often setting up at an event an hour early. He had never let anyone down professionally in the whole time she'd known him. A nauseous feeling of angst was rising in her tummy. There must be some good reason behind his being late? *Come on Jack, let me know what …* She willed her phone to ring.

Claire, the lady in charge of the event, dressed in her glittery black party frock and high-heeled boots, came out of the house once again; brow furrowed and shaking her head. She marched over to Lucy, 'Still no sign of the cocktail bar? No news at all?'

Of course, she had every right to feel pissed off, with her

party bar for the night nowhere in sight. She didn't know Jack, and his usual commitment to his work, after all.

'No, I'm really sorry,' Lucy replied. 'Look, Jack really isn't the sort to let anyone down like this. I'm actually starting to get worried,' she confessed. 'I've never known him be late for a booking, *ever*.'

Who could she ask? Try and find out what was going on. She didn't want to worry his parents. Hmm, what about the guy he lodged with? Yes, Matt, that was it. She'd met him a couple of times when she'd stayed over, and of course with Daisy that time. He was a vet, wasn't he? At the Alnwick surgery. It was only 6:30, someone might possibly still be there. They might have a contact for him there, or she might at least find out his surname so she'd be able to find him on Facebook or something, send a message ... ask if he knew anything, or if Jack had in fact left. Right, she'd try that next.

Lucy fumbled for her mobile, checking again for any missed calls or messages. *Nothing.*

Cocktail Party Claire was now stood by the horsebox, hands on hips, looking for an explanation, but Lucy wasn't a mind reader. 'Bloody hell, I'll have to send one of the guests out to make a trip to the supermarket for some booze at this rate. Or go myself. I really don't know what to do?' The woman was stressing big time, and was of course entitled to be. After all, her campervan bar with its va-va-voom had disappeared, and her big birthday surprise for her husband was about to go down like a wet balloon. 'God, it's bloody freezing out here too.' She shivered. 'Look, I hope everything's okay,' she added, suddenly realising there might be something more to this, 'but it's just ...

Craig's due back from the pub in twenty minutes, and I've got fifty people about to turn up for his surprise party, and no bloody booze.'

'I know, and I'm so sorry. Look, I'll keep trying for you. See if I can find anything out. I'll come and find you as soon as I hear anything. And in the meanwhile, I'm all set up and ready, so at least everyone can tuck into pizzas.'

'Hmm,' was followed by a big frustrated sigh, as Claire retreated to the house, all a-fluster.

Lucy quickly Googled the vet on her phone and was able to find the list of staff. There he was, smiling at her; she recognised the thumbnail of Matthew Taylor BVetMed MRCVS. Typical that he had a common surname. Finding him on social media might well prove a challenge. She'd try and call the vet first, see if they might release his number, or at least let her explain her concern, and they could pass it on.

Her fingertips were trembling as she dialled. She spoke with a lovely receptionist, who explained that they weren't able to give out any private mobile contact numbers, but she took Lucy's details and said she was happy to pass a message on asap, as Matthew was still there, having been working on the surgery team this evening. In the meanwhile, Lucy tried to call Jack's mobile once more. Again, it just rang out, flicking frustratingly over to answerphone. She'd already left three messages, so she rang off.

Her first instinct was to drive over to his house by the route he'd most likely come, but she had a pizza oven belting out at 450 degrees that she daren't leave, and a party of fifty people about to arrive imminently. In fact, some were turning up already. A couple of taxis pulling up beside the horsebox, spilling out their excited guests.

Who might help? Who could she call? Becky? But she already had enough on her plate. And Jack might well have broken down or something, that might be it, and in an area with no signal. Campervan Ruby had been a bit temperamental lately. She needed someone practical.

Olly suddenly came to mind. Yes, she'd try her brother. She scrolled to his name ... called. Thank goodness, he picked up straight away.

'Hey, hi Lucy.'

'Oh Olly, I'm really worried ... about Jack. Can you help?'

'Yeah, of course. What's happened, Luce?'

She tried to get the words out. 'I-I don't know, that's the problem. He ... well, he's meant to be here and he's not turned up. It's cold and maybe icy ... the roads weren't brilliant when I set off.'

'Right ...'

'Or he might have broken down or something,' Lucy continued to explain, trying to still the panic in her voice. 'He was due here to work at this party over an hour ago, and I can't get through on his mobile at all.'

'Okay, so where are you?' Olly's tone was concerned but calm.

'I'm just outside of Belsay, it's a village near to Morpeth.'

'Yeah, I know it.'

'Do you think you could go and check the route from Jack's place over to here? Sorry, I know that's a bit of a pain, but I'm really worried, Olly. It's so not like Jack to not turn up like this. Just to put my mind at rest, while I keep trying to get hold of him, or find out more. I'll message the address and postcode over.'

'Yeah, no worries. I'll just explain to Alice, then I'll set off straight away.'

'Thank you. I might be overreacting, but it's just not like him to be late and not even to call …' Lucy hoped so much that she *was* overreacting. That Ruby would drive in at any moment, and she'd have to call Olly straight back and tell him to call off the search mission.

As soon as she turned off the call to her brother, her phone buzzed to life once more. She looked at the screen expectantly … it was a mobile number she didn't recognise.

'Lucy?'

'Yep.'

'Matt, Jack's mate. My colleague passed on a message to say you'd rung, everything alright?'

'Hi, thanks for calling. Look, Jack's not turned up at this event tonight he's booked for. He was due here an hour ago. Do you happen to know if he actually left your house this evening?'

'Right …' A short pause ensued. 'Ah well, no, sorry – I don't know, I've been working here since two. Hang on, I can ring Jess quickly, try and find out for you. She'll be home. Been there most of the afternoon, as far as I know … she was going to come over early and then cook some supper for us.'

'Okay, thanks. Let me know then, yeah?'

Might he have been struck ill and never left the house? Ruby might still be parked up there? All sorts of scenarios were filling her mind.

'Of course. Will do.' And with that, Matt finished the call.

Lucy vacantly started topping some pizzas, ready to bake, but her heart really wasn't in it. She couldn't abandon the party ship too, though, not yet. Not until she knew anything more concrete, anyhow. But Jack … *Please let everything be okay*, she sent up a silent prayer. Her heart was well and truly being put through the wringer tonight.

Several guests spilled out of cars, making their way into the house, getting ready for the big surprise. Lucy tried her best to look charming and smiley, with her heart somewhere near her boots.

A black Land Rover then arrived … oh heck … with, she guessed, Birthday Boy Craig getting out, just as a call came in from Matt.

It should be balloons and party poppers and excitement, with pizzas served with panache and cocktails all round. But all Lucy could feel was her soul sinking. Craig grinned, curiosity etched over his brow as he spotted the All Fired Up horsebox in his driveway.

Lucy clutched the phone to her ear, whilst trying to keep up some modicum of professionalism, making eye contact with Birthday Boy and mouthing, *Happy Birthday*.

'Matt?'

'Lucy, yeah, he's already left, in the campervan, just after five. Jess saw him go. Said he seemed fine, if a little stressed. He'd had a bit of bother with a flat battery before that, but had got it all sorted with some help from the neighbour.'

Shit, that was over an hour-and-a-half ago. The journey should take thirty minutes tops. Lucy felt a whirr of tension tighten, and then unravel within. Maybe it was just Ruby's battery gone again, stalled en route or something. That was it, she told herself.

'Surprise! Happy Birthday, babe!' Claire came leaping out of the house, making a good pretence of all being well, followed by several friends and family joining in with cries of 'Happy Birthday!'

'Hey, what's all this then?' Craig looked about, nodding towards Lucy's pizza horsebox parked on the driveway.

Lucy forced a smile, but was all too aware of the gaping space where Jack's Cocktail Campervan should have been, all shiny vintage red with its stage lights aglow, and Jack the barman popping corks, party ready and poised to go.

It was then that Olly's call came in.

She fumbled for her phone. Pressing buttons in a panic.

Time seemed to stand still as she heard the words, 'I've found him … Sorry, but it's not good news, Luce …'

❄

Olly had seen the blue flashing lights before anything else, and knew with a strange chill that he'd found the scene of the accident. An ambulance was already there.

He had pulled up carefully to the side of the road, and got out. A ragged intake of breath hit hard, as he spotted the familiar red campervan slanted in the verge, its front end smashed against a tree. *Holy shit! Jack!*

He liked Jack. Had warmed to the guy. He'd made Lucy happy these past few months, that much was obvious.

Olly headed for the blue lights, the green and yellow reflective colours on the ambulance drawing him. He had to find out for Lucy. The back doors were wide open. One of the paramedics was talking loudly to the other, running through some kind of checks on their patient. Olly stood back slightly, letting them get on with their job, overhearing snippets: 'BP is low at 80 over 40', 'likely shock', 'possible internal bleeding', 'broken bones', 'We need to get this guy to hospital, and fast.'

One of the paramedics then turned, heading for the ramp, ready to leap down and slam the back doors. Olly moved in, causing him jump in surprise, explaining that he was a friend, that he'd come looking for Jack. How was he? Could they tell him anything? He explained that Jack was his sister's partner.

'Is he going to be alright?' Olly repeated.

'Ah sorry, mate, we really can't discuss any medical details. And we need to get going here.'

'Can you at least tell me where you're going … which hospital?'

Seeing the crushed look on Olly's face, he patted his arm in solidarity.

'Cramlington A&E, that's where we're headed.' He jumped up into the cab, calling out to Olly, 'He's in good hands.'

Olly stood for a few dazed seconds, as the blue lights flickered and sirens droned into the distance, leaving him to make that awful call to his sister.

Chapter Thirty-One

Her world seemed to freeze.

Lucy had to go. Had to abandon the horsebox, the party, pizzas and all. 'I'm so sorry,' she called, running across to Claire. 'H-he's had an accident … he's in an ambulance. I've got to go … I'm so sorry to let you all down.'

Lucy was already yanking off her apron, her oven gloves, dashing to unhitch the Jeep, ready to leave the trailer behind. Jack was more important than any party.

'Look, please don't let anyone go near the oven at all. You have to be trained to use it,' she warned. 'Just let it go out by itself … I'll be back later … I'm sorry.'

'Oh, no. That's terrible. Can we help at all? Is there anything we can do?' Claire offered, realising the severity of the situation, with husband Craig standing by in support.

Lucy felt a lump rise in her throat at their kindness, despite their special party now being in tatters.

'No, I don't think so. I-I just need to find out how he

is … I'll call. Give you a refund … whatever you need …'
She was already getting into the Jeep.

'Don't you worry yourself about that right now, pet,'
Craig soothed. 'Go on, get to where you need to be …'

And where she needed to be, was with Jack.

❄

The journey passed in a whirl of anxious thoughts and
autopilot driving. Lucy sending up little prayers in her
head. *Please let him be alright. Please let him be alright. Please
let him be alright.* Even giving Jack a stern mental talking-to
at one point: *Don't you give up. Don't you dare let go.*

She wasn't sure of the extent of any injuries. Olly had
only shared that he'd overheard the ambulance team say
there were likely to be broken bones and there was concern
about internal bleeding.

Internal bleeding. Those two words filled her with dread.
That did not sound good. Willing the tears to stay back, she
tried her best to focus on the road ahead. The last thing she
needed was fuzzy vision as she drove.

Olly had told her to go to Cramlington A&E. She knew
the way. Just had to keep going. Keep steady.

❄

Driving along those dark winding lanes, she came across
a road sign: *Diversion.* Damn, it would take even longer
now. Police car there, parked at the roadside, blue light
flashing. Bloody hell, she'd have to turn around. And
then she realised, with the coldest of chills: this was it, the

site. This was where it had happened … She slowed, driving right up to a red-and-white heavy-duty plastic barrier.

That's when she saw Ruby all crushed up and mangled, half off the road and into the hedgerow … the tree that had hit the front end still embedded into the red bonnet, chips of glass from the windscreen scattered in heart-wrenching sparkles over the tarmac.

A policeman started walking towards her … Tapped on her window, 'Sorry love, you'll have to turn around, find another route.'

She couldn't answer for a second or two. Her throat dry, clogged with emotion.

'Okay, yes … uh … it's Ruby … it's my boyfriend's campervan.'

❄

She abandoned her Jeep in the public parking area, and began running for the A&E. Her heart was pounding; the blood in her veins thumping loudly in her head. The sick feeling having never left the pit of her stomach since answering Olly's call … since seeing Ruby like that.

Please let him be alright. Please let him be alright. The mantra was still going over and over in her mind.

In through big glass doors. Bright lights. Chemical smells. People milling about. A toddler crying. Concern heavy like an invisible cloak.

Reception – she'd have to find out where he was, what was happening.

As she headed for the desk, saying Jack's name, which

came out more like a plea than a question, a voice stopped her: 'Lucy?'

Turning, she spotted a tall man with a slight paunch rounding out underneath a navy woollen jumper. A kind face, filled with concern, topped by thinning mousy-blond hair which might have been sandy once, like his son's. He was stood just a few feet away from her, having risen from his plastic waiting seat, looking rather pale. A smart grey-haired woman, her eyes filled with care and hurt, was sat down next him.

'Hello ... are you Jack's parents?' Lucy blurted out. They nodded. 'Oh God, how is he?' Lucy faced them, holding her breath as she waited for their answer.

'He's having a CT scan, love. We'll know more in a while,' Mr Anderson spoke. Steady, steadfast, yet evidently in shock, bless him. He looked shattered.

'But did they say anything? What do they think he's done? How bad is it?' Lucy was scrabbling for clues, still trying to process what was going on.

Jack's mum was giving a supportive smile, but behind her grey-blue eyes (that, oh God, yes, looked so like Jack's) she looked as if someone had taken the wind out of her sails.

Of course, they had been through so much before already ... It couldn't be happening again, not to Jack, not to their other son, that would be too cruel ... it couldn't.

'They think he might have ruptured his spleen. Broken some ribs, there's cuts and bruises apparently, some to his face too,' Simon explained.

Lucy felt a bit giddy. A ruptured spleen was bad. That

must have been the internal bleeding that Olly had mentioned.

She'd watched enough *Casualty*-type programmes to know that it could be life-threatening. And Jack's beautiful face … oh. She wanted to hold him, to help him, but knew she'd have wait, let the hospital team do their job.

'Have you seen him?' Her voice sounded small, fragile.

'No, not yet. A doctor came out to explain the situation when we got here. They've taken him straight to the scanner. Perhaps then into surgery.'

Surgery. Jack laid out on cold metal … green cloth over him. No doubt all wired up. Just a couple of hours ago she was looking forward to a night of catering and entertaining, hearing his banter across the way, with Ruby bold and bright and beautiful. The life and soul of the party. It seemed unbelievable, how life could pivot on a pinhead. And then, finally, at the end of the night they might finally have had chance to chat. She brushed away a heavy tear.

'Here, take a seat, love.' Simon guided her with a calm, caring hand, to the chair next to his wife.

'It might be a while before we hear anything, so can we get you a cup of tea from the machine, or anything?' Denise offered.

They were being so kind, so gracious, yet they must be tearing up inside just like she was. Lucy's stomach was a total whirl. 'Thanks, but I don't think I fancy anything,' Lucy managed to reply. 'It's all such a shock …'

'I can fetch something for us all a little later,' Denise's tone was soothing.

'Umm, it's alright, I can get something for us. In a while …' Lucy realised Jack's parents would also need some

TLC, but she needed to feel more settled before she could stomach anything. Perhaps, when they'd had some news. Hopefully, something positive to cling onto.

'That'd be nice,' replied Jack's dad. The words floating politely.

Suddenly it hit her, what an ironic way to at last be meeting them – in the reception of a bloody hospital. They sat in their own silent worlds for a few seconds, Simon then resuming with, 'So, were you at a function? Was that where Jack was headed with the camper?'

'Yes, a birthday celebration that I've abandoned …' *Oh crikey.* 'I just needed to see him … be with him.'

'Yes, of course,' said Simon empathetically.

The image of Ruby wrecked at the roadside hit her once more. Oh, and where on earth was Olly? Had he followed the ambulance? Gone home? Lucy's thoughts were jumbled.

'We came straight away too,' Denise added. 'They'd found his phone. We're his emergency contact.'

It was hard conversing with their hearts feeling bashed up and their heads so full of fear. So, they rested in silent solidarity for a while.

The clock kept ticking and still no news. Simon went to the desk for an update, but the receptionist just gave a gentle smile and shook her head. 'Nothing new,' Simon reported back.

People darted in and out. Sat waiting. Beepers going off. The reception phone buzzing away. The tap, tap, tap of the keyboard. New patients in, teary relatives. Fear, hope, confusion. Life in the balance. The false alarm. The touch and go. Jack in a scanner right now.

Lucy checked her phone with trembling fingers,

suddenly thinking to update Matt and find out what had happened to Olly. She then saw that her brother had already messaged. He'd headed back home for now, after being advised by the ambulance crew that only family members were allowed to accompany under blue lights. He explained that he hadn't wanted to crowd A&E, but would come along to keep her company at any time if she wanted. She just had to say the word.

After updating her brother and then Matt, she fired a quick message across to Claire at the party, sending her apologies once more, saying they were waiting for news on Jack, and that she'd most likely come and collect the horsebox sometime tomorrow. With a sigh, she remembered how she'd abandoned her pizza station. She added that they could help themselves to the already made-up pizza bases, and feel free to bake them off in the house oven if they wanted.

She had no idea how long ago it was, since she'd dashed off in her Jeep … in a bit of a trance … She glanced at her wristwatch – crikey, that was well over an hour-and-a-half ago now.

Was no news, good news? Or did it mean he had already gone into surgery? *Oh, Jack …*

Chapter Thirty-Two

Time crawled. Lucy went for the briefest of walks, just outside of the A&E doors, to get some fresh air, then back in again. It didn't do a lot to clear the thick head she was now struggling with. But she didn't want to miss any developments, and perhaps, please dear God, the chance to finally see him, hold him.

Quiet spells, followed by inane polite chat, bitter-tasting instant coffee in flimsy plastic cups. Silent, yet massive heartfelt prayers. The three of them sat together. A weird yet comforting kind of shelter in a storm.

And then finally: 'Mr and Mrs Anderson?' A lady dressed in green scrubs came out through the swing doors.

Jack's parents were up off their seats like a shot, with an anxious Lucy close behind.

'How is he?' Denise's voice wavered.

'So, he's had his scan and is being closely monitored.'

He was alive, if he was being monitored … he was alive.

'He took a big impact, however … the next few hours are critical.'

Oh God, what was she saying?

'Come on through. I can take you somewhere a little more private.'

'Uhm …' Lucy politely waited, a few footsteps behind them.

'Oh, are you together?'

Lucy nodded as Jack's father explained, 'Yes, this is Jack's girlfriend, Lucy.'

'Oh, I'm sorry, it's family only just now. I know it's hard, but can you please wait … just a little longer?' the doctor told her kindly, yet firmly.

Where were they going? What was she going to tell them? 'Is he going to be alright?' Lucy blurted out.

'He's stable. But I need to talk everything over with Jack's parents.'

Simon must have seen the panic flash over her face. 'We'll let you know more, as soon as we can, Lucy.'

'I'll wait. I'll be here …'

She wasn't leaving him. She wasn't going anywhere.

❄

Olly phoned about five minutes later to see if there was anything he could do. But without clogging up A&E with extra bodies, options were limited right now. She gave a wry smile as she suddenly pictured the whole family sitting there with her: Mum, Nonna, the works. Olly would most likely have told them by now. They would if they could, she knew that. She'd always have their support.

'Could you order a miracle?' Lucy mooted to Olly aloud.

'I'll try my best,' Olly soothed. 'Have a word with the big man upstairs. It is nearly Christmas, after all.'

'Thanks.' She felt so small, vulnerable, with the doctor still away talking with Jack's parents.

'Well, ring me if anything changes. Or if you want a bed here for the night. Some company … Whatever you need, Sis, we're there for you …'

'I know, and thank you.'

'Take care. Love you, Sis.'

'You too. Bye … and thank you … for finding him.' Her voice cracked.

'Hey, no worries. Chat later, yeah.'

She turned off the call. And she felt small, so very small, in a shifting world that could change in an instant.

❄

A door squeaked open, the same one the doctor had come out from, the sound of rubber soles on lino.

Two figures. Simon, pale-faced, holding Denise's hand.

Oh Jesus! What was it?

Every instinct that filled Lucy was to know and, at exactly the same time, to *not* know.

'How is he?' She was up on her feet, moving towards them.

A butterfly-wing glimmer of a smile spread across his mother's lips, and hope flickered like a candle in the wind within Lucy's chest, as his father said, 'So, it's a bruised spleen. They haven't needed to do surgery, thank heavens, as it's not been ruptured.'

What did that all mean?

'He's been lucky. Several broken ribs too, and he'll be pretty sore for a while. There's a few cuts and bruises, a couple of stitches to his forehead. They're going to monitor him closely overnight, but it sounds like he's going to be alright, Lucy. He's going to be alright,' Simon repeated stoically.

Relief engulfed the three of them. His mum gave a loud sob. Simon's arms were outstretched to them both, as he said, 'Thank God.'

And Lucy felt the warmth and the comfort of his fatherly hug.

Oh Lord, how must it have felt that last time ... when it hadn't been relief but a hammer blow of grief, when they had lost their eldest son? Lucy couldn't imagine what emotions they were going through. How on earth did they manage to bear it? Losing a son, a brother, so young. But you didn't get any choice, did you? Fate could deal the cruellest or the fairest of hands. It was all so damned arbitrary. She understood a little more how life, how emotions, might be difficult for Jack.

'Yes, give it a few more days, well actually a few weeks, and he'll be right as rain,' Simon said, almost like he was convincing himself. The words floating above Lucy and Denise's heads feeling very much like a promise.

'Can I see him? Have you been able to see him?'

'No, not yet. They're having to keep a close eye on him. But soon, Lucy, soon.'

She flopped down into the chair, suddenly overwhelmingly tired as exhaustion mingled with blissful relief.

✳

It was now just after midnight and Simon and Denise had been allowed through to visit Jack briefly, coming back rather emotional but with relieved smiles. Lucy was desperate to see Jack, to hold him, but would have to wait her turn. The nurse who'd walked his parents back over had advised he now needed to rest and get some sleep. She explained kindly that Lucy, not being immediate family, would need to wait until morning for her chance to visit.

Her heart sank, but what could she do? Jack needed that chance to rest and recuperate. He had been through so much. She didn't want to leave the hospital, though, felt drawn to stay near him, even if she wasn't yet allowed to be with him. She sent a 'get well' and 'goodnight' message, hoping his mobile might be near to hand, saying she was right here in the hospital if he needed her, and explaining why she hadn't been allowed in as yet. She finished with:

See you soon. Sweet dreams. I'm here, always. Luce X

✳

Her phone buzzed to life, still clutched in her palm. Bloody hell, she must have nodded off again; last night's fear bleeding out into exhaustion. She had no idea what the time was. Tried to focus. There was a glimpse of daylight outside, and yes, she remembered now, Jack's parents had gone through to see him again, after kindly bringing her an early morning cup of tea and a bacon roll. It had tasted good, surprisingly so in the circumstances, it must have been just what she had needed.

And yes, she should be allowed in to see him soon. Crikey, how long had his parents been in? She was desperate to hear more news on his condition.

Ah. The phone … it was still ringing. She looked at the caller ID: Becky.

Oh, *Becky*. Lucy answered with a frail, 'Hello?'

'Luce?'

'Yeah.'

'I just heard. Oh Lucy, I'm so sorry. How is he?'

Her concern sounded genuine, heartfelt. It was lovely that her friend was back in full support, 'Umm, he's okay, I think. Got through the night alright. Broken ribs, some bruising to his spleen. They just need to keep a close eye on him.'

'Hey, can I do anything to help? Do you need anything?'

'Aw, that's kind. Thank you.' Lucy felt a huge lump in her throat. It had been a long, tough night. And my, she did appreciate Becky's friendship when she needed it most. 'Right now, I don't even know what I need,' she confessed. She'd hardly slept all night. The plastic chairs had numbed her bottom. Her neck felt all cricked. 'But it's good to know you're thinking of me … of *us*.' She paused, feeling the tears jam in her throat. 'I just want to know he's going to be alright, Becks … that's all I need right now.'

'Yeah, of course.'

'Uhm … Who told you? How do you know?' It was only last night when her world had gone topsy-turvy, after all.

'Oh, your Oliver was speaking with Darren. Bumped

into each other at the Co-op this morning. He called me straight away.'

'Oh, right.' She still felt in a daze.

'So, how are *you* doing, hun?'

'Ah, I'm alright. Just tired, worried, it's all been such a shock.' She was trying her best to put a brave face on things.

'Yeah, you will be. Well look, just let me know if there's anything you need, okay? Emergency chocolate supplies. Even if it's just to have someone to chat with to pass some time … okay?'

'Okay … and Becks …'

'Yeah?'

'Thank you.' For reaching out, for being there just when she needed it. Lucy couldn't begin to put it into words.

She heard her friend give a sigh. A sigh that held so much. Until these past couple of weeks, it had been such a difficult time for their friendship. 'No worries, Luce.' There was a beat of silence, before Becky said, 'That's what friends are for. You take care now, hun.'

As she turned off the call, Lucy couldn't help but let out a little sob. Like old times, Becky was there for her when it really mattered. After all their recent ups and downs, their friendship was still strong. It had weathered the storm.

But could Jack make it through and weather his storm too? Lucy's heart felt like it was drowning.

Chapter Thirty-Three

'Lucy? Lucy Brown?' Someone was calling her name.

Lucy stood up nervously. Her right leg wasn't quite working properly, numbed out.

'Hello, would you like to come through and see Jack now?' A nurse approached her. 'He's up on the ward. His parents are taking a short coffee break. They mentioned you were here, waiting to visit.'

'Yes, of course.' She felt a hopeful lift within. 'How's he doing?'

'Pretty good, he's had a stable night. He's been asking for you.'

Oh. Relief and love, and a myriad of tender feelings flooded her. She'd been told the spleen prognosis was positive, and that his ribs would heal in time, but she knew he wasn't quite out of the woods yet. They set off through those heavy grey swing doors, and then took a lift up, the nurse saying how he'd been chatting away about Ruby.

Poor Ruby. Jack probably didn't realise how bad she was.

That image of the crash site would be seared into Lucy's mind forever.

On the ward now, and the nurse indicated which room to enter. 'Far corner, right side,' the nurse smiled kindly. 'I'll leave you to it. But just call if there's anything. There's a button by the bed.'

'Thank you.'

The room was hushed, a four-bedded bay, each section with blue-and-yellow curtains part-pulled around it. Lucy moved forward with expectant caution; hope filling her heart, tinged with a little of the fear that had burrowed there all night.

And ... there he was. Oh my God, his face was bashed up, bless him. Cuts, a couple of stitches above his left eye, bruising.

'Jack,' her voice was a whisper. She tried to hide her shock, but evidently hadn't done a good job of it.

'Bit of a mess, hey?' He tried to smile, which was the sweetest thing, but he seemed sore, tired.

'Yeah, a bit. You look like you've done a few rounds with Tyson Fury.'

'Hmm, feel like it. Might have been better off if I had been.'

'Oh Jack ...' She pulled a plastic seat up near to the bed, taking his hand, where it lay above the covers, in hers.

'Poor bloody Ruby,' his voice sounded a bit raspy. 'God knows what a mess she's in.'

'Hey, don't fret about Ruby ... Look, I know you love that campervan for sure, but let's get you right first.' A tear slid down her cheek and onto his hand. His beautiful warm hand. Feeling his touch once more let loose a landslide of emotions.

'Hey, I'll be okay, Luce. I'll be fine.' The words were positive, yet his voice was strained, like it hurt to talk too much.

'Yeah, you'd better be. Claire and Craig and all the family are still waiting for their bloody party ...' Lucy decided humour was the way to go at this point, or she'd be risking a full breakdown.

'Oh shit, yeah. How was that?'

'A bit awkward, I abandoned ship. Left them all to it. But of course, when they realised what had happened ...'

'Was it Olly who came to look for me?'

'Yeah, I couldn't exactly rush off myself just then, but I was so worried. I sent him on a search mission. Someone else must have got there first, mind you, and thankfully called the emergency services.'

'Jeez, don't remember much ... just the ice ... that awful slide. I knew Ruby had lost it ...' He went quiet. Squeezed her hand a little tighter. 'All I could think was, *Fuck, not me too*. Mum and Dad ... and you ...' Jack's hand was trembling. Shock, and everything his body had been through, kicking in.

'Hey ... it's alright, it's alright,' she breathed. 'We'll get you through this. It'll be okay.' Her heart went out to him. She just wanted to be able to take his pain away. 'You just need a bit of time to rest, to mend. It's been a huge shock.'

'But ... I've been such an idiot. I was going to tell you ... put things right ...'

'It's okay, don't get yourself upset, Jack. Whatever it is,

we can sort it out later. We both need to talk things over …
but not now.'

'No … I have to tell you now. It can't wait …'

Lucy's eyes filled as she looked down at her hands,
somehow entwined with Jack's.

'I should never have shut you out, Luce. And I'm so
sorry I was so shut-off, guarded, and that argument at the
castle … God, it was horrible. I wasn't thinking straight. I
should have believed you about Liam. But it was all so
painful and I thought if I left, it'd be for the best …'

Lucy felt her heart plummet at his words. So, he *was*
thinking of going … of leaving her.

'But I was all mixed up, I'd got it all wrong, Luce. I
couldn't see what was right in front of me. And I'm sorry, so
sorry …' He sounded so damned tired. 'It shouldn't take
something like this to give me that perspective, you know?'

'Don't worry yourself. Just lie back now, Jack. I'll be
here. Shut your eyes, if you need to.' She kissed his bruised
and battered cheek, whispering, oh so gently, 'I love you.'

And he nodded. Closing his eyelids. Giving in to the
warmth of the pillows. His hand still resting there, enclosed
by Lucy's.

❄

He must have dozed. Jack felt his hand gently enveloped.
Opened his eyelids. His face damned sore. His ribs groaning
as he tried to move. And there was Lucy, still at his bedside.

'Hey, sleepyhead.' Concern was etched over her pretty
features, yet she managed a gentle heartfelt smile.

'Still here, then?' His words meaning so much more than the literal. Like they'd be there for each other, in the good times and the bad times to come.

'Of course. How are you feeling?'

'Sore … a bit groggy.'

'Hah, no wonder. You've taken a bit of a bashing, my love. And you're on some pretty strong medication.'

While he was sleeping, the nurse had come across and given Lucy more detail on his injuries; seven ribs were broken, and there were facial lacerations as well as many cuts and bruises. He'd also gone into shock at the scene of the accident. Poor Jack. But the prognosis was good. They were keeping a close eye on him after such major trauma, but in another day or so, if all was well, he might be able to go home. That was such a relief to hear.

'Ah, okay. So, I'm not going to be moving and shaking for a while yet, then?'

'Nope, no way. Bed rest for you.'

'Hmm, that doesn't sound too bad, actually.' He quirked an eyebrow.

Hah, even in hospital he managed to think about sex! *Really.* 'Rest being the operative word.' Lucy shook her head, smiling.

Jack's parents then appeared, edging their way back over to his bay, having purposely given the young couple some space for a while.

'Oh hi, Simon, Denise.' Lucy felt a blush of colour hit her cheeks. Perhaps they had overheard that last snippet of conversation.

'Hello, Lucy love,' Jack's dad answered with a

newfound fondness in his voice. It had been some night for them all.

'Isn't it good to see him chatting and awake?' Lucy continued.

'Hey, I'm here, you know.' Jack laughed.

'Yes, it is good. *Really* good.' Denise smiled softly, as she touched a hand on Lucy's shoulder.

'Well, I suppose I'd better go.' Lucy was aware there should only be two visitors at the bedside at any one time. 'Hospital rules,' she explained to Jack.

'Ah, okay.'

'I'll come back real soon. Be here again for the next visiting hours. Hmm, s'pose I'd better go home and freshen up in the meanwhile.' She hadn't been able to shower or anything, having sat there all through the night.

'Thought things were a bit whiffy round here,' Jack said drily.

'Hey you.'

Jack started laughing, but stopped himself. 'Ah shit, that hurts.'

But it was so lovely to see him jesting, the old cheeky spark still aflame in there.

'Right then …' Lucy rose to stand, though she really didn't want to leave, but knew his mum and dad would want their precious time with him too.

'Thanks for letting me see him,' she turned to his parents. 'For telling the nurse I was waiting.'

'It's the least we could have done,' Simon responded.

'Couldn't have left you sat out there, love. And, we'll keep you posted on any developments,' added Denise kindly. 'Here, let me take your number.'

They exchanged details.

'Now I'm in trouble, my mum and girlfriend in cahoots.' Jack tried to sit up again. 'Ah ... oops, that's sore.'

'Lie back and rest, you,' Lucy chuckled.

It was good to be able to laugh, to smile, to feel that hope was back.

And love and life was there all around them in that hospital bay like a big warm hug.

Chapter Thirty-Four

J ack hated to think of the pain and anguish he had put his parents through. Maybe he should have driven more sensibly that night; he'd known that the roads were icy, after all. It could have all ended so differently, he dreaded to think … *shit*. He'd messed up again. Life was so goddam fragile … so precious. He began to feel a bit shaky, but was trying hard not to let it show.

'Are you alright, Jack?' His mum, still there at his bedside, was evidently in tune with him. He could never get away with much, even as a kid.

'Yeah, just thinking … look folks, I'm really sorry. I'd never have wanted to put you through all that …' His words came out awkwardly.

'It's okay, Son. It was an accident,' his father spoke calmly, reassuringly.

'Something you couldn't have avoided, love. Black ice. Winding lanes. What matters now, Jack, is getting you better,' his mum added tenderly.

'Onwards and upwards, hey, Son.'

'But I always seem to get it wrong.'

'No, you don't, my love.' His mum took his hand. 'Whatever makes you think that?'

'The wrong job, the wrong car – oh God, poor Ruby, she'll be in some state. I've gone and wrecked her.' Oh bugger, his precious Rubes. All those hours he'd spent doing her up, keeping her pristine, and now look what he'd gone and done.

'Don't you go worrying about that. We can get her fixed up again. They've taken her to the garage at Hunter's Hill. It's not the end of the road for Ruby yet, Son, not by any means.' His dad was trying his best to cheer him up, he knew that. 'Anyway,' Simon's tone sharpened, 'what the hell are you talking about, that you're always getting it wrong? You're doing well, have a good business going there with the cocktail thing. Something you love doing. We're proud of you, Son.'

'We only want what's best for you … and what makes you happy. That's all we've ever wanted,' his mum added with a gentle smile.

Were his fears these past years that he wasn't good enough, that he'd never match up to his brother, just that? Fears, not reality?

'We love you, Son.' His dad had a tear in his eye. And his dad was *never* soppy like this. My God, he must have shaken them up. But it was so damned good to hear those words.

'Thanks, I love you too, folks.' He couldn't say anything more as his throat was all clogged up and his own eyes were misty.

His dad leaned over the bed and moved to hug him rather clumsily, all the while his mum still holding his hand, but there was a jolt of pain in his ribcage area. 'Argh.'

'Oh Christ, sorry son.' Simon leaped back.

'It's okay, just my ribs.'

'Bloody idiot that I am.'

The pain eased as his father let go. And they all had to laugh. Though for Jack, laughing hurt too. It was going to be a slow path to recovery, for him and for Ruby, by the sounds of it. But knowing he had the love and support of his mum and dad made that path look a whole lot smoother.

Chapter Thirty-Five

Another dawn, another day, and after taking Daisy for a fresh-air blast of a stroll on the beach, with a maze of memories stirring of her and Jack there on the sands, Lucy was back at Jack's bedside the following morning. The emotional impact of the past two days was still ricocheting through Lucy. An echo of fear lingering, reminding her of how fragile life could be. No doubt Jack was feeling it too.

Sat at his hospital bedside, holding his precious hand, Lucy could still feel the full force of those emotions; the dread at the thought of losing him. Looking at him there beneath the hospital covers, an ache of love surged within her.

'Sorry to have put you through all this, Luce,' Jack's voice was soft, filled with regret. 'And Mum and Dad … ah …' Words failed him then. He choked up.

'We're all just glad you're going to be alright. That's all.' She stroked his forehead gently, avoiding the stitched cut.

'I don't think my mother's going to let me out of her

sight when she gets me back home, is she?' The plan was that he'd go to his parents' from the hospital to convalesce, which made sense. 'It'll be like being a kid again.' He pulled a face.

'Hah, most likely.'

'But hey, I think I've put them, and you, through enough these past few days,' Jack continued. 'I'll have to just toe the line for now.'

'Hah, you'd better.' Lucy gave a smile. 'Oh, by the way, the mobile catering crew's grapevine has been all go. I've had a call from Emma, who sends her love, and promises to send over some chocolate supplies to keep your spirits up.'

'Ah, that's nice.'

'And Ellie and Joe, they've sent a message from the whole castle team, sending hugs and a huge get well soon.'

Jack smiled. 'Yeah, I've had message from burger van Bob. And there's a card from Carrie. She's baking get well cupcakes to bring over for me, apparently. Word of my misadventures must be out on the circuit.'

'That's lovely. Nice to know you've got that support. They're a great bunch.'

It was good to know these newfound friends had their backs.

The two of them chatted on for a while. Lucy ended her visit with a gentle 'goodbye for now' kiss. Jack's after-shave and his smell filling her senses, with a teeny back-note of hospital bedlinen. She couldn't wait to get him out of here and back fully into her arms.

❄

That afternoon, Lucy dropped by at Becky's, wanting to thank her for her caring phone call offer of help. Hoping for a mug of tea, some girlie chat, and a bit of downtime after the high emotions of the hospital, she rolled up at her friend's front door.

Becky appeared almost as soon as the doorbell had chimed. 'Hi Luce. How's the patient doing, then?'

A crumpled-looking Lucy tried to smile, but as Becky folded her into a hug on the front step, that small act of support was enough to let out all the tears Lucy had been keeping back.

'Oh Luce, hun, what's been happening? Is Jack going to be okay?' Becky's face had paled with concern.

'Ah … yes … he's okay, well, he will be soon …' Lucy's shoulders heaved. 'And I'm alright, honestly,' she blubbed. 'It's just … I've been holding everything back.'

'Oh, thank God. Come on in, petal. There's tea, Jammy Dodgers, whatever you'd like. There's bound to be a Dairy Milk or a Crunchie sneaked away in the back of the fridge, too.'

Lucy had to smile. Becky nearly always had a bar of something stashed away from Darren's chocolate-craving clutches. She followed her bestie through to the kitchen-diner. It was bliss just to give in and sink down onto one of Becky's dining stools, while her friend popped the kettle on. The tension of the past couple of days finally beginning to dissolve.

With tea and biscuits to hand, Jack's diagnosis and recovery discussed, and the world put to rights between them, Lucy then remembered her concerns about the state of Becky's relationship with partner Darren. 'So, did you two ever have that talk?' Lucy asked.

'Well, I tried. Last night I finally plucked up courage and broached the issue of his distance. It's like even when he's here, he's not, if you know what I mean. His head's been all over the place.'

'And ... what did he say?'

'He seemed a bit distracted at first. Still insisting it was all to do with work. It just didn't add up, though. I still couldn't help but wonder if he was having some kind of fling. I never imagined that me and Darren would ever get to this. But relationships can change so quickly. It's been a bit scary.'

Lucy nodded in empathy, 'Oh, Becks.'

'And well,' her pal continued, 'I persevered, I asked him outright if he was having an affair, and he looked kind of stunned ... then it all came spilling out. As well as work being crazy busy, with loads of pressure on him, his brother has been having some tests. Well, I knew Sam had had some dizzy spells, and it was obvious he'd been losing a bit of weight lately.'

'Oh no, sorry, I hadn't realised, that must be so worrying for you all.'

'Anyway, his brother had made Darren promise not to tell *anyone* until he'd got the results from the latest brain scan ... until he knew what he was dealing with. But, thank God, there doesn't seem to be anything too scary. He finally heard this morning, it's most likely viral, no sign of any tumours or anything.'

'Phew, but God, that must have been so tough for Darren, not knowing before that.'

'Yeah, and having to keep it all to himself too.'

'Hey, you never quite know what's going on beneath the surface, do you? Everyone's lives, all the ups and down, those curveballs that come crashing in. And hey,' Lucy looked earnestly at her friend, 'I'm so glad, despite it all, we've found our way back to each other, Becks. Talking and connecting is the key, isn't it?'

'Too bloody true, kiddo.'

They raised their tea mugs and mouthed a 'Cheers.'

❄

Half an hour later, as Lucy was heading back outside to her Jeep, Darren pulled up. He got out of his vehicle and she saw he was holding a beautiful bouquet of flowers.

'Oh, hi Luce. Hey, how's Jack doing?'

'Ah, he's getting on okay, thank you. They're hopefully about to let him out of hospital. He's pretty sore, bless him, and will take a bit of mending, but yes, thankfully he should be fine.'

'That's good news.'

'Yeah, really good.' She couldn't wait for him to be discharged. 'Well, they look gorgeous.' Lucy nodded towards the flowers; lilies and roses and more, wrapped in pretty pink tissue and cellophane, their fragrant floral scent drifted across.

'Yeah, bit of making up to do. Work's been manic, been keeping me all hours, and there's been lots going on … I think I need to apologise to Becky.'

Becky had told Lucy in confidence about his brother and their rocky patch, so she merely gave an understanding smile. 'Ah, well, they are gorgeous. And a lovely place to start, I reckon. Best of luck.' Lucy was so relieved to hear things were now looking up for her friends' relationship.

'Thanks … Oh and, Luce, I'm glad you and Becks seem to have patched things up. She seems so much happier now you're back in touch. More her old self.'

'Yeah, I'm happier too. We go back a long way. It's been hard these past couple of months.' Lucy gave a wide smile. 'Bye, Darren, I'll let you get on in. Looks like you've got an important job to do.'

'Yeah, cheers, Luce. Oh, and tell Jack I'll be ready to cheer him up with a pint or two when he gets out and about.'

'Will do. And actually, I think me and Becks are already on to that one.'

In fact, Becky had just bitten the bullet and asked them round there for New Year's drinks as a couple.

Lucy was still smiling as she got into the driver's seat. Seeing the flowers, and with Darren's and Becky's explanation, it seemed very much like Becky's fears for her relationship were unfounded. And as for the girls' friendship, well that was definitely back on solid ground.

All she needed now was to get Jack back to full health, and then see where their own relationship might be headed …

Chapter Thirty-Six

'Are you sure you're up to this?' Lucy checked, as they strolled slowly along the sands with Daisy trotting along at their heels.

It was the morning of Christmas Eve. Jack had been out of hospital for five days now, having been given pretty much the all-clear as long as he took plenty of rest and recuperation.

'Yeah, honestly, I need the fresh air. Having been cooped up in that hospital, and then at Mum and Dad's this week … I feel like I've turned into an old man in a care home or something … They've been great, to be fair,' he added, 'but I just need some space. And, I think *we* need some time just for us, too.'

'Yeah, this is lovely. Just the two … well,' she glanced down at Daisy, 'three of us.' She'd visited his family home every day since he'd got out of hospital, but this was the first time they'd been together alone. She gave his woolly-gloved hand a squeeze, having made sure he'd wrapped up well for his first outdoor trip since the accident. 'You mustn't overdo it, though, not until you've had chance to heal properly. What did they say at the hospital?' she reminded him.

'Ah, just to take things steady for a bit.' Jack slowed, pausing near the shoreline to look out over the rolling pewter-grey waves.

'Well, we'll not go too far, then.'

They were both dressed warmly, in thick coats, scarves, hats, boots. Lucy didn't want to take any chances when she'd picked him up from his parents' house in Alnwick for their short walk on the beach. With his broken ribs and bruised spleen, Jack was still unable to drive, and even if he had been, poor old Ruby was going to be a long while yet at the repair garage. She'd taken even more of a bashing than her owner.

Jack's thoughts must have drifted to Ruby and the accident too. About what would happen next … 'Wonder when I'll be able to get back to work? Soon, I hope. Can't stand all this doing nothing. I've got bookings coming up. Already had to miss a couple. But then … bloody hell, how can I run a Cocktail Campervan without a camper? Without my gorgeous Ruby?' The reality of his situation was beginning to hit home.

'Hey, there's no rush,' Lucy soothed. 'You've got to get yourself right first. That's the most important thing.'

'I know, but in a couple of weeks' time, into the New Year, I'll need to start up again. I've still got some dates in the diary to fulfil. I can't let everyone down. I've managed to build a really good reputation. And … I need to earn a living. Statutory sick pay isn't going to get me far.'

'I suppose not, but hey, you need to step back for a while at least, Jack. You need to make sure *you* get right first.'

'I know, I know. But Ruby needs a full overhaul, and there are vintage parts that aren't easy to find – a whole new front end, for one. I've spoken with the garage. It might take months, not weeks, to find a good match. I need to get her put right, or else I don't have a business to go back to, Luce.' He sounded despondent; it was all flooding in.

'Maybe you could try using something else as a bar. Set up a stall, I suppose.' Lucy realised that sounded feeble.

'It's not the same though, is it? Bit soulless that, a bit of tarpaulin and a table. Ruby was so cool. The Cocktail Campervan … it was all about her shiny red charm, the chrome, the lights, her vintage style … her character.'

'Yeah, she was … *is*,' she corrected herself, 'a real gem.'

There were a few beats of silence between them as they strolled.

'Anyway, what have you asked Santa for?' Lucy asked Jack, switching tack as he was beginning to sound a little down.

'Ah … other than a fully restored Ruby …' he stalled. In a few days' time, he'd know if his *real* Christmas wishes might yet come true. A plan was forming. Everything had been shaken up and settled with new clarity since the accident; like the glittering flakes in a snowglobe. 'Nothing much really, bits and bobs,' he continued coyly. 'Think my parents have done enough with looking after me this past week or so, without having to splash out on any expensive gifts. You?'

'Oh, I'm not too worried. It's always nice to get a few

little surprises, but Christmas time, well it's more about being together, seeing the family, and enjoying the day, isn't it?'

'Yeah, I suppose.' They walked on, over the damp golden sands, both mulling things over. Daisy stopping to sniff at some seaweed and a crab shell. Jack's mood had dipped. He looked sombre.

Lucy suddenly had a light-bulb moment, 'I've got it!'

'Yeah?'

'Yes, how does a Cocktail Horsebox sound? Just until Ruby's all fixed up, of course. We can join forces. Some nights as a bar, some as the Pizza Horsebox and hell yes, sometimes both. Let me help you out.' She was concerned he'd try to rush into working too soon, and make himself more poorly in the long run, but she could keep an eye on him that way, make sure he wasn't overdoing things. 'Yeah,' she continued, feeling buzzy about the idea, 'for events I'm not booked at, we can take out the oven and use the space for your bar stuff. And, if it's a joint booking – well, we'll work it out. I'll definitely have space for some drinks and things in the pickup. What do you reckon? A bar in a vintage horsebox, that sounds pretty cool too.' She was delighted with her plan.

Jack was nodding, trying to take it all in.

'And I'm sure the event organisers would go for it, once we explain. Then you can still keep your existing bookings. Pizza and prosecco, the perfect combination, don't you think?' She was feeling animated now. 'And hey, I bet you'd sell loads of those Morpeth Mules too.'

He frowned for a second, not getting it.

'Mules, horses, a horsebox.'

'Hah!' He laughed. 'You sure about this, Luce? It sounds a lot for you to take on, too.'

'Of course I'm sure. And hey, aren't we a team now? Isn't that what it's all about?'

Jack was staring at her. Seemingly thinking.

Had she said too much? Been assuming things again? *Are we a team?* She began to fret. When he got better, was he actually planning on staying around? Or with Ruby out of action, might his backpacking dreams come back to the fore? Lucy still wasn't sure.

Jack's smile then widened. 'Yeah, Luce, that is actually a great idea.' And he was almost, almost about to pick her up for a twirl, when he realised that he couldn't, his outstretched arms dropping swiftly. 'Ah, no, my ribs and all that … Soon, though.' And they'd be able to do far more that a beachside twirl too, thank heavens. It had been far too long since he'd been able to share her bed. But he suddenly felt tired; the exercise and the fresh air catching up on him. 'Can we just sit somewhere for a while, Luce? I'd like that,' Jack suggested, feeling the strain on his bashed-up body.

'Okay.'

So, they strolled back up the beach to settle on a large smooth-surfaced rock in a sheltered spot, where they could look out over the expanse of the bay. This was Lucy's beach at Embleton, and the view here – whatever the season or the weather – was always stunning. Today it was grey sky, grey sea, but not dull in any way at all, with the waves dancing in, in a surge of white froth, and a low rumble like thunder as they broke on the shore. Little grey-and-white seabirds stood dipping their beaks in the sands, the gulls circling above. The air fresh and smelling of salt and sand.

'Hah, this is where it all started,' Jack noted, his tone poignant. 'You and me ...'

'Hah, yes, you and your Morpeth Mule cocktails, getting me tipsy in the sunshine. It was a darned sight warmer that day, mind you.' Gorgeous happy memories came flooding back. The day it all began ... when Jack had surprised her with beachside cocktails, and they'd ended up chatting for hours, sat in the sun-drenched dunes.

'It was a good day.' Jack smiled.

'A very good day.' Lucy agreed, wistfully.

'I'm glad you said yes, that you stayed a while that day,' Jack continued, suddenly sounding thoughtful.

'Yeah, me too. Oh God yes, do you remember me falling off that put-me-up chair in the dunes?' She gave a goofy grin.

'Yep, into my open arms,' he finished with a broad smile.

They had stayed long into the evening, chatting, getting to know each other. What they had had these past months was fun and romantic and wonderful, yet it seemed so fragile, too.

Sometimes you had to risk your heart. Take a chance on love. And whatever might happen between them from now on, she knew she'd never regret that decision to stay that day. But there was still that question lingering in her mind, since she'd seen his open laptop that day.

It was time to take her own advice. To be honest and open. Even if the answer was not what she wanted to hear.

She turned to face him. Taking in that handsome face, those slate-blue eyes, with their cheeky sparkle, the sandy-blond, slightly scruffy hair. The face she knew she had fallen in love with. She took a deep breath. 'Jack ... are you still thinking of going away?' Her voice sounded small, fearful. 'Heading off abroad?' she clarified.

Jack quirked an eyebrow as he gave a small frown. 'Luce, what are you talking about?'

'It's just, well, a few weeks ago ... I couldn't help but see ... it was up on your laptop ... when I called by that day.' It had been looming in her mind ever since.

Confused furrows crossed his brow.

'New Zealand?' There, she'd said it. The furthest place in the world he could have chosen to go.

'Ah ...' He suddenly looked serious.

So, there *was* something to it.

'Yeah, I was having a look,' he admitted.

Lucy felt her heart contract. The wanderlust must have been kicking in for him again, after all. Those ideas of coupling up with the horsebox for Team Pizza and Prosecco, it was all some silly pipe dream.

'Well, I often get itchy feet this time of year. After Christmas and New Year, then come the really quiet months for The Cocktail Campervan. There's the odd booking, but business kind of disappears in Jan, Feb ... even March can be a bit of a trial. After all, who wants much in the way of outdoor catering just then, to be fair?'

'Oh ...' Lucy was waiting with a lump in her throat for what Jack was leading up to.

'So, I figure that's the best time to get away. Head off for some new adventures. Once I get myself up and running again after this little run-in, that is.' His tone was too bright, too breezy.

'I see ...' Lucy swallowed hard. Felt herself grip his

hand tighter, as though that action might just help hold onto him for a little bit longer. She could see their world of two slipping away. 'Right.' She turned her head as a little plink of a tear hit her cheek. Bit down on her lip. He'd not promised her anything. She had no right to ask him to stay.

Lucy gathered herself and sat looking out to sea. Someday soon, he'd be thousands and thousands of miles away.

'Hey, it might just be some silly idea, I don't know. Like you say, I need to get myself fixed up first.' He turned to face her, seeming to sense her unease. Took her face in his hands so gently, and gave her the tenderest yet most passionate of kisses, that stirred so much feeling within her. She held onto him, her fingertips running through his hair, tracing the nape of his neck, her lips tasting his, filled with the feeling that she really didn't want to let go.

As they reluctantly pulled apart, Jack grinned, saying, 'Don't think we could have got away with that at my parents' house, do you?'

Lucy had to smile, 'Maybe not quite such a smackeroo, no.'

Daisy joined in with a happy woof.

'Look, I've been thinking,' Jack took up, 'do you want to come over for some drinks ... maybe some supper, tomorrow evening? To Mum and Dad's, I mean.'

'Christmas Day?' This seemed pretty significant.

'Yeah, I know you've got plans with your own family through the daytime, and I know you've already met Mum and Dad now – weirdly, in the hospital – and seen them when you've visited this week, but, well ...' his words trailed. 'Well, I'd like you to come over.'

'Okay.' Was this some kind of recompense for him planning on fleeing the country in a few weeks' time, she wondered? Then told herself off, for over-analysing. After all, she'd been waiting for this moment for weeks and weeks. To be meeting the parents in a lovely sociable way at last, and that Jack was asking. 'Yes, I'd love to.'

And they sat holding each other as close as they could, without crushing Jack's healing ribs, their bodies resting together, seeking shelter. It felt so very precious.

And maybe, just maybe, Lucy prayed, after going off on his travels, having had his freedom, he'd find a way back to her.

Chapter Thirty-Seven

'It's Christmas!' Lucy shouted.

Daisy looked up with a *What's the matter with you?* kind of expression, though her tail did join in with an involuntary happy wag. It was just the two of them at home in the little cottage that morning, snug and cosy in the double bed.

There was a stocking to open for the Dachshund, with dog treats, a pâté-style lunch sachet and a new stylish navy neckerchief with snowflakes on. Daisy was very interested in the dog treat bag (turkey tasty bites) and had to try one immediately, of course. It was Christmas, after all.

'Well then, Daisy Doo, it's a quick breakfast for us, then we're off over to Olly's.'

The Jeep was already loaded with gifts for all the family, plus a little something for Jack and a hamper of local goodies she'd hand-picked from the village shop and Driftwood as a thank-you to Denise and Simon too. She was slightly nervous about the 'meet the parents' Christmas supper – even though she had, of course, already met them at the hospital and visiting this week – but this was on a more formal footing. Despite that flutter of anxiety, she had a feeling that today was going to be a good day.

❄

It was gorgeously festive over with Olly and the gang. The Christmas lights were on and so welcoming: warm-white twinkly strands strung along his front windows, and there was a cute wooden reindeer all lit up stood beside his garden path too. Freddie was waving excitedly at the window.

'Happy Christmas, Freddie!'

Her nephew came bundling into her arms at the front step.

'Santa!' was all he answered with a beaming smile, taking Lucy's hand to lead her into the living room where the big tree laden with baubles and tinsel and coloured lights twinkled, and where there were still a few gifts left unopened – rather amazingly, with a toddler around.

Daisy enjoyed a sniff about beneath the branches, causing a small pine-needle shower.

'Oops, come on Daisy, out from there,' Lucy warned.

With hugs from Alice and Olly, Lucy was welcomed in a festive wave of goodwill.

Nonna and Sofia arrived soon afterwards, laden with gifts galore, all wrapped up beautifully in silver star-patterned paper with red bows and curling string, and fancy tags. Sofia loved making Christmas into a work of art.

After a toast with Buck's Fizz, the gifting began. Freddie

was spoilt rotten, opening parcels in a ripping frenzy of Christmas wrap – which is of course absolutely as it should be on Christmas Day – with new toys, sweets, and clothes. His favourite being a little Thomas the Tank Engine train set that Lucy had bought him, which she was thrilled had hit the mark.

Lucy received some gorgeous bath bombs and a voucher to visit the Alnwick Gardens, a new hat and scarf set – hand-knitted by Nonna – and a pretty top from her Mum, which she was delighted with. Freddie had painted a picture for her too, of a blobby-shaped Santa with a brown blobby reindeer; it made her smile so much. Now that was going to be pinned to her fridge door back in the cottage, for certain.

Later that morning, Dad and partner Jo dropped by for coffee and mince pies for an hour or so, bringing yet more gifts, and a bottle of champagne to leave with them to enjoy with their Christmas dinner. He and Mum had made their own lives over the years, and were pleasant to each other. At times there could still be a trace of coolness between them, the rift many years ago having gone deep, but which they were happy to put aside on days like today for the sake of the family. That was what was important.

The traditional turkey dinner, cooked as a joint effort by Olly and Alice, was delicious, and was finished off with delightful Christmas pudding (bought by Lucy at the Claverham Castle Christmas Fayre from the Pudding Pantry stall!), and yet more mince pies (made by Nonna) served with a dollop of thick clotted cream, and a Santa-shaped chocolate bar for Freddie. With stomachs groaning but happily full, they spent the rest of the afternoon slumped on the two sofas in the lounge watching the *Paddington Movie*, much to Freddie's joy.

Lucy took a little fresh air and a walk around the block with Daisy as dusk rolled in. The Dachshund was now sporting yet another of Nonna's knitted creations; this time a bright-red elf-style suit which was all wrapped up for her along with a small bone-shaped toy. Hah, Lucy's little helper, lol! Though Lucy wasn't quite sure how much 'help' she was at times – well, perhaps on the cuddles and emotional crutch side of things, yes. And then it was time to go. Time to join Jack and his family.

With hearty hugs, and 'Merry Christmas' all round, a chorus of 'Thank yous' and 'See you all soons', they set off. Lucy's heart giving an excited yet anxious lift at the thought of being able to see Jack and his family on this special Christmas Day too.

❄

Lucy approached the red-painted wooden door of the large semi-detached house, where a traditional fir-and-holly-style Christmas wreath hung in welcome. She rang the doorbell with a feeling of slight trepidation. This felt like a significant step, and Lucy was also well aware that this was never an easy day for any of Jack's remaining family, not since his brother Daniel had passed away so suddenly and tragically all those years ago.

'Hello, hello, come on in,' Denise greeted her at the door with a warm smile.

Simon was there too, offering to take her coat. And then Jack came through, meeting her at the living-room door, dressed rather unexpectedly in a 'robin' festive jumper, which made her smile.

'Hi, you.'

'Hey.'

She wondered how he might be feeling, after being so reluctant at one point for this meet-the-parents gathering But rather than seeming uneasy, he gave a gorgeous grin as he said, 'Happy Christmas, Luce.'

'Yes, Merry Christmas to you all.'

'Hope you've had a lovely day with your family?' Denise asked. 'Where were you now … over in Rothbury?'

'Ah, that's where my family are from, yes. But we were actually here in Alnwick at my brother's place. Just off Allendale Drive. Mum and Nonna came across too, and my dad dropped by. It was really lovely, thanks. And you …?' she asked politely, as Simon ushered her through to the lounge, where Jack gave her a quick kiss on the cheek, and they then sat rather rigidly at first beside each other on the sofa.

'A quiet one, but nice, yes.'

Lucy wasn't quite sure what to say. It would be a tough day for them, always. Lucy's eye was drawn to the photos on the mantelpiece. The pictures of the young man who looked so very much like Jack in the ones beside him, perhaps a bit taller. And her heart went out to them all. She wondered whether to say anything, to acknowledge their ongoing grief, but on a day like today, would that make things easier for them or more difficult? It felt somewhat like the elephant in the room at that point.

Luckily, Denise saw where her gaze had fallen. 'Yes, that is our Daniel. He was such a lovely young man.'

'You must all miss him terribly,' Lucy acknowledged, her throat tightening with emotion.

'We do …' Simon took up, 'but life does move on, it has to. And, there's always something to look forward to.'

Lucy admired his stoic positivity, knowing there was still such a sense of loss behind those words.

'Yes, you've got to catch the light where it falls, Lucy,' Denise added gently.

What a lovely saying, thought Lucy. Hopefully, in time, she might turn out to be Jack's ray of light. They certainly all needed a little sunshine in their lives of late, Lucy included. She smiled, feeling the warmth of Jack's body beside her.

'Hey, where's Daisy?' Jack checked.

'Oh, I left her in the Jeep for now.'

'Oh, don't be silly, she can come on in.'

'Yes, we've heard all about her.' Jack's mum smiled. 'A real character, by the sounds of it.'

'Well, she certainly is that.'

Daisy was made to feel welcome too, and soon settled down on the sofa with the two of them. In fact, since Jack's accident, with him convalescing, she'd actually seemed to have softened towards him. It was often his thigh her chin sought to rest on. His hand she pawed for a stroke.

They spoilt Lucy with a delightful supper of carved roast ham, cranberry-topped pork pies, salads, and a gorgeous local cheeseboard with grapes, apples and chutneys. Jack's parents had evidently gone to a big effort. Lucy's stomach was already groaning after a full turkey dinner and pudding, but she was far too polite to decline. Jack made himself useful opening a bottle of champagne for them all, followed by a glass of merlot with the cheeses. He hadn't lost his barman touch by any means. A homemade fruit-and-cream-topped pavlova followed, with Lucy fit to burst at this point, but so grateful for their warm hospitality. And the four of them sat for a while contentedly chatting at the dining table, with a happy Daisy scouring for crumbs beneath them. Lucy was relieved that it seemed to be going so well.

'It's so lovely that Jack has finally brought a girl home to meet us,' said Denise, the champagne loosening her tongue a little.

Lucy and Jack felt a ripple of awkwardness at this point, giving each other a look across the table.

'Mind you,' added Simon wryly but not unkindly, 'I'm not sure we would have had the benefit of your company, had Jack not had his accident … when we've all had to meet up anyhow.'

'Okay, Dad, Mum. Thanks for that.' Jack rolled his eyes, yet managed a smile.

In fact, Lucy had been wondering the very same thing too. However it had come about, Lucy was very grateful to be getting to know them. They seemed to be good people, who'd had to cope with so much these past few years.

They were sat at the traditional wooden dining table, the family furniture solid and made to last – and it was obvious their love was too. Lucy realised that she was looking forward to getting to know them all even more in the coming weeks. Hopefully she'd get that chance.

The conversation turned to Lucy's business, with Simon asking what work she'd done before. After she'd said she'd been based in Morpeth previously, Denise had asked how she liked living by the sea. It was a polite, friendly conversation but it did feel a little like twenty questions to the already nervous Lucy. She realised that she wanted them to like her. And, she wanted Jack to be able to feel at ease with her there. If there was going to be some kind of future for them, the seeds of it would need to be planted here. She glanced over at him, his eyes had a hint of sparkle, his smile genuine. He seemed to be comfortable, at least right now, with the situation.

At the end of their extended meal, Simon raised his glass. 'Merry Christmas, Lucy.'

'Yes, Merry Christmas, love,' added Denise.

'Cheers, Lucy.' Jack's smile was warm and tender, and his eyes seemed to be saying so much more.

'Happy Christmas to you all! And thank you, it's been a wonderful evening.'

And she raised her wine glass to meet theirs. It made her think of a 'cup of good cheer'. Hah, must be all those Christmas songs and carols she'd been listening to lately. She felt mellow and happy. It had been a perfect 'Meet the Parents' supper after all.

❄

They stepped outside into the back garden, for a little bit of time out and a moment to themselves.

'Aw, that was a lovely evening. Your parents are great, Jack.'

'Yeah, they're pretty good.' Jack was nodding thoughtfully. 'They like you too, I can tell.'

'Phew! Well, we did kind of get to know each other really quickly at the hospital that night.'

'Yeah, of course.'

And the words took them back to that awful time, the feelings of fear, of standing at the edge of an abyss, and thankfully being able to step back from that cliff-edge of loss.

And then there was no more need for words. In the frosty night air, Jack took a step forward, taking Lucy slowly and gently into his arms. Nothing was going to stop this moment, even if his ribs were groaning a little in protest.

And their lips met, making their whole bodies light up. Their love bright and tender, and quietly passionate, between them. With senses igniting one-by-one, until Lucy felt a bit giddy. A Christmas kiss like no other.

❄

Denise had offered for Lucy to stay over, so she could enjoy a Christmas tipple or two. And as Lucy lay in her single bed, an hour or so later, thinking what a wonderful day it had been, her phone pinged from the bedside table. She reached over, and opened the message.

Jack:

Missing you already. xx

She smiled in the dark.
Another ping. Jack:

When I feel better I want to do all sorts of things to your gorgeous body … but not tonight. Can't promise I won't cry out in pain rather than ecstasy, lol. xx

And she laughed out loud in the dark.
Then she messaged back simply but truly:

I love you. Merry Christmas. x

Jack's reply was a heart emoji and two kisses. But for such a long time, he still hadn't said those words.

Chapter Thirty-Eight

Twixtmas soon arrived. Jack was back at his parents' house after a short but lovely walk along the riverside at The Pastures in Alnwick with Lucy. His mum was still insisting that he stay with them for a while longer yet, so she could keep a close eye on him whilst he was convalescing. Honestly, he felt he'd morphed into a strange mix of his teenage self and the elderly man he might one day become (sore ribs, sore back, grouchy!). But actually, he did appreciate their support and care. And a regular supply of good home cooking was a huge bonus, he had to admit. He was feeling stronger by the day.

It was a mid-afternoon and the watery winter sun was dropping low in the sky. Jack sat quietly in the wingback chair that had once been his late grandad's, overlooking his parents' garden. A rose bush surprisingly still had a few last frosted pink blooms, clinging on. A red-breasted robin hopped about in the border. Night would come soon, shifting into another day. Every day that everyone took so much for granted. With that accident … Jeez, he might not have been here to see it all. He might have lost everything in that split second of impact. The reality hit him. And again, that awful, striking sense of loss for his brother. His time had come way too soon. Daniel, his big bro, who'd scarcely stepped into his adulthood.

How life could change in an instant. Ice on the road. A heart shutting down. That's all it took, one moment. But, as he sat there, he realised too, that that's all it took to take life by the balls and turn things around. He'd wasted time, being scared, holding back …

There was something he needed to do.

❄

There was a knot of anxiety in the pit of Jack's stomach. He *so* needed to get this right. He'd checked the contents of his rucksack – twice – before Lucy had arrived to collect him. And Matt had had his instructions too; he bloody well hoped his mate had got it right. Frustratingly, with the pain in his ribs, he was still unable to drive himself following the operation.

It was now New Year's Eve, the sky a swirl of grey cloud matching the swirl of emotion building inside of him. He was doing the right thing, definitely. He just hoped the master plan went well. They pulled up at the grassy parking spot that he indicated, halfway up the moorland hillside. A few hardy sheep eyed the two of them as they got out of the Jeep. The breeze was fresh, but not fierce, thankfully. The view stunning across the green-and-brown patchwork of fields in the valley, and up towards the higher hills of the Cheviots with their dusting of snow in the distance. The last day of the year was pulling out all the stops for him; he was feeling hopeful.

He hoped to goodness he'd remembered the landscape of this hill correctly from his hike up here a month or so ago ... the position of the sole fir tree that was all part of the plan.

'You okay climbing up here?' Lucy looked a little concerned. This was a bit of a hike, not particularly far, but still, for someone with broken ribs and not long out of hospital ...

'Yeah, yeah, I'll just take it steady. No worries.' He was resolute. He had his sturdy walking boots on. Today was the day. He couldn't wait any longer.

They chatted on the way up the steep, stony track.

'I went to see Ruby the other day,' Jack spoke, sounding a little sad. 'Dad took me down to see her at the garage. She was in a bit of a bad way, bless her.'

'Do you think they'll be able to fix her?'

'Yeah, it might take a while, but she's been moved to a specialist garage down in Gateshead, one that restores VWs. I had a good insurance plan in place, thank heavens. But it's going to take some time to get her right. To even find the right parts.'

'I bet that was hard, seeing her again. Like that ...'

It had been. Partly to see the state his vintage campervan was in – all his hard work in renovating her having been destroyed in that instant – and also to realise what might have happened to him, a few centimetres the wrong way, a different impact ... It was difficult to contemplate. Today was not the day for dwelling on the negatives, however. It was time to look forward, to look up. 'Yeah, it was tough. But we'll get her fixed up, back to her former glory, for sure. Lots of TLC, and a hunt for the right parts. Even Bob from the burger van is helping out. He gave me a call to see how I was getting on, has a mate that deals in vehicle parts and has loads of contacts, apparently. Yes, The Cocktail Campervan will be back soon. My gorgeous Ruby will be all sparkly and just like new.'

'Of course she will.'

Jack paused for a breather as the path levelled out, halfway up the slope, taking in the view.

'It's beautiful here, isn't it ...' Lucy gazed down over the valley, across banks of heather and gorse, down to fields of peeking-through winter-sown crops and grassy meadows where cotton-wool sheep grazed, and up again to the high hills of the Cheviots, under a sky of grey and blue broken by shafts of white-golden sunbeams.

'Yeah.' Jack was lost to nervous anticipation once again, his stomach on spin mode. They walked on once more, steadily. Then he spotted it. *Cheers, Matt, phew.*

'Oh, look,' he tried his best to sound carefree, surprised, 'someone's dropped something.' It was actually tucked beneath a small rock. A sheet of plain A5 paper. Of course, he couldn't bend down to the ground himself very easily to reach it.

'Oh, hang on.' Lucy crouched down and picked it up. She began to read aloud: '*You are the rush of the sea, The hush of the hills, The calm to my storm.*' That was it. No other words. She looked up. 'Oh ... wonder how that got here?'

'Strange, yeah. Someone must have dropped it and not

realised,' Jack said, trying to sound nonchalant, his pulse racing, heart thumping.

'Hmm … and just a few lines. That's all? Odd.' Not wanting to leave rubbish on the hillside, Lucy tucked the sheet of paper inside her coat pocket.

They set off again, walking about fifty metres up the rugged moorland path between low bushes of winter-brown heather. Jack then paused to take a breath beside the bare branches of a small hawthorn tree. Hooked onto a twig was another piece of paper, with the exact same writing as before.

'Oh look, another one. Snagged in the little tree here.' She plucked it from the branch.

'Ah, right …'

She read aloud once more: '*Life has changed so much since I met you. You give me roots, let me keep my wings. You make me smile, make my soul sing.*' She paused, taking in the words, 'Ah, that's so sweet. I wonder how they got here … why?' She took a closer look at the lines of poetry. There was in fact something vaguely familiar about the handwriting.

Someone who wrote poetry … hmm. She furrowed her brow and looked towards Jack.

He seemed easy-going about it all, however. 'Uh, must have fallen out of someone's pocket, maybe,' he said, all nonchalant.

Again, she tucked the note into the pocket of her coat, where it sat alongside the first sheet of paper. 'Curious. Someone's obviously dropped them.'

'Yeah, wonder what that's all about?' Jack played along.

The next climb was a bit steeper. Jack's breath was a little ragged with the effort.

'Are you alright?' Lucy placed a gentle hand on his arm.

'Yeah.'

'Want me to carry the rucksack?'

'Nope, I'm fine.'

'What on earth's in there, anyhow?' Her brow creased.

'Ah, just some light refreshments,' he breezed out in reply. Hoping his racing heart and the flush of his cheeks didn't give him away.

Lucy shook her head at him, whilst smiling. 'O-kay.'

They set off again up the last rocky, peaty slope of track, where she took his hand to steady him over the steepest part. A final rugged stretch, a short climb and then they were at the top. A pile of stones marked the summit. The view from here was glorious, a full 360 degrees. Across to the peaks of the Cheviot Hills, Holy Island to the north, Bamburgh Castle and the coastline, where they often walked, and down towards Lucy's village of Embleton. You could just make out the ruins of Dunstanburgh Castle there too, away in the distance. Hills, sea, sky … stunning.

It felt wonderful to be alive. Jack couldn't help it, he gave Lucy a big, rib-crunching, heartfelt hug.

'Amazing, isn't it.' Jack smiled right through the rib pain.

'Beautiful.'

And they stood and gazed about them, taking in the dramatic, winter-moody scene on all sides. And then … gentle white flakes began to fall from the sky. Just a dusting of them … snow. The hush of it. So delicately pretty and icily tickly as it landed on eyelashes. They stood poking out their tongues, feeling its icy touch. Laughter. A tender kiss.

This was the time … absolutely.

Jack took a breath. 'Right then,' he announced, 'I need you to wait right here. Just for a couple of minutes.'

'*Really?* What's going on, Jack?'

'It's fine. All good. Just wait and see. I just need to get organised.'

She shook her head, grinning. What crazy scheme was he up to now?

'I won't be long, I promise,' he called out, already making his way down the sheep track that he'd memorised which zig-zagged between the low heather. 'Just stay there. I'll call you when I'm ready.' Jack was feeling a weird champagne-fizz mix of tension and excitement now.

He slipped down away from the summit, his heart beating like a hammer, stopping just over the first brow, a spot where Lucy could no longer see him. Yes, this was the place. He undid his rucksack and set to work.

❄

Well, life was never dull with this guy, she had to admit, even a walk in the hills was taking an unusual turn. Lucy stood, feeling a bit daft yet smiling to herself, at the top of the hill. Taking in that glorious view. Waiting.

'Ready!' His call carried from a rise in the hillside. She spotted the top of his sandy-haired head and his arm waving. He probably had a glass of fizz or some special cocktail lined up, she mused. An early New Year's celebration?

'On my way.' She was grinning as she approached a sheltered spot just down past the rise. A-hah, just as she imagined, there was a half-bottle of champagne with two flutes laid out on a small picnic rug.

'Aw, this is amazing. Thank you.'

Jack was looking really nervous. His eyes darting towards a tree – a fir tree – that was in fact the only tree on this part of the hillside. Elsewhere, it was all low bracken and heather. Light glinted off something … oh, a bauble …. and tinsel. Hah, he'd made a Christmas tree for her. Brilliant!

'Oh, Jack …'

'Take a look,' he motioned towards the tree.

She spotted a strand of silver tinsel, a gold sparkly star hanging on a string, and a silver bauble. 'Yeah, it's really pretty.'

'A *closer* look.'

Oh, there was another small square of paper, dangling from a branch.

'Go on, read it.'

'So, the poem … it was you!' Lucy exclaimed, rolling her eyes with a grin. 'You could have fooled me!'

She unhooked the sheet of paper from its washing-line peg.

'*Thank you for filling the hole in my heart. And this is where our together journey starts …*'

'Aw …' Her eyes had gone all misty.

'And look …' Jack was grinning now, pointing.

And, there was another bauble, clear Perspex. It was hanging on a silver string and had … *LUCY* etched on the side. There was something inside it. She stepped closer. 'Oh.'

'You can open it.'

'I can?' She was intrigued and stepped forward to pluck the festive ball from the tree. Her heart rate now pulsing in her chest, almost a match for Jack's.

The bauble had a clasp, and it opened out into two hemispheres. *Oh …* there was a small grey-velvet box inside. Lucy wasn't sure what to think. A late Christmas gift, perhaps? How sweet. She held her breath as she looked at Jack with a curious smile.

Slowly, she opened the box. Inside was the prettiest necklace with the most beautiful piece of turquoise sea glass as its pendant, set in a delicate silver surround. The glass was shaped like the crest of a wave.

'Oh, this is so beautiful,' her voice was tender, filled with love. 'It's just like the arc of a wave.'

'Yes, it made me think of the coast, made me think of you … *us.* I never had chance to buy you a gift in time for Christmas.'

Oh crikey, that's not what he was meant to be saying at all. He'd had it all worked out in his mind and now it had gone blank. It wasn't merely a Christmas gift …

Jack took a slow breath. 'Lucy … okay, this might sound a bit corny, but I feel like I'm on the crest of a wave with you … and maybe we can roll ashore together, come back home together …' He paused to look right into her gorgeous dark-brown eyes. 'And soon, we can set sail and go on some new, amazing adventures together too.'

He dug into his pocket, and felt for the envelope. It burnt under his fingertips.

'What are you saying, Jack?'

'Well, I was thinking about us going off and doing some travelling … seeing the world a bit.'

'Us? You mean *together*?' Lucy's eyebrows arched.

'Yeah, what's up? Don't you fancy it?' He felt a bit panicky. Had he misjudged things?

Lucy was stood with her mouth open, unable to speak.

'And … oh, if you've not got the savings, don't worry. I've earnt really well these past few years. And it would just be for a few weeks; we'd be back for the spring, for our businesses,' he clarified. 'It'll be brilliant. A whole new adventure. What do you reckon?'

She was still in shock. He wanted to travel *with her*. And typically for Lucy, her sensible side was thinking about all the implications. 'Ah, maybe … it sounds good,' her tone was cautious. 'I'd have a few practicalities to sort out. Like finding somewhere for Daisy to stay …'

But already Lucy's mind was coming up with a plan, with her mum as base camp and Olly as support. Daisy loved going to them anyhow, and she'd be spoilt for sure.

'Life's for living, Luce. I've learned that much.' Jack was smiling hopefully. *Carpe diem.*

Of course, Lucy thought. The accident with Ruby … What had happened to his brother … it could all get taken away so easily. And yes, she realised, yes, she would *love* to travel … and *with Jack*. She let out a little squeal. 'Yes … that sounds amazing. I've only ever been as far as Italy.'

Travelling … *together*. A smile like warm honey spread over her lips.

Jack then slipped the envelope into her hand.

'What's this?' Today was layered with surprises.

Lucy fumbled as she opened it. A printout … tickets … it was only bloody well two tickets for New Zealand!

'Oh my God, Jack, this is just crazy … but wonderful.'

She turned towards him, tracing her fingertips gently over the scar of his stitched cut on his forehead, down his nose to touch the cute V of his lips. He'd made it through the accident, and he was here with her today, and he'd still be with her for days and days to come. His warm welcoming mouth was waiting for hers as she leaned forwards, where they met with a passionate, and oh-so-tender kiss, filled with the hopes of their future dreams, and the taste of their adventures to come.

As they gently parted, Jack held her gaze, still feeling the need to say more. 'Luce, these past weeks, with the accident and everything, I've learned how truly precious life and *love* is. I don't want to waste another second. Lucy, I want to be with you …' It was all spilling out now, his heart on his sleeve, risking such a huge bashing, but he couldn't seem to stop. 'Maybe, when we get back from our travels, we can get a place of our own together, or if you can't bear to part with Cove Cottage, we could stay there? We can work all that out. Just say you feel it too, Luce, that we can do this, that you're in … that ours is a forever kind of love.'

Oh, my goodness. Lucy was wide-eyed and trembling, taking all of this in.

There was a nanosecond before the words flew out of her mouth: 'Yes, yes, of course I'm in.' How bloody amazingly crazily wonderful. 'Woohoo!' She flew at him, squeezing him in an excited hug, unfortunately managing to once again crush his healing ribs.

Wow, it was a yes! Jack was thrilled and relieved, but, 'Ouch. Ribs, Luce.'

'Oh God, yes, sorry.'

'No, I'm sorry, I should be whirling you around in my

arms … and much more. Soon, my love. When I'm back to full capacity.' He gave one of his cheeky winks.

'Absolutely. There'll be plenty of time for all that.'

And they had all the time in the world. Time for lovemaking, homemaking, building a life together, sailing the ups and downs, setting off on wonderful adventures, riding the storms and the crests of the waves. Then he reached to place the sea-glass necklace around her with happily trembling fingers.

Jack picked up the bottle of champagne that he'd carried all the way up the hill, and with a huge, happy and relieved smile, and with his typical barman flourish, popped the cork. 'Happy New Year, Lucy. I can't wait to spend it with you. Here and in New Zealand, and in all the other adventures yet to come …' He grinned broadly as he poured out two glasses with fizz.

'Oh,' she was feeling overwhelmed, 'Happy New Year. Thank you so much. Cheers, my darling Jack.' Lucy lifted her glass, feeling on top of the world … well, she *was* on the top of a moorland hill with a view to the Cheviot Hills and the stunning North Sea coast of her beautiful Northumberland. And that was as good as anywhere in this world.

'To us! Cheers. I love you, Lucy Brown.'

Those words filled her heart and her soul.

'I love you, too.'

They clinked glasses.

Wow, fizz and a future together! Now *that* was the best New Year's gift ever.

Jack's poem

You are the rush of the sea,
The hush of the hills,
The calm to my storm.
Life has changed so much since I met you.
You give me roots, let me keep my wings.
You make me smile, make my soul sing.
Thank you for filling the hole in my heart.
And, this is where our together journey starts . . .

Acknowledgments

Every book is helped on its way by a team of wonderful supporters.

Thanks to Mum and Dad for always being there for me, for encouraging my love of reading from an early age, and for their pride and support in every step of my writing journey.

My talented editor, Charlotte Brabbin, for polishing this story and making it shine, and the team at One More Chapter and HarperCollins for backing it and sending it out into the world with a smile, big thanks. The cover design for this series has been gorgeous, so thank you to illustrator Hannah George and cover designer Lucy Bennett. And, of course, thanks to my lovely agent, Hannah Ferguson; much appreciation for all your ongoing advice and support.

My friends, and especially those in the Romantic Novelists' Association, your support is always treasured. And cheers to all those who help to spread the word about my books – Chatton Village Store, the bookshops (especially

Forum Books in the North East of England), the libraries (thanks particularly to Michelle Watson at Northumberland Libraries), and to my fantastic readers and the book bloggers whose lovely reviews and comments never fail to bring a smile to my face.

Research-wise, several people have helped with this book, giving up time to answer my many questions, so big thanks to Min at 'Minnie's Mobiles', Graeme at 'Fizz on the Tyne', Richard at 'Crusts and Castles' and Dr Hannah Lee for the medical info. If I've got anything wrong, then it's down to me!

Last, but never least, to my family: Richard, Amie, Harry, Toby and Rowan, thanks for supporting my dream of being an author even when it means life at home gets pretty hectic. For the cups of tea, glasses of fizz, caramel shortbread – all essential writing fodder – and for being my cheerleaders, thank you.

Best wishes to you all,
Caroline x

A Letter from Caroline

Thank you so much for choosing to read *Mistletoe and Mulled Wine at the Christmas Campervan*. I hope you've enjoyed spending time with Lucy and Jack and, of course, the delightful Daisy Dachshund whilst touring the fabulous Northumberland coast and countryside with campervan Ruby. Hopefully you've been curled up with this novel with mulled wine, cocktails and mince pies to hand!

If you have enjoyed this book, please don't hesitate to get in touch or leave a review. I always love hearing my readers' reactions, and a comment or review makes my day and can also make a real difference in helping new readers to discover my books for the first time.

You are welcome to pop along to my Facebook, Instagram and Twitter pages. Please feel free to share your news, views, and recipe tips, or why not drop by to read about my favourite cocktails, latest bakes, see Jarvis (my crazy-lovely spaniel), and find out more about the inspirations behind my writing. It's lovely to make new friends, so keep in touch.

Thanks again. Take care!

Caroline x

Facebook: /CarolineRobertsAuthor
Instagram: @carolinerobertsauthor
Twitter: @_caroroberts
Website: http://carolinerobertswriter.blogspot.co.uk

Recipes from the Christmas Cocktail Campervan

Luscious Limoncello Fizz

1 serving – Nonna's favourite!

- 40ml limoncello
- 125ml prosecco
- Twist of lemon zest

Pour a 40ml shot of limoncello into the bottom of a flute-style glass.

Top with chilled prosecco, stir gently, and garnish with a thin twist of lemon zest.

Simply perfect!

Toffee Apple Cocktail

- 25ml caramel syrup
- 25ml cinnamon syrup
- 100ml apple juice
- 40ml brandy/calvados or apple schnapps
- apple slices and/or cinnamon stick to garnish

Pour a measure of brandy into a whisky-style glass.

Add the caramel and cinnamon syrups, then the apple juice. Stir.

Add an apple slice and cinnamon to garnish. Can be served on ice, or, as an alternative, warm it through gently.

Enjoy!

❄

Non-alcoholic Apple Pie Cocktail

Thanks to Min of Minnie's Mobiles.

- 25ml caramel syrup
- 25ml cinnamon syrup
- 100ml apple juice
- soda water
- apple slices (dipped in lemon juice to stop them browning) and/or cinnamon sticks to garnish

Fill a tumbler glass with ice.

Pour in the caramel and cinnamon syrups, then the apple juice.

Top up with soda water.

Add the garnish.

Enjoy!

❄

Jack's Merry Christmas Mulled Wine

Serves 6.

- 750ml bottle of red wine
- 1 large cinnamon stick
- 2 star anise
- 4 cloves
- 250ml water
- 2 strips of lemon zest and 2 strips of orange zest
- orange slices to serve
- 4 tbsp caster sugar

Put the wine, water, spices, zest and sugar into a large pan.

Warm gently on a low heat for about 10 mins.

Remove from heat and leave to infuse for a further 30 mins.

Re-warm gently to serve.

Pour into heatproof glasses or mugs. Decorate with a slice of orange.

❄

Claverham Castle Irish Coffee

- 150ml freshly brewed black coffee
- 40ml Irish whiskey
- ½ tsp brown or caster sugar
- 2 tbsp double cream, lightly whipped

Pour the hot coffee into a heatproof glass (or mug).

Add the whiskey and sugar, and stir until dissolved.

Gently float the cream on top by spooning on carefully. (This is easier than the traditional way of pouring it over the back of the spoon!)

Sip and savour!

❄

Cranberry Crush Mocktail

- 125ml cranberry juice
- 125ml soda water (or lemonade)
- mint garnish

Half fill a tumbler glass with crushed ice.

Pour over some cranberry juice, and top up with soda water.

Serve with a sprig of mint to garnish. Refreshingly festive.

❄

Lucy's Turkey and Trimmings Pizza

This is actually Caroline's version of the recipe, not Lucy's – as Lucy would be making her own dough and using the San Marzano tomatoes. But this one is quick, easy and very tasty indeed! Makes one large pizza – enough to serve two people with a side salad.

- 1 x 385g (or similar) pack of ready-made fresh pizza dough
- 25g seasoned butter (add salt and pepper to some softened butter)
- tomato paste – 150g passata, 3 fresh sage leaves chopped and 1 tsp chopped parsley, stirred together
- 150g grated mozzarella and 75g grated cheddar
- toppings: cooked turkey breast (approx. 150g); mini balls/chunks of pre-cooked stuffing; pre-cooked pigs in blankets (sausage-and-bacon wraps); and red onions, thinly sliced
- cranberry sauce (to garnish)

Pre-heat oven to 220°C (fan 200°C)/Gas Mark 7.

Roll out your ready-made dough to a large circle or oval. (Or if you're going for added drama, cut it into a Christmas tree shape!) Lay it on a pizza baking tray (ideally) or a large flat baking tray. Spread with your butter and cook for 6 mins, which will start crisping the pizza sides.

Spoon over your tomato sauce evenly, taking it almost to the sides.

Add half the cheese and then your festive toppings. Sprinkle with the rest of the cheese.

Bake for a further 10–12 mins until golden, crispy and the cheese is all oozy and melted.

Drizzle with cranberry sauce (optional). (Mix the cranberry sauce with a little water and warm it to make it runny.)

Delicious!

❄

Driftwood's Boozy Brownies

- 185g unsalted butter
- 185g good-quality dark chocolate
- 90g plain flour
- 45g cocoa powder
- 3 large eggs
- 275g golden caster sugar
- 150g white/milk chocolate chunks
- 100ml Baileys (or you could try Alnwick dark rum)

Preheat the oven to 160°C/fan 150°C/Gas Mark 3. Grease and line a 20cm non-stick square baking tin.

Melt the butter and dark chocolate together, either carefully in a microwave or in a bowl over hot water. Set aside to cool.

Break 3 large eggs into a large bowl and tip them into the golden caster sugar. With an electric mixer on maximum speed, whisk the eggs and sugar until they look thick and creamy. You'll know it's ready when the mixture becomes pale and about double its original volume.

Stir the Baileys (or other alcohol) into the cooled chocolate mixture and gently fold through the eggy mousse.

Combine the cocoa and flour. Hold a sieve over the bowl of eggy chocolate mixture and sift the cocoa-and-flour mixture, shaking the sieve from side to side, to cover the top evenly. Gently, fold in the cocoa-and-flour mixture. Then fold in the chocolate chunks.

Pour into the baking tin and cook for 30–35 mins. Then take it out of the oven and test by inserting a cocktail stick into the middle. If it's a little sticky that's fine, as it will firm up as it cools.

Allow to cool in the tin, then turn out and cut into approx. 12 squares.

❄

Nonna's Panforte

Somewhere between confectionery and a cake!

- Butter for greasing
- 300g whole almonds, hazelnuts and pistachios, toasted
- 50g candied peel, finely chopped
- 250g dried fruit, chopped (apricots and dates)
- 50g plain flour
- spices: 1tsp cinnamon, ¼tsp ground cloves and ¼tsp ground nutmeg

- 125g runny honey
- 150g caster sugar
- icing sugar to dust (1 heaped tbsp)

Line a springform cake pan with either parchment paper that has been well greased and floured, or edible rice paper (this is easier).

Tip the nuts, candied fruit and dried fruit into a bowl. Sift over the flour and spices. Mix together.

Heat the honey and sugar in a medium saucepan over a medium heat. Bubble 3–4 mins until the sugar has melted. Pour the hot liquid over the fruit and nuts, and swiftly stir to mix.

Working quickly, scrape the mixture into the cake pan with the back of a wet metal spoon to flatten it.

Immediately place the dirty pots and bowls in hot soapy water, as they are so sticky.

Bake in a slow oven at 150°C/fan 130°C/Gas Mark 2 for 35 mins.

Let it cool for about 15 mins and then remove from the pan, using a palette knife and/or fish slice.

Remove the baking parchment (if you used rice paper, you can leave it on). Cool completely on a wire rack, then dust generously with the icing sugar. Cut into 12 wedges to serve.

Keeps in an airtight container for up to 2 weeks. Ideally, wrap each slice in baking parchment.

Buon Natale!
Merry Christmas!